THE TOTALLY GNARLY, WAY BOGUS MURDER OF MUFFY MCGREGOR

T E D D Y   D U R G I N

ISBN: 1533324360
ISBN 13: 9781533324368
Library of Congress Control Number: 2016908390
CreateSpace Independent Publishing Platform
North Charleston, South Carolina

CHAPTER 1

"If my life was a movie, Siskel and Ebert would give it thumbs down."

It was probably the truest thing Sam Eckert said to his two friends, Chip Roundtree and Buddy Bradford, on that fateful day in the summer of 1986. A week removed from their last day of sophomore year, the three high schoolers sat at their usual table in the Laurel Centre Mall food court in suburban Maryland, having lunch.

"Gene and Roger would never give your biopic 'thumbs down,' Sam," Buddy assured.

"Siskel would," Chip said deadpan.

"OK, yeah," Buddy conceded. "Gene probably would. He's such a bastard sometimes. But Roger has never needed a movie to work entirely for his thumb to be turned up. And God knows Sam's life hasn't worked entirely."

"Thanks," Sam frowned. "Thanks for that."

"I'm serious. Roger would appreciate the journey you've taken to get to this point. I mean, sure. You *are* one of the only kids in school who lives in an apartment and not a house. And you don't play any sports. You've never made the honor roll. And you have all that bushy, curly red hair that looks like a nightmare to comb."

Chip joined in, pointing to Sam's mid-section. "And he already has a gut at 15."

Sam winced, as if physically wounded. "This is not changing the reviewers' opinion," he protested.

Now, of course, you've heard that every child is special. Every kid is remarkable. Well, most people had to look really long and hard to find what was special and remarkable about these three. Chip was unique only in that he was the lone black kid in a nearly all-white Catholic high school. Tall for his age and wiry, he looked like he could play multiple sports and play them well. But he couldn't. Not a single one. He didn't even have any interest in athletics. He was much more into music and the pop culture of the time. Chip's mother had died when he was very young. Three years old, in fact. Car accident. He didn't talk much about it to his two buddies or, really, to anyone. It had been just him and his dad for as long as he could remember.

Buddy had two fantastic parents, both of whom were alive and well. His father and mother ran the local two-screen cinema in the relatively small town of Laurel, and they as a family were always getting to see the latest movies early before anyone else in town. As a result, Buddy would have a brief window of time to spout cool and funny lines to his class-mates before anyone knew they weren't his own. A few weeks earlier, for instance, he was "feeling the need ... the need for speed" and offering the girls in school the choice: "Take me to bed or lose me forever." His face was still red from a couple of the cheek slaps.

This week, the wannabe Top Gun was wise beyond his years, interject-ing lines like "A lie becomes a truth, Chip-san, only if the person wants to believe it" and "Sam-san, what the heart knows, the head sometimes for-gets." Sure enough, "The Karate Kid, Part II" was about to hit screens that Friday, and Buddy was throwing out brand-new Mr. Miyagi quotes whenev-er he could ... even if they made no sense in the context of the conversation.

As for our lead boy, Sam? He's the one who will have the most inter-esting story to tell once this summer is over. Sam was both a Lutheran and a child of divorce, which made him stand out doubly so at Our Lady of Sorrows High School. For Catholics, divorce has long been a no-no. It's marriage to the death for the most devout. There were so many two-parent households at Sam's school in 1986, he often referred to himself as Rudolph the Red-Haired Protestant never allowed to play in any Catholic reindeer games. If there was Holy Confession during school hours, he had to wait in the pews with the one Muslim classmate, Amar, while all of his classmates lined up to tell all to the priest.

But it was that feeling of being an outsider, coupled with their complete lack of athleticism, that made Sam and Chip best friends. And their encyclopedic knowledge of motion pictures is what drew them to Buddy. They were probably the only kids in school who never missed an episode of "At the Movies With Gene Siskel and Roger Ebert."

It was this love of the syndicated film review show that was propelling their discussion this very morning. "My point is," Buddy continued, "Gene Siskel and people like him, they're elitists. Just like three-quarters of the dipshits we go to school with. They can't appreciate what someone like Sam has had to overcome in his life. Like a wise man once said, 'Sam-san, for person with no forgiveness in heart, living is worse punishment than death.'"

"Stop ruining all of the good, new Miyagi quotes!" Chip yelled, reaching across the rickety food court table to give Buddy a quick shove.

Dark-haired and rather gaunt, Buddy was one of those kids you could glance at and immediately tell what he would look like at 30, at 50, even in old age. Rather comically, he raised his bony arms to show Chip a karate chop pose and then froze in that position for several seconds. Sam chuckled, but then went on with his lament as Buddy slowly dissolved back into a relaxed, sitting position. "Roger would only appreciate what I've had to overcome because he was once a young, fat bastard like myself."

"And a life-long titty fan," added Buddy, "like yourself."

"True. I still can't believe he wrote 'Beyond the Valley of the Dolls.'"

"God bless that movie!" Buddy exclaimed. "Wall to wall breasts! Do you remember that scene where the one chick--"

"I don't know why we're even discussing this," Chip interrupted. In truth, he hadn't seen the movie and wanted to stop Buddy before he started really rambling. "No one's putting my man's life up on a screen. And, even if they did, today definitely wouldn't make the final cut."

Chip and Sam had come to the mall that day to get summer jobs. Chip had just finished his first and only interview, having been hired on the spot as a part-time cashier and stock boy at Harmony Hut, Laurel Centre Mall's main music store. The three had gathered to toast his success over some Orange Julius and Roy Rogers fast-food and to pump Sam up for his interview in less than a half-hour.

"So, are you gonna tell us where you're interviewing, Sam?" asked Buddy. "You've been all secretive and shit for a week now."

Sam bristled at the question. Maryland in 1986 required anyone under the age of 16 to obtain a special work permit if they wanted to get a job at a store or restaurant or most other businesses. Even then, most of the mall's retailers preferred their employees be at least 16 years of age. Chip had just turned 16, and Buddy would forever have work at his parents' cinema. Consequently, Sam didn't have many options. He had one "in," courtesy of his mother. And there were definitely pros and cons for a boy his age with his particular tastes.

"16 Plus," he mumbled softly in reply.

"Where?" Buddy and Chip asked in unison.

"16 Plus!"

Both boys hesitated for a couple of seconds, then together busted out laughing. 16 Plus was the one store in the mall that catered specifically to plus-sized women and girls. "Samuel," Chip chortled, "aren't you already unpopular enough?!"

Buddy added, "Yeah, seriously, dude. I know you've always had a thing for the Omega Mu's. But this is going a bit too far, don't you think?"

"Oh, no, no, no," Chip followed. "Who he has a thing for is Barbara Jensen. And with the basketball booty on that girl, 16 Plus has got to be one of her stores!"

Sam had indeed had a crush on Barbara Jensen since the 7th grade when she was the first girl in their class to develop cleavage. And he was overjoyed when she was among those who made the jump from the local public school to Our Lady of Sorrows when they graduated junior high.

Sam always had an eye for the large girls ever since his heavy-set mother, Francine, subscribed to BBW, Big Beautiful Woman magazine when he was just eight years old. For years, it was the only thing there was to read in the Eckerts' bathroom while sitting on the toilet. The fact that Barbara was a genuinely nice person up until this past school year was a bonus. But then she started hanging around with the likes of Muffy McGregor and Elena Eveler -- vapid, mega-popular cheerleaders, who liked to keep around a girl or two not nearly as pretty or as thin. Barbara's whole attitude and disposition had changed. So, Sam's goals were simple and twofold in applying to 16 Plus. One, be there when she came into the store to shop. And, two, get her to go to just one movie with him before the end of the summer when neither one of them would have to answer for it the next day in school to their friends.

Francine Eckert was a regular customer at 16 Plus. In fact, she was quite possibly their best customer, always having at least two items of merchandise on layaway and always one of the first to take advantage of the loyalty coupons the company mailed out each month. They owed her at that store. Sam was counting on that.

"Yeah, yeah. Guilty as charged," he said sheepishly. "Look, it's just a stock-boy position. I'll probably always be in the back. You'll rarely see me out on the floor. And ... what can I say? Big women need love, too."

"Yes, they do," Chip replied. "And clothes. Well, having just obtained a position myself in the retail trade just over an hour ago, I can definitely give you some advice on what to expect in your interview. Be prepared for some hard questions."

Sam was a bit nervous. He had never interviewed anywhere before. "How hard?" he asked Chip, tugging at his clip-on necktie which was starting to feel like a noose around his neck. The metal clip dug into his Adam's apple, making it hard to swallow.

"Oh, you won't believe what Chet over at Harmony Hut asked me. He wanted to know where I thought 'black music' would be in 10 years? Like, in 1976, who could have predicted L.L. Cool J and Run-DMC?"

Buddy chimed in, "Yeah, my dad, even when he's hiring lowly ushers or the new popcorn guy, he always likes to ask the 'crystal ball' questions.

'Where do you see yourself in 10 years?' 'Where you do see movies in 10 years?' Man, I hope we get new 'Star Wars' movies in 10 years. That's what I would answer."

"Yeah, and you'd be unemployed," Chip cracked. "Be glad your daddy is a business owner. For the rest of us, we have to actually ace the interview process."

"What else did you get asked?" Sam questioned.

"I got asked some messed-up questions. Like, 'Do I know the breakdown of how many albums are sold today on CD as opposed to LP and cassette tape?' There was another one sort of like that. Let me think. Oh yeah! 'Why did 8-tracks fail?' I just winged it. He also was really excited when I told him I went to Catholic school. Wanted to know if any of the girls will be coming by in their plaid skirts and button-ups. Like, hello! School's out for the summer, dude."

"The perv!" Sam exclaimed.

"Yeah, for real. Oh, and he wanted to know if I ever had a problem being on time. Punctual is the word he used. For a second, I thought he was calling me a punk."

Sam suddenly jumped up. "Shoot! What's the time? Almost noon? Gotta go. My interview's at 12!"

"Smooth move, Numb Nuts," Chip chided. Then, pointing to his friend's obvious clip-on tie, slightly wrinkled khaki pants, and Oriole orange dress shirt, he added, "And, hey, awesome K-mart outfit. Or is that Zayre's? Very cool threads, Samuel. Love the tie!"

"Yeah, Sam, remember" Buddy added, yelling over the bustle of those around them eating, drinking, and searching for empty seats. "Every employer's crazy about a sharp-dressed man!"

"Dicks! Both of you!" Sam yelled back, as he made his way to the escalator to the left of the food court. He brushed past several standing shoppers as he made his way down to the mall's lower level where 16 Plus was located.

———

"So, are you a chubby chaser, Sam?"

That was the first question Collette Stephenson, manager of the Laurel Mall's 16 Plus, asked the boy in his interview. For some reason, a strange mix of fear and titillation swept over him. She asked it very direct, very matter-of-factly. And in Sam's 15-year-old mind, he couldn't help but briefly wonder, "Is she flirting with me? Am I going to be her stock boy-boy toy?"

Sam had watched too many unscrambled Cinemax and HBO late-night movies at that point in his young life. As with most teenage boys circa 1986 or even 1486, pretty much any situation where a female spoke to him became a possibility for sexual intercourse. And, to be fair, there really was only one way to describe Collette. She was a big, blonde beauty! She was imposing, for sure. A husky woman who would be out of most mortal men's leagues if she were just a few inches shorter and a few pounds lighter. Sam certainly found her intimidating. Sexy as all Hell. But mostly imposing, especially as she repeated her last question to him.

"Samuel Eckert, I asked you a question. Are you a chubby chaser?"

"Pardon ma'am?

"Oh, you heard me. I'm asking if you like your women large?"

"Well, I--"

"I mean, why else would you apply here as opposed to the dozens of other 'cooler' stores in the mall? I know, I know. Most of them want their seasonal workers 16 or older. You'd think with a name like 16 Plus that we would, too. And, yes, I know your mom is one of our most frequent customers. My sales associates get dollar signs in their eyes whenever they see her coming."

"She could do a lot with the employee discount, Miss Stephenson," Sam said. He was suddenly very aware of the slight quiver in his voice.

"Yeah, but let's be honest. You don't care if she saves an additional 20 percent. You know, I've seen you around before. When you come shopping with your mom, you never actually come into the store with her. You either go up to the Time Out arcade or you go hang out with the old folks on the benches outside J.C. Penney's or Hecht's. If you don't want your little school friends to see you for the 15 or 20 minutes your mom browses in here, why would you want to be seen actually working here?"

Sam tried to stiffen up, give his voice a deeper and more steady tone. "Well, I'm applying for stock boy, ma'am. I'll be in the back most of the time, right?"

Collette leaned back in her office chair. She had an inkling there was more to this job opening for the boy than he was leading on. She had been with 16 Plus for several years and had never hired a male before in any capacity. No one with a penis had ever applied, in fact. Was she off base? Did the kid just want to make a little extra money between mid-June and Labor Day? Or was there something more?

"Most of the time? Yes. But not all of the time. In addition to keeping the stock room clean and maintaining our layaway stock, you'll be responsible for vacuuming the store's floor, keeping behind the counter swept and clutter-free, untangling hangers, and we'll need an extra set of eyes out front the weekend the mall does its Sidewalk Sale promotion. This job will be like spending a couple of months at your strict, German grandmother's house. You'll be seen, not heard. But you *will* be seen."

Sam pondered this for a moment. He was already unpopular enough at school. Chip was going to be at Harmony Hut, which was pretty much the greatest store in the mall back in the '80s for a teenager to work at except for maybe Spencer's Gifts or Chess King. And Buddy was going to be a fixture at his parents' movie theater, selling popcorn, tearing tickets, and putting up posters. They were both going to come out of this summer and into junior year of high school so much cooler than when they started. But a stock boy at a clothing store for plus-sized gals? He was taking a big risk for even a brief moment with Barbara Jensen. And he was only going to be part-time. What if she came in when he wasn't working there? He wouldn't even know.

Still, it was a chance he was willing to take. And, for some reason, he felt compelled to tell Collette right up front. "OK, there *is* this girl."

"Ah, now we're getting somewhere," Collette smiled, pleased that her intuitions were on the mark. Pointing to Sam's belly and barrel chest, she cracked, "A large girl for a large boy, huh? What's her name?"

"Barbara Jensen."

"Barbara Jensen. I know her. Well, I actually know her mother. She shops in here almost as much as your mom does."

"What about Barbara?"

"Unfortunately, she prefers to shop at our Columbia Mall branch two towns over. I was manager there before they transferred me here, and she used to come in once or twice a month. You see, Sam, most big girls your age won't shop at the 16 Plus nearest them. They don't want to be seen by their other classmates. On the positive side, we have some lovely and quite large Columbia girls who come in here all the time. If you like the plumpers, you'll like them. And you'll see Barbara's mom in here from time to time, for sure. Who knows? Maybe if you get in good with her, you can get in good with Barbara."

"Does this mean I'm hired?"

Collette stood up. Suddenly, she didn't seem nearly as intimidating to Sam. Extending her hand, she replied, "You're timid. You have no experience. And you haven't been able to avert your eyes from my cleavage for more than 15 seconds this whole time. Against my better judgment, yes, you are hired. Welcome to 16 Plus! Let me show you around."

When she said "Let me show you around," she did a certain flip of her hair which put her at an angle that for some reason was familiar to Sam. He had indeed been having a problem making eye contact with her throughout the interview, mostly because of her ample bosom. Suddenly, he found himself looking more at her face. He had seen her before. And not just from a distance while he waited outside the store for his mother to finish her shopping. Up close, she looked very familiar. And then it hit him.

"Oh my God!" he exclaimed.

Collette had opened her office door to walk him back into the store, but then she suddenly shut it. "What? What's wrong?" she asked.

"You! You were a BBW model! December edition! The Christmas issue ... uh ... uh ... 1980! Right?!"

"You read Big Beautiful Woman Magazine?"

"Of course!" Sam replied, then quickly realized how weird that sounded out loud. "I mean, uh, my mother does. She's had a subscription ever since I can remember. She loves all of the clothing ads and 'How-to' articles. Not to be crass, but it's been my can reading since I was, like, 8. She keeps her most recent back issues in a basket next to our toilet and the rest in storage in her closet. Never throws away an issue!"

Collette was briefly speechless. What an odd boy this was in front of her. "I don't know whether I should be impressed by this or deeply disturbed," she said. "And, for the record, it was the 1981 holiday issue."

"Well, I was close. Oh, man. You in that Mrs. Santa nightie. That was HOT! Do you know how many times--"

"No, I don't. And I don't ever want to know. Come, Sam. Let me show you around."

CHAPTER 2

Collette and her assistant manager, Julianna, showed Sam everything he needed to know to be a good stock boy that afternoon. Julianna was shorter than Collette, but was a solid and substantial woman in her own right. Having just been called out by Collette for his wandering eyes, Sam tried to divert his gaze away from her cleavage as much as he could. But his efforts made both women giggle at times during his brief orientation. "Eyes here," they kept telling him in an almost motherly way, pointing their index and middle fingers to their own eyes.

The two ladies introduced him to the 16 Plus layaway system, which was really just three long shelves of boxes filled with merchandise that people couldn't afford or didn't want to buy right away, but could have stashed for a later purchase within a set amount of time. He would be responsible for tagging each box and cataloging it. They showed him the proper way Collette liked the store's floor swept and its carpet vacuumed. They introduced him to the sales associates working that day, Judy and Deirdre, both attractive and just slightly overweight women in their early 20s. Sam was having a pretty wonderful afternoon, by his standards.

Lastly, Collette showed him the mall's trash room situated in the bowels of the shopping center, the parts of the complex shoppers rarely saw. It was there that he would take each day's garbage and place it into one of the two large dumpsters for when the trucks would come, open the big metal doors leading to the outside back of the mall, and empty the containers with their large metal arms.

The trash room definitely stank. That day, there was a weird citrusy smell in the air that made Sam want to gag, but it seemed to have little effect on Collette. "Basically," she said, "you just hoist the bags up and into the cans. Put some shoulder into it to get them over. The last thing you want is a bag coming back down at you and splitting open. And don't shut the lids. They're too hard to open, and you'll just piss off the next stock boy or girl who also has to get rid of their store's trash."

At that moment, almost on cue, Muffy McGregor entered the room with two large, plastic bags of trash from her sales associate job down at the Wilson Suede & Leather store. By almost everyone's assessment, Muffy was physically attractive. Blonde, beautiful, and curvy, she was a head-turner. She was also your standard, spoiled rich girl, a popular pom pom cheerleader at Sam's school who was dating the starting quarterback, Brent Fitzpatrick. She had barely acknowledged Sam's existence for the past two years, and she didn't acknowledge it that day either.

"And speaking of pissed-off, little stock girls about to get rid of the mall's trash." Sam was surprised to hear those words coming out of Collette's mouth. He had never heard anyone dare talk to Muffy McGregor like that.

Muffy was having none of it. "Shouldn't you be over at the food court's trash room, looking for any meat still left on the bones?"

"Oh, please. Bitch, I could pick my teeth with your legs."

"Go choke on a Twinkie, heifer!"

"Go choke on the blood of your family's hired help, whore. Or better yet, just GO!"

Muffy let out an audible scoff. Turning, she muttered as she exited the room, "I am SO out of here!"

Sam was pretty taken aback by the rapid-fire exchange he had just witnessed. He'd heard of catfights, but had never seen one quite so vicious and up close. "Wow, that was pretty hot," he marveled. "Did I notice some sexual tension there?"

"No," Collette answered quick and decisively. "You didn't. And please tell me you don't find that one attractive in any way!"

Sam was quick to answer. "I don't," he said. "But I can't speak for every other guy at school. They're all in love with her. She, of course, only dates jocks. Right now, she's going with Brent, our quarterback. Actually, he's also our point guard and starting pitcher."

Collette was eager to wrap things up. "And thus concludes your tour and orientation, young Sam. Any questions?"

"No, ma'am."

"Then be at work bright and early tomorrow morning before 10 a.m. The main entrance doors near Time Out will be unlocked. I'm sure you know, we get a lot of retirees who come for their exercise early before the stores open. You'll have to wade past them."

———

After his interview and brief orientation, Sam made a beeline for some of those old-timers. He actually enjoyed hanging out with the senior citizens who spent their days walking the mall, sipping coffee, eating at the food court, reading the paper, and generally gossiping on the large, cushioned benches positioned throughout the mall. They came in packs of two, three, as many as six or seven from the assisted living home that was located across the street from the shopping center. Sam didn't know either of his grandfathers or his father's mother. They all either died before he was born or when he was very young. His one surviving grandma lived in Tucson, far away, and he rarely saw her.

So, he loved hearing the stories about World War II and growing up in the Depression that the seniors would sit around and tell. Mostly, he loved hearing about all the gossip of the mall. Those old folks seemed to know everything that went on.

The biggest gossiper of them all was Mel, a short, stout man who was always seen with his taller, thinner, old war buddy, Rodney. Mel was from Maryland, born and raised. But Rodney had recently relocated to the state from Pennsylvania after his wife died. He was lonely, and Mel had raved about the Glory Days Seniors Home. On this afternoon, they appeared to be in deep conversation on the benches outside of The Hecht Co. department store with Mervyn Rabinowitz, the town's private investigator who always came to Mel and his friends for information when he was on a case. Today, he was just there to bitch about his marriage.

"You got a 'Wake up, Handsome, I love you?!'" the small, bushy-haired, late forty-something man asked Mel incredulously.

Mel smiled broadly. "Yes, sir, I did. My sweet darlin' says that to me every mornin'. Aw, what's wrong, Merv? Didn't you get a nice 'Good morning, Sleepy Head?' too?"

"Oh, I got a 'Good morning.' But it was a 'Good morning, you rancid sack of old Jew water.'"

Rodney chimed in. "Poor Rabinowitz."

At that, Mel noticed Sam lurking nearby, listening in on the conversation. "Hey, Sam! Did ya get the job?"

Sam briefly wondered how Mel knew he had a job interview that day, but he knew better than to ask. There really wasn't much that went on at that mall that particular man didn't know about. Who got hired. Who got fired. Who was interviewing with whom. Who was sleeping with whom. Mel knew the different rents the retailers were paying. He knew which merchants were vacating spaces, and which ones were coming in to replace those going out.

Rabinowitz loved Mel because he could always come to him to see which cheating spouses were meeting their secret lovers on any given day. After all, few people noticed the "old fogies" sitting on their benches, listening to all of the various conversations with their hearing aids turned up. Mel would often see a cheating wife or philandering husband meeting up with an affair during the week only to see that same cheater at the mall on Saturday or Sunday afternoon with his or her spouse and kids. It was that kind of swinging town back in '86.

Today, though, had been a relatively boring one at Laurel Mall. Nothing but scenes from Rabinowitz's marriage and speculation as to which kids were getting which summer jobs. "Yeah, I got it," Sam proudly answered. "You're looking at the new stock-boy of 16 Plus!"

The three older men whistled and applauded. "You must be in hog heaven, boy!" Mel exclaimed. He had a voice that sounded like John Fogerty singing ... only he wasn't singing.

"Hey, come on, sir. No fat jokes."

"Yeah, lay off the kid," said Rodney, his mouth full of food.

"What are you eatin' there?" Mel asked, slightly annoyed at his friend's lack of manners.

"What I eat every day. Roy Rogers. Yesterday, the Double R Bar. Today, bacon cheeseburger. Food for the soul."

Mel turned his nose up. "Not even Bag Lady Betty outside the mall would chow on that stuff every day. You know you're eatin' Trigger, right?"

Just then, Chip spotted Sam and came over to get him. "I thought I'd find you in the ICU. We gotta get going. Buddy's mom is picking us up outside of Time Out in 15 minutes."

Chip felt uncomfortable around the old timers. The '80s were becoming a progressive decade. But he found most senior citizens anything but. Sam insisted that Mel and his bunch were different, a good-natured group. But Chip knew they came of age in a time when black people weren't thought of as equals. He just was never quite sure where he stood with old, white folks. So, he tried not to engage them.

As Chip turned on his heels to leave, though, he was greeted with the sight of Brent Fitzpatrick and most of the football team's offensive line ... four of the biggest, young white kids you'd ever want to see. Brent asked Chip the same question he asked him every year at this time. "Hey, Chocolate Chip. Are you playing football in the fall?" They were under the impression that because Chip was black, he was naturally gifted at sports.

"No," he replied. "My dad wants me to concentrate on my studies, but maybe next--"

Brent cut him off. "Then forget you then!" And with that he and his crew walked on. Brent would then not speak to Chip until just before basketball tryouts in November. And then he'd ask the same question. "Are you playing?" And Chip would tell him "No." And Brent would move on. It was the dance they did every year.

"Damn," said Rodney, who had observed the exchange. Turning to Mel, he cracked, "I thought we licked the Nazis years ago. Looks like some Hitler Youth survived."

"Yeah," added Mel. "You and he are gonna have SO much to talk about at the 20-year reunion."

Chip couldn't help but chuckle.

"Hey, Chip is it?" Rodney then asked, a bit sheepish. He wasn't used to talking to young black youth anymore than Chip was used to talking to sixty- and seventy-something white men. Nevertheless, he felt the urge to relate.

"Yes, sir?"

"I want you to know," Rodney said, with the utmost seriousness. "I completely respect what those Tuskegee Airmen did in the war."

"Oh ... uh ... thank you?" Chip didn't quite know how to respond.

Just then, it happened. The explosion! Mel, Rodney, and Rabinowitz could see it from their sitting position just over the shoulders of Chip and Sam out the mall's side entrance windows. A bright ball of fire and debris. It was just as the sliding doors from the parking lot were opening to let in some mall patrons. It was a car, a car that just suddenly blew up. The sound was deafening, and it made the whole mall shake. Many people instinctively dropped to the floor. That's certainly what Chip and Sam did. Those closest to the doors were lucky they weren't hit by bits of fiery shrapnel that blew into the mall. Screaming and people shouting swear words and exclamations were immediate.

"Holy shit!"

"Oh my God!"

"Fuck!"

"What the hell just happened?!"

It took less than a minute, though, before those exclamations were replaced with:

"Who's car was that?"

"Was anyone inside?"

And "Someone call the police!"

Mall security was the first to respond, as Laurel Centre's half-dozen or so guards rushed from all over the property to the vehicle now completely engulfed in flames. A crowd formed almost immediately as the security personnel tried to get people to step back in case another explosion was to follow. It did, and people started screaming and ducking for cover all over again.

By that time, the mass of patrons both near the door leading out to the parking lot and those who were brave enough to draw close to the flaming car outside was so thick that Sam and his friends couldn't make out anything that was going on with the vehicle.

"By crackey, it's been a long time since I heard or seen a 'splosion like that!" Mel said, his heart racing. "Everybody alright?"

Sam, Chip, Rodney, and Rabinowitz nodded in the affirmative. Rodney had been to war, but the other three had never been this close to such an event. And the immediate chaos was highly disorienting. Sam's ears rang. Chip felt dizzy and just a touch nauseous. Rabinowitz's temple throbbed from where he hit his head on a bench when he dove for cover.

Rodney steadied the P.I. and helped him sit down. "I'll tell you what," he said. "If someone was in that car, they ain't alright?"

Multiple sirens could be heard in the distance, as the local police, fire, and rescue squads were not far from the mall. It was hard to tell what was headed the mall's way. Cop cars? Ambulances? A fire truck? It sounded like all of them. Numerous vehicles could be heard screeching out of the parking lot, too, to beat the inevitable gridlock that was about to form.

From out of the chaos, a single mall security guard emerged. Walking at a hurried pace and out of breath, the out-of-shape man was speaking loudly into a walkie-talkie, giving someone in authority on the other end an update on the situation. "Yes, sir! There was definitely someone inside! All authorities have been notified, and multiple sirens are en route. The vehicle? A red Pontiac Fiero. Yes, I recognized it, sir. It's parked in the same spot just about every day. More than likely a mall employee!"

Hearing the make and the model of the vehicle, Sam's heart seemed to skip a beat. "Pontiac Fiero?" he exclaimed. "Oh my God, I think that was Muffy McGregor's car!"

Chip couldn't believe it. "No way!"

Mel was equally shocked. "You mean that little tease who works at the Suede & Leather shop? What a looker. How can you be sure?"

"My dad's one of the grease monkeys over at the Lube Job across town. One time I stopped in to see him, and Muffy was there with a brand new red Pontiac Fiero that her parents gave her for her Sweet Sixteen."

The five fell silent, contemplating the cheerleader's possible grisly end. By that point, the smell of the burning car and the body roasting inside had wafted into the mall and met their collective nostrils. Finally, it was Rodney who spoke up. "What a world. What a wicked, wicked world."

———

Fortunately, Chip, Sam, and Buddy were to be picked up on the mall's south parking deck on the opposite side of the shopping center. That upper deck was eerily quiet. There were still a few sirens that could be heard in the very distant background. But other than that, most of the activity was on the north side of the mall.

The three boys sat on the curb waiting for Mrs. Bradford to pull up, none of them knowing quite what to say. At that point, they didn't know for sure it was Muffy who was in the car. But word had already spread that she had clocked out early for the day from her part-time job after her last chore -- getting rid of the morning's trash in the garbage room.

Sam wondered if that was the last time she talked to anyone. How sad if it was. It was such an ugly exchange between her and Collette. He wondered how Collette felt and if she regretted her brief spat with the girl. "I had just seen her," he muttered to his two pals. "I mean, literally, I had JUST SEEN HER!"

Chip shook his head. "It had to have been her. On my way to get you from the feebs, I passed right by her. And she was totally headed for the parking lot. I don't know why I noticed, but I did. She had keys in her hand. She was walking hard, too."

The three went quiet again. Even though Chip had indeed lost his mom at an early age and three of Sam's grandparents had passed away over the years, death was still something that seemed very distant and removed to the boys. Certainly, they never knew anyone their own age who had died or been killed. They were among a generation that didn't even have to think about their classmates being drafted to war. Vietnam was more than a decade over. They only knew Korea from re-runs of "M*A*S*H" that aired each night on the local UHF channel. And World War II was quickly becoming national fable.

Every once in a while, they'd hear of some teenager getting drunk and wrapping his or her car around a tree. Or, there was some kid in the next town over or the next state over who died of a drug overdose. It didn't mean much, except the inevitable assembly and lecture at school in which an expert was brought in to preach against the dangers of booze and getting high. But a classmate being blown up in a car?!

Buddy tried to bring some levity to the situation. "Well, there's at least one cool thing about this. Look at all the TV news vans here."

Amid the chaos, the mall's property management team was having the press vans park on the south parking deck. It took a little while, but the news crews from both nearby Washington, D.C., and Baltimore had made it to their small town about equidistant between both cities.

"I wonder if NBC 4 will send Arch Campbell?!" Buddy asked excitedly.

"The film reviewer?" Sam replied. "No way. Not even if Muffy had been killed in your dad and mom's movie theater."

"Actually, I already saw the Channel 4 van," Chip said. "Looks like they sent that new lady reporter. You know the cute and chipper one."

"Ah, Katie Couric," Sam said, with a slight hint of marvel. "I wouldn't mind having her at 6 and 11!"

Both Chip and Buddy looked at him with disgust.

"What?!" said Sam, not ashamed of breaking the tension. "You can't expect me to stop being a dude!"

His two friends looked at each other and shook their heads. "I guess not," Buddy replied, chastisement clearly in his voice.

Chip also looked at Sam with disapproval. Then, a slight smile cracked his serious demeanor. "Now, if we're talking Maureen Bunyan of Channel 9, I'd like to provide her with some exclusive coverage. You know what I'm sayin'?! I'm always up for some Bunyan!"

Chip and Sam broke into a fit of giggles. Buddy wasn't having any of it, though. "You ghouls!" he exclaimed. Then, getting up, he announced, "I'm walking away. God's now preparing two very special bolts of lightning for you two hyenas, and I don't want to be anywhere near either of you when he sends 'em down."

Sam and Chip pressed on. "Channel 9 must be like porn for you," Sam said to Chip.

"Oh, you know it. They got some fine-ass soul sisters on that broadcast. Bunyan. J.C. Hayward. Andrea Roane. And you could eat a meal off Phyllis Armstrong's ass!"

The two boys broke out into full hysterics, bumping shoulders, giving each other high-fives. The two hung off each other like a couple of old drunks, both practically in tears as they continued to crack wise on the local lady newscasters. It was all a direct result of the tension they were both feeling. They needed the release. Buddy just peered into the distance, hoping the two would calm themselves down by the time his mother drove up the ramp. She was obviously stuck in the traffic that was starting to snarl around the mall.

The only other person who was anywhere near to witness this embarrassing display was a single, random young man with a camera. He got about five feet away from Chip and Sam and snapped their picture twice, which, for some reason, caused the two to laugh even harder. The man then scurried off into the mall. At the time, Chip and Sam didn't think much of this seemingly random incident.

They really should have.

CHAPTER 3

Sam found it hard to sleep that night. He stayed up much later than he wanted to, considering he was about to start his first job ever. He just couldn't pry himself away from watching local news coverage on the Baltimore and Washington, D.C., channels. Laurel was indeed equally distant from both cities and Sam's small bedroom TV could pick up both markets' broadcasts.

The reports left no doubt that Muffy had died just starting her car. Even worse, the town's police suspected foul play. Even though the '86 Pontiac Fieros had a few recalls and reported engine problems, it was looking more and more like someone had tampered with her car and that she had been murdered.

It was weird for Sam to see places that he was familiar with on TV. The town, the mall, the parking deck. It was even weirder to see people he actually knew interviewed on camera, like Rodney getting face time and muttering "It's a wicked, wicked world!" and Brent, Muffy's boyfriend, who tried mightily to muster a tear when interviewed but just couldn't.

And when there was no more news to be had at 10 and 11, Sam laid in his bed with the radio on softly. There really was no "death channel" to turn to for sad music, so he listened to the local Top 40 stations; Q107, mostly. As hard as he tried, Sam couldn't really bring himself to actually be sad. Muffy never gave him the time of day. And he always thought she and her popular clique were responsible for turning Barbara into a status-obsessed hanger-on, one who also barely acknowledged Sam's existence in the hallways and classrooms of school this past academic year.

Sam did think of Barbara, wondering how she was dealing with the news. Surely, she must have heard by now. He had her number from the school directory. But his procrastination started at about 8 p.m. and lasted well into the night, way past a decent hour to call her. Just after midnight, Q107's overnight DJ played Phil Collins "In the Air Tonight," introducing it as a dedication from "Muffy's friends." And he wondered if Barbara was somewhere with those friends, calling the station, requesting the song, and probably drinking themselves into a teen stupor.

It was not a good night, but Sam eventually drifted off.

———

He woke up the next morning just before 9 a.m. to the sounds of women cackling in his apartment's living room. Sam's mother, Francine, worked six days out of seven at the local old folks' home where Mel, Rodney, and his cronies lived. But today was her day off, and she had her two best friends, Mindy and Cindy, over for morning coffee. They all lived in the Steward Towers apartment building. Francine was the only plus-sized woman of the three. Mindy was in her early 30s, a waitress at the local Toddle House restaurant. Everyone said she looked like the singer, Juice Newton, but she didn't see it. Cindy, meanwhile, worked as a security specialist for the Hecht Co. department store in the mall. She also had turned 30. But most people took her for younger on account of her cute, pixie-ish haircut and build. Better women would have been talking about U.S.-Soviet tensions or the growing crisis in South Africa or even Muffy's possible murder. Not these three.

"Oh my God!" Mindy exclaimed. "Five words, ladies. Five words! Bobby Ewing ... in the shower!"

The three squealed with glee. Cindy, Mindy, and Francine had been huge "Dallas" fans over the years, ever since the "Who Shot J.R?" craze. And their coffee klatches after each season's cliffhanger were among their most animated. This was their first get-together after the most recent cliffhanger in which Pamela Ewing woke up the morning after her wedding to Mark Grayson to find her supposedly dead husband, Bobby, in her shower all soaped up and wishing her a simple "Good morning."

"What does it mean?!" Cindy asked aloud. "How could Bobby be in that shower?! Katherine hit him with the car a year ago. We watched him die!" She then sprawled herself across the cushions of Francine's couch in a goofy re-enactment of the rundown. Then, in a mock dying voice, she mimicked the character's final words. "Be ... good to each other. Be ... a ... family!"

"What if Bobby had a twin we never knew about?" Francine posed. "Maybe they were separated at birth, and Jock and Miss Ellie never knew they had two babies."

Mindy was quick to interject. "Well, I guess that would be the most obvious way to bring him back. At least he'd be a real Ewing. But the tabloids all seem to think he's going to be a bad guy, that he's some schemer who's been surgically altered to look like Bobby."

"Oooh, I read that, too!" Cindy stated. "The *Enquirer* claims they found script pages in a trash dumpster outside the studio, and one of the scenes was Fake Bobby having the bandages cut off his face and him looking in a mirror and saying something like, 'My God! I look just like him!'"

Francine shook her head. "I still think he's a long-lost twin. That's what everyone wants."

"No!" Mindy replied emphatically. "Everyone wants Bobby back. Yeah, it's great to have Patrick Duffy back. But people want Bobby Ewing back, and I just don't see that happening."

"I don't care how they bring him back," Cindy said. "Just as long as that gorgeous man is once again on my TV every Friday night at 9."

At that, the three ladies realized Sam was awake and stirring, lumbering half-awake from his bedroom to the apartment's small kitchen. "There's my working man!" Francine said with pride. "I was just about to wake you up. You can't be late for your first day. By the way, how long do you have to work there to qualify for the employee discount?"

"I didn't ask, Mom."

"Well, be sure to ask Collette today. She's too awesome to stay at our little Podunk store forever, and I don't want to lose my 'in' now that I have one. Oooh, and also ask her if we can use your employee discount with any of my coupons, OK?"

Sam poured himself a glass of milk and some dry cereal in a bowl. There was something about sugary Trix that always seemed to comfort him. As he started to munch away, he became acutely aware that Francine and her friends had completely stopped chattering. The three sat still, sipping their coffee.

"Ladies, I didn't mean to intrude on your very important adult conversation. Please go on with your theories. I think you're all wrong, by the way. I read in the *Inquisitor* that it IS Bobby and that the whole last season was just a dream."

A stray thought of Muffy roasting in that car fire then crossed his mind, and Sam added wistfully, "If only life worked that way, huh?"

Francine got up from her recliner and walked slowly over to her son. "Oh, Sam. We're out here talking about soap-opera cliffhangers and retail discounts, and you're hurting, aren't you? We heard about your friend. How awful. No wonder you were so quiet last night. Are you OK, sweetie?"

The two embraced, and both Mindy and Cindy offered their condolences as well. He briefly wished the other two ladies had gotten up and given him hugs. But that was just the 15-year-old monkey in him talking. "I'm OK. Muffy and I, we weren't friends. In fact, I don't think it was possible for her to even glance my way without looking like she vomited a little in the back of her throat. She wasn't the nicest of girls, Mom. Of course, I never wished fiery death on her."

"Well, if the news is right, it sure sounds like someone wished her dead."

Just then, there was a hard knock at the door. Sam had been expecting Chip, as it was to be his first day of work, too, and they were going to walk the six blocks to the mall together. There was some discussion that the stores wouldn't open on account of the tragedy. But Sam hadn't received a phone call from Collette. So, he assumed he was to report for duty.

Chip apparently hadn't been called by his boss either. He was dressed in his Harmony Hut vest, with freshly pressed khaki pants, a fitted shirt, and his new name tag pinned to his lapel. Sam immediately noticed his friend's rather frantic, intense state. He was just a bit out of breath, sweating even, a slightly crazed look in his eyes.

"Have you seen it?!" he asked urgently.

"Seen what?"

"IT!"

Chip held a copy of the local weekly newspaper, the *Laurel Times*, in his hand. Chip's dad, Vernon, sold advertising for the publication. So, they would always get one of the first copies of each week's edition quite literally hot off the presses. Apparently, the publisher deemed Muffy's death so major, so newsworthy, that he assembled his staff to rush-print a special overnight edition of the paper. It was only a few pages, as the editors, writers, and production staff had worked all night on it.

"Wow, a Special Edition? Pretty impressive for the old hometown rag."

Chip's intensity didn't wane. "Look closely at the front page," he said, through gritted teeth.

Sam's eyes were immediately drawn to a large photo of Muffy in the left column. It was her last yearbook portrait, and she looked perfectly made up as always. "Yeah, there she is. I have to admit, Muffy could take a good picture. Wherever she is now, she's gotta be happy they used that shot."

Chip put his hand on the side of Sam's face. It was cool, a bit clammy, and trembling ever so slightly. Chip directed Sam's eyes to the right column of the front page, to a second photo just as large. "I don't think Muffy, wherever she is now, is very happy with the other photo," he said, anger now seeping into his tone. "I know I'm not!"

Then, Sam saw it. It! Everybody has three or four moments in their lives that they will remember clearly, vividly, for the rest of their days. For many, it's their first kiss or saying "I do" or the first time they heard their baby let out a cry in the delivery room. For Sam Eckert, it was the first time he ever saw his picture in a newspaper. There he and Chip were, sitting on a curb outside of Laurel Centre Mall, laughing their fool heads off. And over what? Which one of the local female newscasters they'd like to boink?

It took a few moments for Sam to even register that that was him and Chip in the picture. "What?" was the only word he could muster at first. He squinted at the photo for at least a few seconds, briefly wondering when it was taken before realizing it was just yesterday. That one random man with his one random camera.

"Oh. Oh, no, no, no. Oh, sweet Christ, no!"

The first cohesive, coherent thought he had was Brent Fitzpatrick was going to pummel them. He was literally going to pound them both until they were as flat as a Looney Tunes cartoon character who had just been run over by a steamroller. There wouldn't be any blood, any brain matter. They would just be stomped flat, face down, until dead.

Laughing mere minutes after the guy's girlfriend had just perished in a ball of flames? So wrong. What did Buddy call him and Chip? Ghouls. Yes, that was the perfect description, Sam thought. He was a ghoul.

The photo was truly awful. Chip was doubled over, in mid-guffaw, holding his stomach. Sam was draped over him like a touchy-feely drinking buddy, his face lifted straight to the sky, to the heavens, open-mouthed and just wailing with laughter. Sam was ashamed, mortified. Chip just held the paper completely still in his face, the photo seemingly getting bigger and bigger every second it was in front of him.

And then Sam read the caption below the pic. It was so unbelievable, he had to read it twice. In fact, it was so unbelievable, he had to read it aloud. "Two friends grieve over the loss of their fallen friend?"

Chip could only nod silently. His emotions were so raw at that point that his bottom lip was quivering.

Sam repeated the caption, putting special emphasis on the words "grieve" and "friend." "Two friends *grieve* over the loss of their fallen *friend*?!"

"No matter how you read it, it's all levels of messed up," Chip bemoaned.

By now, Sam's mom's interest had been piqued, and Cindy and Mindy had risen from their seats in the living room, as well. "Honey, is anything wrong?" Francine asked.

Sam immediately snatched the newspaper out of Chip's hand and folded it over several times as if he was rolling it up to swat a bad dog's nose. He didn't quite know what this meant yet, but he knew it wasn't good. "Uh, no. Everything's cool, Mom. Chip and I just have some things to discuss before work. Dude things. We'll be in my room!"

Sam grabbed Chip by the arm to lead him into his bedroom. Chip turned to go with him at first. But then he looked back at the three grown-ups and thought to ask, "Do any of you read the *Times*?"

All three shook their heads "No."

"Good!" Chip replied. "My dad works there, and he says print is dying anyway." The ladies all nodded "Yes." And Chip then followed his friend into his bedroom and shut the door.

———

"Two friends grieve over the loss of their fallen friend?!?!"

Sam couldn't stop reading that line. The photographer, obviously new and inexperienced, didn't even stop to get Sam and Chip's names. If he had, they never would have given him permission to use the shot.

"You can keep reading that line over and over, fool. But the words ain't gonna change."

"But ... but ... we're laughing our asses off in this photo!"

Chip grabbed the paper from Sam's hands. He stared once again at the photo, trying to see it from the perspective of someone who had no idea when the shot was taken and what he and Sam were actually doing in it. He closed his eyes for a few seconds, then opened them again. Finally, he was able to see what the caption was directing the reader to see. It didn't look like they were laughing. It looked like they were crying. Even worse, it looked like they were bawling in grief-stricken agony.

"Man, it does kind of look like we're tearing up in that pic. If my dear old Auntie Angela saw this, she'd say, 'You boys was ugly-cryin'!'"

"This is bad, Chip. This is really bad. I don't care what the caption says. People are going to see that it's us laughing."

The two sat down at the foot of the bed in unison and stared a bit more at the photo. They didn't even think of reading any of the Special Edition's articles or tributes to Muffy. The journalism staff had gathered quotes from their school's principal and teachers, Muffy's friends and family members, and some of her co-workers at the mall. Her photo had appeared numerous times over the years in cheerleading spreads and in a few local print ads when she was younger and a child model. Those pics were grouped in a photo montage on the third page.

But Chip and Sam didn't turn to that page or any other. They could only stare at their embarrassing photo. "I don't know," Chip finally spoke up. "The only other person who knows the truth about this is Buddy. And he's not going to say anything."

"Maybe you're right. I hope you're right. How do you think we should play this?"

Chip thought for a moment, then answered. "I don't think we have to play it one way or another. First of all, we're lucky it's summer vacation. By the time we go back to school after Labor Day, no one's going to remember this newspaper. And, two, no one our age even reads the paper anyway!"

"This is true," said Sam, relief suddenly washing over him. "So, you're thinking we're home free?"

"Home free!"

———

Sam and Chip arrived at the mall just like their respective bosses asked them to, a few minutes before 10 a.m. when the stores would lift their grates and open officially for business. The almighty dollar ruled, and mall management decreed that all stores were to open except for Wilson's

Suede and Leather. The official statement was it would be "business as usual" to honor the victim. The executives, of course, theorized that with all the free publicity being generated across all news outlets, people would come to the shopping center in droves just for the curiosity factor.

They were right. The mall was already teeming with people, and not just the employees who were arriving early. There were the usual senior-citizen "mall walkers." And there were indeed throngs of people who saw the reports on TV and had to come to the center just to be where news had happened and was still happening. The news crews themselves were also back, interviewing people both inside and outside the shopping center.

It was less than 30 seconds upon entering that Sam and Chip realized they weren't "home free." Collette was the first person who came up to them. She was running late in getting 16 Plus open for the morning. Building management had surprised her by not shuttering the mall for the day, and she was not happy. Even worse for Sam, she appeared openly disappointed in him. "Nice picture in the paper, Sam," she grumbled. "Do you think you can pull yourself together and make it through a full shift today?"

"Yes, ma'am. Of course. I'll be right there."

"I can't believe they're making us work today! I can't believe it!"

Jason Mumma was the second to spot them. The beefy boy sported a tight, military-style crew cut because his hair would be too wavy and unkempt otherwise to mimic any of the popular hairstyles of the mid-1980s. So, he went with the Army look that he figured worked in any decade and made him look truly tough. He called it his "asshole cut."

Mumma was the school's defensive tackle during football season, its starting power forward in basketball season, and the backup catcher in baseball season. He also was one of the cockiest kids around, the kind of boy who seemingly lived for towel-snapping teammates in showers and punching underclassmen's groins in the hallways. His victims likened him to "Biff Tannen on steroids."

Sam was too big to physically push around. And, by 1986, times had changed to the point where even kids in a majority white Catholic school didn't attack a good kid like Chip with racial slurs and physical abuse. But for most bullies, homophobia was still an acceptable go-to form of harassment.

"Well, well, well!" Mumma called out, swaggering over to them with his buddy and eternal hanger-on, Dave Garbarino, by his side. "Look at these two limp-wrists. Awesome picture in the paper, ladies!"

Sam, who was almost as big as Mumma, felt like using his girth for once. But he had no fighting skills. Mumma was all muscle and always, ALWAYS ready to fight. "Get out of our way, Mumma," he did manage to mutter.

Mumma wasn't backing down, even putting his hand on Sam's chest to keep him from advancing. Out of loyalty, Chip stayed close to his friend.

"I can't believe you two knob goblins cried for the camera," taunted Mumma. "The bitch had it coming, if you ask me. So, like, when you got home last night, did you lick each other's pussies?"

Sam was about to come back at him when, from out of nowhere and to his extreme surprise, Brent Fitzpatrick intervened. "Back down, Mumma! These are my boys!"

"Your boys? Since when?"

"Since right now. Get out of here, and don't talk to them again. You got that!"

Like dutiful foot soldiers, Mumma and Garbarino did as they were told. Brent was the one kid in school the bullies didn't dare cross. He was known as the Golden Boy. Only 16, Brent had the body of a man and was the physical equal of any teacher, coach, or administrator. And he had indeed been Muffy McGregor's handsome, arm-candy boyfriend since the last Homecoming.

Watching Mumma and his friend retreat, Sam let out a slight exhale and said, "Thanks, Brent. That was about to get ugly. But, uh, yeah. Since when have we been 'your boys?'"

"Since this," he answered, holding up the front page. "Dudes, I didn't even know you knew her. I'm, like, so touched by this. I'm feeling it. I'm feeling some mighty love for you two right now."

At that, Brent gathered both of them to each of his pectorals and brought them in for an embrace. "Cam, Chocolate Chip. You're with me now. OK? One-hundred percent."

"Oh, well, that ... that's great, Brent. It's Sam, by the way. My name is Sam."

"Yeah, and just Chip for me. You can leave off the Chocolate part."

Brent made an awkward attempt to give Chip the "brother's hand-shake." It didn't really take. So, he pulled him in tighter for a second hug, still grasping his hand and still grasping Sam and holding him tight against his other breast. "You got it, my brother. Even though you're not on my team, you're on my team. Neither one of you is ever going to get picked on or beaten up by guys like Mumma again. I'll see to that."

Sam looked up at him, admiration in his eyes. It actually felt quite wonderful being in Brent's arms. "That's so cool," he purred. "It's like you're Jerry Dandridge and we're Evil Ed."

"What?"

"Nothing."

Brent slowly eased up on the hug, and Chip and Sam resumed their slow walk to their new jobs. Brent stayed with them for a bit. He seemed lost and unsure of where to go. Sam could see that the guy was a bit of an emotional wreck. His eyes were red and puffy. He had a slight sniffle. He just seemed utterly dejected and wandering. Brent had never been nice to either of them, not once in two years of high school. Brent's family moved to town right before freshman year, and he was instantly liked and adored due to his athletic prowess. Very quickly, he became the top dog in school.

Regardless, Sam felt sympathy for him that morning. Now, he really felt bad about the photo. In fact, he was surprised at how bad he suddenly felt about it. Chip, though, beat him to the punch in offering Brent condolences. "I'm real sorry about Muffy, man. You guys were like the king and queen of the school. It's hard to imagine you without--"

"I can't imagine it, bro!" Brent interrupted him, breaking into a cry. "I don't want to imagine it. Aw, man! Why couldn't I have been crying like this when I was on the news yesterday?! Did you see me? Not a single tear. I looked totally bogus. What the hell's wrong with me?!"

"Brent, you were in shock," Sam said, putting his hand on his new pal's shoulder. "You were in a daze. Don't beat yourself up. Let's hold each other a little more. Come in for the real thing."

But Brent turned away. "I can't help it, man!" he raged. "I look at this picture of you two, and that should have been me next to her on that front page. That should have been a picture of me crying like a butthole! I loved her, man. I LOVED HER!!!"

"Of course you did."

"I should have been on that front page, bro! Whenever there will be school events, years from now, honoring Muffy, they're going to have this front page on display. And it'll be all big and blown-up and poster-sized. And there you two will be, crying for my girl, for all time. Should have been me! And her mom and dad? I know them. They're gonna frame this and they're gonna put it on their wall at home, maybe even in Muffy's bedroom. This front page is for all-time, brothers. You know that, right?"

Sam's throat was dry. "Yeah," he rasped. "We're starting to know that." He looked at Chip, but Chip couldn't even look at him. He was in an almost stupor-like state, muttering the name "Maureen Bunyan " quietly over and over again.

Brent was too lost in his own despair to notice. Suddenly, he turned in the other direction and started walking away from them. "I'm going for some air. I love you, guys! You *will* be at the funeral."

Chip snapped out of his trance. "No, I don't do funerals!" he blurted out. Sam glared at him, and Chip shot him a stern look back. Then, Chip realized one very important nuance. "Oh wait. That wasn't a question, was it?"

"We'll be there for you, Brent," Sam replied, before leading Chip off in the opposite direction. "Hugs, bro!"

Chip was incredulous. How could Sam even think of attending Muffy McGregor's funeral? She wasn't either of their friends. In fact, he was pretty sure she was borderline racist. Chip let his feelings be known when he was sure they were out of earshot of Brent.

"There's no way -- NO WAY -- I'm going to that funeral! And you shouldn't even think of going either." A small smile came over Sam's face. Chip noticed a defiant, almost greedy glint in his friend's eyes. It was a look that made him very nervous. "Sam, what are you thinking?"

"Dude, I'm just going to say it."

"Oh, don't say it."

"This could be our ticket to popularity!"

"Oh, God, you said it. No, you mean this could be your ticket to dating Barbara Jensen. Oh, and by the way. If you wanna be cool, don't reference 'Fright Night' to a jock. Really, Sam? Jerry Dandridge and Evil Ed?!"

Chip was right. Sam was already having visions of walking back into school in September, high fiving Brent Fitzpatrick in class right in front of Barbara, and her suddenly seeing him in a whole new light. A light they could share together. In that moment, Sam was thinking Homecoming, prom, marriage, kids, the whole shebang.

He and Chip were about halfway to 16 Plus and almost in front of Harmony Hut when Sam stopped walking, clutched Chip's forearm, and drew close to his friend. Lowering his voice to an almost whisper, he said, "Look, that's a messed-up photo. There's no doubt about that. But it's obviously out there. We can't take it back. But what if we were to parlay this into something good, something positive. Like Father Henry is always saying, 'Turn that minus into a plus.'"

"He was talking about Christ and the cross!"

"The same rules apply here."

"No, they don't. They couldn't!"

"Look, man, we've been pigeon-holed for two years now. Cliques formed that first week of freshman year, and we didn't fit into any of them. This is our 'in!' This is the second chance that every outcast, marginalized, spat-upon dweeb teenager dreams of! To have school let out for the summer and then to come back in the fall as a totally reinvented person with friends and parties and chicks! Don't you want to reinvent yourself?"

"I'm the Black Guy, Sam. I'll always be the Black Guy. I can't exactly reinvent that. But you know what? I actually like being the Black Guy. I'm pretty good at it. It comes naturally to me. And you're insane if you think one photo in one stupid newspaper is going to make you someone who you aren't."

But for the next five or so minutes, Sam and Chip did pretend to be people they weren't as classmate after classmate came up and embraced them. And, with each one, Sam grew more and more sure that the good life awaited both he and Chip come the start of junior year. Maybe sooner. Seniors gave them pats on the back. Incoming freshmen wanted to know their names. They got two separate invites to lunch at the food court from girls. The principal's secretary even recognized them, gave them each kisses on the cheek, and a card with the name and phone number of a grief counselor the school was recommending to students in mourning.

Without classes to go to, many of the students and staff of Our Lady of Sorrows were converging on the mall, visiting the scorched spot where Muffy had lost her life, and leaving flowers and other keepsakes. And everyone who came up to Sam and Chip that morning asked the same thing.

"You *will* be coming to the funeral, won't you?"

CHAPTER 4

Of course, Sam and Chip attended Muffy McGregor's funeral. They really had no choice. It was at Pumphrey's Funeral Home, the place where pretty much every kid in town's grandparents were eventually put on display before being laid to rest. The only thing Sam ever looked forward to when going to this place over the years was the little mint tray the Pumphrey family kept on a table near the front door. The mints were so good, and you couldn't find them anywhere else. They would just melt in your mouth when sucking on them. But they'd melt at the perfect pace, and the mints never became too much that you wanted to spit them out.

Everyone had fresh breath when attending a Pumphrey's funeral. And everyone did on that gray June day. There was Father Henry, the high school's resident chaplain, who was going to conduct the service. He was a mountain of a man, well into his 70s, but still quite healthy. Powerful even. There were Muffy's parents, Skipper and Kitty, dressed to the nines, as always, and looking like a First Family. They were flanked by their other children, 14-year-old Wink and 12-year-old Bunny. The names were silly to most, but they did fit each of them as the McGregors were obscenely wealthy.

Sam and Chip were glad a crowd of mourners was gathered around the family so they didn't have to offer awkward condolences to their faces. They really shouldn't have been there. It was incredibly awkward for both teenagers. But, for Sam, it was a chance to gauge just how "in" with the "in crowd" he and Chip had become.

Brent was the first of their classmates to see them. By now, tears were flowing out of the jock like timed waterworks. He was practically a fountain that afternoon. "Dudes!" he blubbered. "You made it! Thank you so much for coming."

Brent seemed to thank everyone who entered the funeral home for coming, even though it really wasn't his place. He was just the boyfriend, after all, and not part of the family. It seemed very presumptuous even to those who were sympathetic to his grief. But no one advised him otherwise, so he practically parked himself at the front door of Pumphrey's and didn't miss a single arrival that afternoon.

After Sam and Chip, there were several of Muffy's aunts, uncles, and cousins who arrived. Sam recognized a few mall employees come in, too, but no Collette. Strangely, there was Mervyn Rabinowitz, the P.I. who went right for the mint table, then largely stayed off to the side the whole time observing the different mourners.

And, of course, there were Muffy's friends. Sam felt an immediate rush in his chest when he noticed Barbara among them. The curly, blonde-haired teen wore a black, sleeveless dress that Sam recognized from the rack at 16 Plus. In fact, Collette had dressed one of the mannequins in that very same outfit on his first day of work. Barbara looked great in it, too, Sam thought. But he also thought better to go up and tell her. That would have been more than awkward. So, he just stared at her for a few seconds at a time, hoping she'd glance over and they could make a connection. She never once looked at him.

The atmosphere was more than a bit strange for a funeral. The various TV news crews kept a respectful distance, but all the Baltimore and Washington network affiliates were there filming from across the street. Inside the church, there was the usual crying and hugging and people leaning on each other and sharing memories of the deceased that you would expect at such a gathering. But there were also questions, some whispered, some not. "Could it have really been murder?" "Who could have done such a thing?" "Why Muffy?"

Then, of course, there were still some who questioned if it was a problem with the vehicle, a defect, that caused it to explode. This led to Sam and Chip hearing murmurs of "Why did Skipper buy her that car?" and "No kid that age should drive a vehicle nicer than mine!" and "I've heard those Fieros have had problems from the get-go. Didn't Skipper and Kitty do their research?"

Soon, though, the Catholic funeral mass started, and everyone took their seats in the same groups and cliques as always. Sam and Chip sat in the back row, as removed as they could be. After three hymns and a couple of Scripture readings, Father Henry took the pulpit. He based nearly his entire eulogy around the theme of penance, of confessing one's sins to him and to God and then embracing voluntary self-punishment to achieve absolution. He shared with those gathered that Muffy had recently gone to confession and had received such absolution. But he then warned that she left behind family and friends and co-workers who were living in a time where people were growing increasingly disconnected from God.

Sam marveled as the man really got into his sermon, spouting such paraphrased Biblical verses as "Unless we do penance, we will perish!" and "Those who seek penance shall fall into the hands of the Lord, not into the hands of men." Sam was tempted to lean over and whisper to Chip that Muffy was rumored to have fallen into the hands of quite a few guys over the years. All he had to do was look at his friend with a small smile and a mischievous glint in his eye for Chip to whisper, "Ain't nothin' funny, stop smiling." The very last thing they needed was to start another round of giggles.

Father Henry closed with a call to action. "Bring forth therefore fruit worthy of penance!" he hammered. "True repentance requires fruit. It requires outward acts. This do in remembrance of Him ... in remembrance of Muffy."

The priest then opened the service up to anyone who wanted to come forward and say a few words about the dearly departed. Muffy's father was quite eloquent, talking about his first-born in glowing terms as only a fawning, adoring dad could do. Her mother remembered a rare girl's weekend away the previous summer, where it was just her and Muffy. She recalled feeling at the time that her teenager was "slipping away" from her, but the trip had brought them back together as mother and daughter.

Barbara was next. She didn't share a memory or a thought. Instead, she tearfully recited the lyrics of Phil Collins' "Against All Odds (Take a Look at Me Now)." Her eyes traveled longingly from the page to Muffy's coffin and back to the page as she read: "You're the only one who really knew me at all. So, take a look at me now. There's just an empty space. And there's nothing left here to remind me, just the memory of your face. And you coming back to me is against all odds, and that's what I've got to face."

Brent followed. He didn't really have anything prepared. So, at first, he just awkwardly piggy-backed off of what Barbara had to say, "Yeah, she was the only who ever knew me at all, too. How can she just walk away from me? Or, drive away from me. Well, I guess she never got to drive that day, did she? Aw, man. I'm just ... I'm just fumbling this whole thing, aren't I?"

You could feel the awkwardness in the room. Nevertheless, several of the mourners muttered support for the boy.

"No, you're fine."

"Keep going. Just let it out."

"You can do it, Brent."

Those who knew him best feared that he would start talking in sports clichés. Sure enough, he did. "Muffy didn't fumble. She never dropped the ball. She gave 110 percent every day, every play. People said that she was my cheerleader. No way, man! I was hers. You hear that? I'm not ashamed to admit it, y'all! I was her cheerleader. I had on a big old skirt and pom poms for that girl! And every day, I cheered for her! I was, like, M-U-F-F-Y! Why? Because she was awesome. You all saw her. She was AWE-some!"

Then, Brent went quiet for a few moments. He lowered his head, as if in quiet prayer. When he lifted it, he scanned the entire gathering, every face. He tried to have a different expression for the first few people he looked at. Was he done talking, Sam wondered. Did he have anything else to say? Was he ever going to step down off that pulpit?

Maybe if Sam and Chip hadn't sat in the back row, what happened next wouldn't have happened. Maybe if they had sat with the crowd, somewhere in the middle of one of the rows, Brent would have looked right past them. But he didn't. "Now," he said, his eyes suddenly trained on them, "now I want to bring up two most excellent friends of Muffy's, and I want them to say a few words."

Chip's hand literally went to Sam's thigh. "Oh, no he isn't," he said under his breath.

"You know them less from school and more from the newspaper," Brent continued. "Sam ... Chip ... dudes? Come up here, boys. We all want to hear what you have to say!"

For a moment, Sam half-expected the mourners to start clapping in support. But the room was quiet, deathly quietly. He reached out to take Chip's hand to lead him up front, but Chip slapped it away. Only those closest to where they were sitting saw that brief physical exchange and squinted at the two in reaction. As they made their way to the pulpit, both boys felt weak in the knees. Neither had ever stood in front of such a large gathering before and spoken.

And, really, what did they have to say? Muffy truly meant nothing to either of them. It was sad that she was gone. You couldn't help but feel for her family and those closest to her. And there was the whole loss of youth and innocence thing. But when it came down to it, Muffy had always been a real bitch to both of them. There just wasn't a personal connection there.

But at least one of them had to say something. They both looked out over the gathering. There must have been 20 rows of chairs, with a dozen people to a row each. Some even stood in the back of the room, as the place was that packed.. Sam whispered to his pal, "You got anything?"

Chip, exceedingly bitter that Sam had brow-beat him into coming, quietly muttered, "I don't know. How about, 'Welcome to Fright Night ... for real.'"

"Ah, man. That's cold-blooded. So, it's like that?"

"Yeah, it's like that. It's exactly like that."

By this time, some audible murmurs started arising from those who had come to pay their respects. Both boys sensed they were perplexing the crowd and broke off their brief bickering. Chip nudged Sam to the podium. The sudden lurch forward briefly caused his nose and chin to tap the extended microphone. Sam struggled for words. For a brief moment, he actually thought he could muster tears. He wanted his mother. He wanted a ride home. Then, he said the only thing he could think of in the moment. Thinking of his mom, her shows, Bobby Ewing ... what were those final words he said last year when he died?

"Be good to each other," Sam said, trying to adopt Patrick Duffy's death-throes stammer. "Be a family."

———

Sam and Chip had to endure many things that day. The funeral. The cemetery. Looking the McGregors in the eye and lying about how much their Muffy meant to them. They tried to get out of the reception afterwards back at the family estate. But like the funeral, person after person said to them, "You're coming back to the house?" Sometimes it was with a question mark, sometimes not. They couldn't not do it.

McGregor Manor, as the kids at school called it, was everything Sam and Chip had heard about and more. Located on several acres in West Laurel, neither boy had ever been there before. They'd never been to any of Muffy's parties, and neither one of their parents had ever gotten an invite to any of Kitty McGregor's charity functions. The home was ornate, but still tasteful. Parked cars wound their way around a large, circular driveway out front and spilled out onto the tree-lined, perfectly manicured Melbourne Drive.

Sam kept looking for an opening to talk to Barbara all afternoon. He felt like such a heel that that was his one overriding thought. But he couldn't deny it. Chip, meanwhile, still couldn't believe that no one could see that he and Sam were laughing in the newspaper photo and not crying. Not a single person even suspected. His dad was right. People really will believe whatever they read. If it's in a newspaper or a magazine or scrolled across a TV screen, it has to be true.

It was a warm, very humid East Coast day, and the air conditioning that hit people in the face as they came in the front door caused some to gasp, some to sneeze, but most to just go "Ahhhhhh!" Sam and Chip stayed together, close to that front door in the home's marbled foyer. They stayed together, that is, until Sam saw Barbara.

"Just go," Chip sighed.

Sam hadn't been comfortable all day, and he certainly wasn't feeling particularly confident approaching his crush. But he figured if ever he had a chance with her, it was going to be now, today, in this place, at this time. She was very sad faced. Barbara was always a serious girl. But coupled with grief, she was even harder to approach. Sam started with a basic compliment.

"I really like what you said at the funeral, Barbara."

The girl hadn't even noticed his approach. "What? Oh, Sam. Yeah, thanks."

"No, I mean it. I'm a big Phil Collins fan. I don't think I'll ever be able to listen to 'Against All Odds' the same way again. It's always been this great love song, but you ... you turned it into something else."

"It's still a great love song," she said softly, staring blankly past him.

She wasn't giving him anything back. She hadn't commented on that terrible newspaper photo. She didn't return his compliments. Did she like what he had to say at the funeral, he wondered. Sure, it wasn't much. "Be good to each other. Be a family." Yikes, now that he thought about it, he sorely wished he had a do-over. He was about to wish the same after this conversation.

"Love your dress by the way!"

Barbara finally engaged. "You love my dress?"

"Yeah," he replied, a broad, silly smile coming over his face. "It's a 16 Plus, right? I work at the one in the mall. It's on our back mannequin."

Barbara bristled. She looked around quick to see if anyone heard what Sam had just said and was relieved that everyone within earshot was either too into their own conversations or too into their drinks and food. "Shut up," she said, in a low and embarrassed growl. "I do NOT shop at 16 Plus."

Sam immediately went on the defensive. "Oh, hey. No, I know that. You shop at the Columbia branch, though, right? That's cool."

"No, I don't!"

"It's cool, it's cool," he assured, panicking as only a 15-year-old boy can. "Look, if you want, I think I can get you my employee discount. I bet it's also good at Columbia. We could maybe go shopping there together sometime?"

Barbara went from embarrassed to full-on outraged. Sam was surprised at how formidable she was when mad, like a really mean teacher or a lady cop. "I don't believe this!" she spat. "Are you hitting on me at my best friend's funeral?!"

"No! No, of course not! I just thought--"

"You thought wrong. Now, get away from me. You're a parasite."

Before Sam could do as he was told, Barbara moved on to another room in the house where there were fewer adults and more of her classmates. Sam could hear several of them greet her enthusiastically from where he was standing.

He looked over at Chip, who had watched the whole sad and pathetic exchange. Chip could only shake his head and turn away to one of the numerous food tables spread throughout. The McGregors certainly knew how to put on a good spread. The caterers had been setting up the whole time while the family was at the funeral and burial. Sam made his way over to one of the serving stations where baby crab cakes and bacon-wrapped scallops awaited. Also there was Rabinowitz.

"You alright, kid?" he asked. "That was brutal."

"Rabinowitz, what are you doing here?"

"Yeah, I know what you're thinking. There's Mervyn Rabinowitz ... putz ... schmuck to the world. What's he doing hobnobbing with the rich and powerful of Laurel? Shouldn't he be sifting through their garbage cans or taking pictures of them though their windows?"

Sam took a pause. Rabinowitz had real issues. "I wasn't thinking any of those things actually," Sam said. "You just look as out of place as my buddy and I do. Are you a family friend?"

"More like a family employee. The McGregors don't have much faith in the local Barney Fifes. They're already dissatisfied with the way the police are handling the investigation. So, they've hired me to see if I can find out who killed their daughter. Hey, nice speech at the funeral, by the way. When someone asks you to 'say a few words,' they usually don't mean that literally."

"Yeah, yeah. I know. So, it's really murder and not some car malfunction?"

"Oh, no doubt about it. It was murder, good and proper."

"Wow."

By this point, Chip had strolled across the room to join them. He also knew Rabinowitz as the town's not-so-private, private eye from all the time he spent scoping people out at the mall.

"Hey, Chip," Sam said excitedly. "You're never gonna believe this. Rabinowitz here is on the job. He's been hired by the McGregors to find Muffy's murderer, and he's scoping out suspects right now!"

Chip was immediately concerned. "Wait, you mean the killer could be here, in this house, right now? It could even be someone we know?!"

Rabinowitz shrugged. "Could be."

The two boys pondered this. Suddenly, everyone in the room seemed just a bit different. Sam and Chip looked at each person with suspicious eyes. And neither kid felt safe.

———

It took a while, but Chip and Sam were finally able to extricate themselves from Muffy's wake. And they went where all teenagers in their predicament would go in 1986. Back to the mall. The mall food court, to be exact. And Buddy was there to meet them, eager to hear everything that went on without him.

They told him all about how hyper-emotional Brent was. How he brought them up to the pulpit to give a speech. How Rabinowitz was there and on the clock. Mostly, Sam talked about Barbara.

"I struck out, man," he lamented, his mouth full of McDonald's. "I totally whiffed."

Buddy thought for a minute. He usually had some words of wisdom, and they were usually from some movie. He knew just what to say. "You know what you did wrong? Sounds like you put on an act. But Barbara's a modern woman. Don't try put on an act, Sam. You can't do that to a modern woman."

"What?"

"Oh, it sounds like you had your plan of attack. But that won't attract the modern woman. You're an old-fashioned man, and she understands the things you, sir, were doing."

"Buddy, what the hell are you talking about?"

Buddy started laughing. "It's this song in this movie that's coming out on the 27th."

"Any nudity in it?" Chip asked.

"No, but it's funny as Hell. High-larious! Danny DeVito, Bette Midler. It's called 'Ruthless People.' My dad and I previewed it this morning before the theater opened, and the studio sent us soundtracks in the mail a week ago. There's a Billy Joel song on there called 'Modern Woman' that I've been listening to the last couple of days. It's gonna be his top seller of all time, Sam. Of all time! You gotta hear it. It totally applies to you and Barbara."

"Is there at least a panties scene in the movie?" Chip pressed.

"You want to see Bette Midler in her panties?"

"Of course not. But there's gotta be other chicks in it."

"Yeah, there are. But, uh, no panties. Oooh, but we do have the trailer for 'Howard the Duck' attached! And, in it, you get a sweet, sweet shot of Lea Thompson crawling around on all fours in her panties! It's gonna be the greatest!"

Chip sat back in his chair, shaking his head. "It won't beat the greatest panties scene in movie history," he declared.

Buddy nodded his head in reverent agreement. "True," he said. "But nothing will ever top Ripley in her panties at the end of 'Alien.'"

"They were SO tiny! They couldn't have been comfortable."

"I know! That whole time she's avoiding the alien, getting attacked by Ash, setting the ship to self-destruct, going back for the freakin' cat! And she's running around in THOSE panties?! They didn't even cover her--"

"A woman is STILL dead, people!" Sam interrupted.

There was something about their trivial conversation that really got to the boy. Or maybe it was just the whole day. Had he been taking Muffy's death too lightly? Should he have been laughing and cracking jokes outside the mall that day? Was popularity in school so important to him that he would keep up a lie for the next two years?

He should have had more to say at the funeral. He shouldn't have tried to use the wake to hit on Barbara. And he shouldn't be sitting here chomping on a Quarter Pounder with cheese and listening to these two boobs discussing Great Moments in Movie Panties History.

"Relax, Sam," Chip said. "We got through the funeral. It's not like we have to go back to school tomorrow and keep dealing with all this. Let's just coast now 'til September."

Sam pondered this for a few moments. His sudden, intense seriousness had put a halt to his friends' trivial musings. They looked at each other, wondering what would be a safe subject to talk about. Finally, Sam spoke up. "I don't know if I can do that."

"Do what?" Chip had never seen his friend so serious. Something had definitely changed in him and changed fast.

"I don't think I can just 'coast,'" Sam answered. "I don't know. Maybe it was something Father Henry said. All that stuff about penance and making things right. This is bad to say, but ... man, I've never really paid attention to any of his sermons before. My mind's always wandered at church."

"And today?" Chip asked.

"Today was different. It felt like it was really about me, about us. We've done some wrong here, Chip. OK, I've done some wrong here. Things like popularity and a girlfriend and acceptance, they get handed to kids like Brent and Muffy and Mumma. But, for whatever reason, guys like me and you have to earn it. And to earn it, I think I have to do what Father Henry preached. Seek penance. Seek absolution."

Chip didn't tell his friend that he hadn't really listened to Father Henry's eulogy. Like Sam, he also rarely paid much attention in church. He always found Catholic masses too structured. It was so easy to get used to their beats and snap to attention when the service called for it. But he knew enough about penance and absolution from religion classes to know those were roads that were often very hard to take.

"And how exactly are you going to seek all that?" he asked.

From out of the corner of Sam's eye, he noticed Rabinowitz lurking about. The detective appeared to be looking for someone specific, and it didn't take him long to find the object of his search. Mel and his buddies from the old folks' home. They were having coffee and cinnamon rolls a few tables over. "Of course!" Sam almost cried out. What better people to go to for information on the inner workings of Laurel Mall than Mel and his cronies. They lived for such gossip and scuttlebutt. And if anyone had an idea at this early stage who killed Muffy, it would be them.

But then Sam thought to himself, "What if it wasn't someone associated with the mall who was Muffy's murderer? What if it was someone out of Rabinowitz's wheelhouse? Someone younger. Someone not from the mall, but from school. Rabinowitz was going to need someone who knew Muffy's friends; who could talk to people her age; someone suddenly popular, but still under the radar, who could maybe get answers."

Sam suddenly knew exactly what his penance would be. "Gentlemen," he declared. "I'm going to find out who killed Muffy McGregor!"

CHAPTER 5

As Sam made his way to where Rabinowitz was in the food court, Buddy and Chip sent him over with a veritable serenade of warnings like "You're crazy!" and "No way!" and "If you tell Rabinowitz our secret, I'll never forgive you!" But Sam didn't care. And he didn't listen. He was determined, quite possibly more determined than he had ever been about anything in his 15 years. He was not to be dissuaded in any way.

Rabinowitz, of course, did his best.

"Kid," he said, after Sam had pulled him aside to one of the other food-court tables and delivered his sales pitch. "Private investigating ain't what you see on TV. Believe me! This ain't 'Magnum P.I.' This ain't 'Matt Houston.' This ain't 'Mike Hammer' or 'Riptide.' Do you see a mustache on this face? No. Do you see Rabinowitz motoring around town in an amazing, red Italian sports car? No. I drive a Datsun."

"Sir, I understand that. But--"

"When you see me walking around the mall, spying on pathetic adulterers and philanderers, do you hear cool TV theme song music in your head? Do you hear the 'Magnum' theme? Of course you don't. You probably hear carnival music. You and me, boy? We ain't Hardcastle and McCormick. We ain't Simon and Simon. I'm not Spenser: For Hire, and I'm not Remington Steele. I'm not even Paul Williams from 'The Young and the Restless.'"

"OK, now you're reaching. I don't even know who that is."

Sam was amazed at how worked up Rabinowitz was getting. He seemed to enjoy his tirade. His words seemed rehearsed almost, like he'd just been waiting for a kid or some other commoner to ask if he or she could help out on one of his investigations. Or maybe he had indeed rattled off this whole speech before.

The man raged on. "I think you're the one who's reaching, Sam. Private investigating is a whole lot of drudgery. It's waiting around in your car for hours, hoping your target shows up with his girlfriend on the sly. It's hoping there's enough light left in the day to get a good photo of them locking lips from a block away. It's getting to dumpsters before the garbage man does and unwrapping every crumpled-up note and discarded piece of paper you can find, hoping that it'll be a phone number or an incriminating charge slip. Do you ever see Remington Steele stumbling out of the garbage, down on all fours, gagging, and trying not to puke? It smells in there. Worse than you can imagine. Of course you don't see Mr. Pierce Brosnan doing that. Private eyeing is about--"

"Alright, alright," Sam interrupted. "I get it. I really do. I'm not asking for a badge and a permit. I just want to help you. I don't even care if you take all the credit if I somehow come up with something that leads to the killer. I don't want credit. I just want..."

"What, kid? What do you want?"

"This is just something I need to do. No offense, Rabinowitz. But if Muffy's murderer is one of my classmates, there's no way you're going to find that out. Look at you. You can't relate to today's teens. But I can. I know all of the players. This will free you up to work all the other angles. Maybe Muffy wasn't the target at all. Her dad is certainly rich. And he's probably pissed off a bunch of people in his lawyering business to get to be that loaded. Or maybe Muffy had some stalker who followed her around the mall? I don't know. But if it was somehow, somebody from school, I can help you with that. I know I can."

Rabinowitz considered what he was saying. Somewhere in the middle of the boy's spiel, he started to make some sense. But what if things took a serious turn? What if there was a real killer on the loose, and something happened to the kid on his watch? Would he be liable? Still, he liked Sam's instincts. He had thought of both possible angles that he just mentioned, too, especially someone connected to Muffy's dad who was an attorney for the local law firm of Dietrich, Ferro, and Spunkmeyer before starting his own practice. High-powered lawyers in small towns always have enemies, Rabinowitz thought. His brother was such an attorney in upstate New York, and he had people who absolutely despised him.

Then again, Muffy was quite the looker. And from everything he had gleaned so far, she wasn't the nicest person. She could have thoughtlessly rejected any number of mall lurkers who frothed at the mouth for her, who saw her day-in and day-out in those sexy Wilson suede and leather outfits. Or, it could have been some poor sicko who never had the courage to work up the nerve to talk to her, who ultimately decided no one could have her.

But someone from school? Some petty classmate who was bitter that Muffy was so popular or so pretty or so rich? Or some rival cheerleader whose perky, little nose had been pushed out of joint because Muffy "made varsity" and she didn't? Or some nerdy girl who was jealous Muffy walked around school with the best jock on her arm? The possibilities were endless, and Rabinowitz's acid reflux flared in his gut just thinking about all of the pathetic scenarios.

He hated his high school years. Just hated them. And none of the cases he had worked over the years had ever brought him in contact for very long with teenagers. He really couldn't stomach the teens of 1986, with their ridiculous hair, gaudy clothes, and awful music. They flooded the mall every day. They were the waiters and waitresses at all of his favorite greasy spoon restaurants around town. They were the little assholes who skipped school and ruined the matinee movies he tried to take in at the local cinema on days where his case load was light and he didn't want to go home. How he despised their seemingly endless snark and complete inability to whisper.

Rabinowitz sighed. He couldn't believe he was actually considering the boy's request. "Meshugenah," he mumbled.

Sam didn't understand. "Pardon?"

"Meshugenah," the P.I. repeated, louder and more clear this time. "It means crazy. I must be meshugenah to even be considering this. But you actually have a point. Two things, though. One, I fully expect the cops will close this case quick and this will all be a moot point. And, two, I highly doubt anyone at that hoity toity school of yours has the skills to rig a car to blow."

Sam had already thought of this. And his reply was quick and assured. "Nah, they'd pay someone to do it for them."

Rabinowitz nodded and smiled. "Exactly!" he exclaimed, tapping Sam's chest with his index finger.

"So, where do you think I should start?" Sam asked. "Half the school was at the funeral. Did anyone there raise your suspicions?"

Rabinowitz thought about asking Sam the same question. He wondered how effective the boy would be in getting any information. He always thought he was one of the school's fringe kids. Not quite a nerd or an outcast. But he had observed the school's cliques many times at the mall. The jocks, the preppies, the brains. Sam didn't seem to fit into any one of them. But maybe that was his hook. Maybe he was just ordinary enough to fit in with all of them, Mervyn considered. Or none of them. Either way, he could hopefully come in under the radar. The danger, of course, would be asking the wrong person the wrong question at the wrong time. Rabinowitz ran that risk himself.

"Alright, kid. Just the school angle. And I mean that. I'll handle everything else, especially anyone connected with the McGregor family and law practice. These are people who are out of even my league. In fact, I may already have a lead."

"Oh yeah. Who?"

"No one you need to ever know about it. Believe me. As for the school, I'd definitely start with that babbling boyfriend of Muffy's. What was his name? Bent?"

"Brent," Sam quietly corrected him.

Sam bristled at the thought. While he felt some shame for using Muffy's death to get in good with the popular crowd, he couldn't help but feel some trepidation over questioning his new buddy, the Golden Boy of the school, about his dead girlfriend. That and the guy was 200 lbs. of pure muscle. In his emotional state, if he thought for a second that Sam was implying that he had anything to do with his beloved's death, Sam could only imagine the beating he would receive.

"Yeah, Brent," Rabinowitz said. "Brent Fitzpatrick. Big, oafy son of a bitch. He'd be the first person I'd have a sit-down with. And any friends of hers, too. Like close friends. Best friends. Anyone who would be jealous or envious of Muffy for whatever reason."

Ugh, Sam thought. That meant Barbara, too. Maybe this wasn't such a good idea. Rabinowitz noticed his sudden ambivalence. "Hey, Sam. You don't have to do this. Maybe you should leave it to the professional."

Sam's mind was a bit of a jumble. But the only thing that seemed to bring any clarity was being part of a solution for once. Mostly, he just kept hearing Father Henry's words of warning from the pulpit.

"No," he spoke up. "I want to do this. I just wanted your opinion on where to start."

Just then, Mel and Rodney walked by on their way out of the food court and back to their benches. "Well, I for one am going to start my mall sleuthing with these two gents," Rabinowitz said, pulling his chair out to block their path. "Mel, you were saying something earlier about an argument you had witnessed?"

Mel took a sip from his coffee. He had helped Rabinowitz with many cases, and he was only too eager to share what he knew in this matter. "I didn't actually see the argument. Gertrude Gerhardt, that German mustachioed frump from back at the Home, was the one who saw it. She parks herself outside the Friendly's every day, because she likes to see all the little ones with their ice cream. Well, she told Mabel Sue who told my Mrs. that Muffy last week got into an anything-but-friendly argument outside the Friendly's with that hunky, lunky, peacock-struttin' dude who manages the Harmony Hut."

Sam's ears perked up. "Chet?"

"Yeah, that's the cat. Well, Gertrude swears it was a lovers' spat. And she said that Muffy was trying her best to calm him down and stop him from making a scene. But Chet was madder than a hornet in a syca-more tree."

That's when Rodney chimed in. "And you know that Muffy was at least 10 or 12 years Chet's junior at the untimely time of her passing. So, we're talkin' some serious jail bait if what Gertrude saw was so."

"Juicy!" Rabinowitz exclaimed. "Sirs, you do not disappoint."

Mel accepted the praise. Rolling his eyes playfully, he replied, "Well, now. This is, of course, all rumor and conjecture and innuendo."

"Yeah, gossip and buzz and chit-chat," Rodney added, with a mischie-vous grin.

"But we believe it!" the two old men said in virtual unison.

Rabinowitz immediately turned to Sam, whose mind was reeling at the possibilities. Was Muffy cheating on Brent with Chet? Did Brent know? Did he only recently find out? Who else saw this supposed spat? And did it even happen? Half these seniors who flock to the mall from the Home each morning have terrible vision. How would this Gertrude Gerhardt know a Muffy from any number of other blondes who work at the mall?

"Well, Sam. Looks like you really do have to start with your friend, Brent, huh?" Rabinowitz needled.

"Yeah, I guess so. The problem is, school's out for the summer. It's not like I can just see him tomorrow, for sure, and strike up a conversation."

Just then, Sam heard his name being called from a bit of a distance away. The voice was instantly familiar, although Sam could hardly believe the timing. It was Brent, flanked once again by members of his offensive line. It was the first time since the murder that he almost looked like his old self again. And if he was his old self and this was a week ago, he would be calling Sam's name just so Sam could rise up, answer him, only to have Brent yell back something wise and memorable like "Screw you!" just for the amusement of his jock buddies.

But this time was different. He called out "Sam!" excitedly, like he hadn't seen an old friend in many weeks. "Brent?" Sam answered back.

"Party at my house tonight!" the quarterback announced. "You're coming!"

Again, it wasn't a question.

———

Chip got the same loud and boisterous invite from across the food court, too, and he really had no choice but to attend. He and Sam could hear songs from Van Halen's "5150" album from two blocks away as they approached the Fitzpatrick house. That's where Chip had his father drop them off so they wouldn't be seen driven to the party by a parent in a 10-year-old station wagon that emitted a most awful odor while idling at traffic lights and in driveways.

"OK," Vernon Roundtree said, as the boys exited his car. "Have your little narrow behinds to the rendezvous point by 11 o'clock. Oh yeah. That's right! Extraction is at 11 sharp. That's p.m., gentlemen! And you both better be there. I ain't missing Johnny for anyone. He's got Lou Rawls on tonight."

Chip and Sam walked hurriedly to the house, which sat on a cul-de-sac in one of the older neighborhoods of Laurel. The homes were mostly split-level, single-family residences that most locals referred to as "Brady Bunch houses." And Brent's family dwelling indeed looked a lot like that of Mike and Carol's on the classic TV sitcom. At least from the outside.

As Chip and Sam made their way through the open front door and into the home's living room, they saw a number of familiar faces from the school's "in crowd" lying about on the floor and stairs and draped across the matching, floral-patterned couch and love seat. Most were drinking from plastic cups that almost certainly contained beer or some other alcoholic beverage, probably from the large punchbowl on the dining room table. Few looked up from their booze and conversations to even notice they had arrived.

Chip and Sam were so entranced staring at all the details and people of the room, they almost tripped over a boy and a girl making out on the floor by Brent's mother's corner curio cabinet. The two young lovers barely looked up.

Unfortunately, the first person to say anything to them was Jason Mumma. And, Jason being Jason, it wasn't very nice. "Shit!" he exclaimed. "I guess I'm gonna have to get used to your two faces!"

Chip and Sam could both smell the alcohol on the boy's breath. "Nice to see you, too, Mumma," Chip replied with a frown.

"Actually, I'm surprised to see you here," Sam said, immediately probing. "Didn't you think of Muffy as a bitch who got what she deserved?"

"She did, but that don't mean I can't drink to her. Best thing that ever happened to me was that little skirt breaking up with me freshman year. Now, let me guess. You two twats were invited by Brent, and you came to join his little harem."

Mumma motioned to the small set of stairs of the split-level that led down to the home's family room where Brent could be seen sitting on a sofa surrounded by four girls from school. Muffy's friends and rivals had not waited long to descend on the jock, offering him their comfort. He had girls on either side of him, stroking his dark, wavy hair. One girl was on the floor, at his feet, with her hand on his right knee. Sam was a bit dismayed to see that the fourth member was Barbara who was sitting on the recliner facing Brent, a sad and sympathetic look on her face.

Mumma continued, "Alright, here are the rules for you two. If there are only two beers left in any cooler, they ain't yours. You leave them. Don't stare at anyone making out. Don't talk to any of the cheerleaders or any of the pom-poms. None of them are drunk enough yet. And, most important of all, do NOT talk to me!"

And with that, Mumma turned away from them and waded back through the crowded house, out the sliding glass patio door in the kitchen, and into the backyard where more teenage, Catholic debauchery was being had. Chip grumbled to Sam, "So, how's that newfound popularity working out for you?"

"Can it, bro. We're here to do a job."

"No, you're here to do a job. Remember, I'm fine just coasting. Chillin'. There's no killer here, man. Just a bunch of killer a-holes. If it was anybody from school, I bet it was that French, suave bastard, Fabrice. I never trusted him."

"The foreign exchange student? Nah, he went back to Paris when the school year ended."

"Well, it's not one of these mouth-breathers. And I'll tell you what. It ain't my man Chet either. That dude's an awesome boss. He's giving me free CDs, like, every day! They kick the shit out of 8-tracks and cassette tapes. And, by the way, he gets more tail than a toilet. Hot chicks come into our store every day asking for him."

"Had Muffy had been one of them?" Sam replied.

It was a question that Chip didn't have an answer to. He had started his job after Muffy was killed, and he never saw her in the store at any other time. She could have had a crush on him that went bad. Chet was one of those Don Johnson types. Handsome face, slicked-back Pat Riley hair, the perfect amount of beard stubble at all times. He didn't go for the "Miami Vice" pastels either, but instead preferred a wardrobe of cool grays and blacks. He probably even looked great in the '70s, Chip thought. He probably had a young Robert Redford thing going.

"Maybe," Chip conceded. "I'll tell ya what. Just this once, I'll go feel Brent out on this, if only to clear Chet's good name. Why don't you--"

"Go feel Barbara out?"

Chip chuckled. "Yeah, out. Not up."

———

Chip waited until there was a spot on the family-room couch for him to sit down and have his chat with Brent. The girl on Chip's right side had gotten up to get another drink, and the girl on the floor at Brent's knee had sprung up moments earlier when her boyfriend entered the room from outside. It was only the one girl, Elena Eveler, and Barbara left. And, hopefully, Barbara would soon find herself chatting with Sam. For now, though, she sat there quiet, not saying anything.

"How you doin', buddy?" Chip asked.

Outside, they could all hear a dozen or more kids scream-singing Van Halen's "Summer Nights" in drunken unison. Brent looked pained. The party was getting more and more loud and boisterous. "Maybe this was a mistake," he said in a tired voice. "I thought a party would do me good. My parents went away for the weekend. Our neighbors went with them. I slipped fifty bucks to our other neighbors to not call the cops. We practically have the night and the cul-de-sac to ourselves. But nothing's helping. I still feel awful."

Brent then looked over at Barbara and sang drunkenly off-key, "Take a look at me now!"

Barbara gave him a small smile. Then, she quietly got up, a tear forming in one of her eyes, and made her way over to the beer keg in the corner of the room.

Chip waited until Barbara left to resume his conversation with Brent. He noticed Elena had fallen asleep on the quarterback's shoulder, snoring a bit, a beer bottle still in her right hand. By the dozen or so empty bottles on the table in front of them, he surmised that wasn't the first she had downed. Brent was looking a little bleary-eyed from drinking, too. He could barely keep his head upright.

"I hate to see you like this, Brent. I wish there was something I could do," Chip said, looking for some turn of phrase that would turn the conversation to Chet even in an offhand way to see how he would respond. Then, it hit him. "Hey, do you like music?"

Brent sucked on his beer like a baby on a bottle. Swallowing, he answered, "Yeah, who doesn't it?"

"Well, I just got hired at the Harmony Hut in the mall. Why don't you come by sometime next week, and I'll hook you up with a couple of CDs."

"Harmony Hut?" Brent slurred.

"Yeah, you know, the music and record store. You come by on Monday or Tuesday when it's slow, and I'll take you in the back room. You won't believe some of the promotional stuff my boss gets from the record companies, stuff we don't even put out for sale. Posters and T-shirts and music samples."

"Your ... boss?"

"Yeah. Chet. Good man. Cool guy."

"Chet?! Chet ... Robitaille?!" Brent made a move to get up, but fell back down to the couch. He landed on Elena's head, who had fallen to the cushions when Brent arose. He lurched forward, briefly bumping heads with Chip. Then, in a surprisingly coordinated motion, he grabbed Chip by the shirt. "You work for Chet Freakin' Robitaille, that lying sack of shit?!"

Chip winced at the pull. Adjusting his body so that Brent only had shirt and not skin or what few chest hairs he had, he answered, "Uh, yeah. I do. Something wrong, Brent? You got a problem with Chet?"

Brent suddenly got a strange look on his face, like he had let a secret slip from his lips. He rose up and, this time, he managed to successfully make it to his feet. He stumbled the first two steps, but then righted himself. He started to walk away in a slow, measured pace, heading towards the steps that led back up to the kitchen and living room level of his house. As he made it onto the first step, he looked back at Chip and said cryptically, "I got no problems with no one. Not anymore."

———

The downstairs beer keg was empty, so Barbara exited for one of the two outdoor bars Brent and his buddies had set up in the backyard. Sam followed her out there, making little effort to hide the fact that he was essentially stalking the girl, waiting for an opening. When she saw him, she just sighed. No frown. No rolling of the eyes. Just a long, annoyed, highly audible sigh.

"I deserve that," Sam said. "That and probably a whole lot more."

At this point, he thought, there was no point in being shy or timid or holding anything back. He'd known Barbara since junior high. He could remember playing tag and dodgeball and Capture the Flag with her and the other kids back on the playground. He recalled going to birthday parties at Shakey's Pizza and Farrell's Ice Cream where she was present. It never stung that girls like Muffy didn't give him the time of day. But it hurt like Hell that Barbara was now like that. He tried to remind her of the old days.

"Come on, Barbara. How many years we got between us? We got a lot of years. What can I say? I'm a buffoon." When she still didn't look at him, he figured the most direct route was the best. "Alright, I'm sorry I tried to hit on you at your best friend's funeral! Do you forgive me?"

Barbara shook her head. She always found Sam to be a fairly simple boy. And she liked that he didn't have much in the way of filters. She was still navigating the "in" crowd herself, and she had dropped a number of friendships when Muffy and Elena and the others took a liking to her. She briefly thought of asking Sam's forgiveness, but she wasn't willing to go that far. She would only say, "You *are* a buffoon." But she said it with a slight smile.

The fact that the corners of her mouth were raised ever so slightly was the most encouraging sign Sam had seen from her in months. "Yeah," he replied, "but I'm most certainly NOT a parasite!"

Finally, she looked at him. "Yeah, that was kind of harsh, wasn't it? Sorry for that."

Sam muttered a quick "Apology accepted," but then he fell quiet. There was an awkward silence that followed, as Sam fumbled for the next thing to say to her. He didn't want to utter something stupid again that would be perceived as a come-on. So, maybe he should just quit while he was ahead, he thought. Then again, he wasn't really at the party to beg her forgiveness. He was there to start putting together a puzzle. Was Barbara part of that puzzle? He couldn't bring himself to believe that. There was no way.

But as the seconds turned into at least a minute with nothing said, Sam started to grow a little desperate. He said the only thing that popped into his head. "I should never have tried to put on act with you. You can't do that to a modern woman."

Barbara laughed immediately. "Modern woman? Me?"

"Uh ... well ... yeah. You bet you are."

Barbara turned almost flirty. "Modern woman," she repeated, her eyes suddenly dancing a bit. "Yeah, I am! Thanks, Sam. So, what does that make you?"

Sam struggled to recall the rest of the lyrics that Buddy had not so smoothly worked into their conversation earlier. What was the term he used? "An old-fashioned man, I guess" he said.

They chatted for a few more minutes, mostly about Muffy, recalling her beauty and her many accomplishments. When they were finished and Barbara went off to be with some of her girlfriends, Sam found Chip inside still in the Fitzpatrick house's family room. Sam wasn't even ashamed that he hadn't asked Barbara anything about the murder and if she knew anything more than she was letting on. He was just so happy to report: "Dude, I think I just made some progress with Barbara!"

Chip, though, was still deep in thought about his odd, intense exchange with Brent minutes earlier. He sat on the family-room sofa, drinking a beer of his own, Elena Eveler still passed out next to him and now in a full snore. He looked up at Sam, then took a gander at Brent's last school photo that was framed and displayed on his parent's downstairs hearth. In a low, wistful tone, Chip said to Sam, "Unfortunately, I think I just made some progress, too."

CHAPTER 6

Sam was still thinking about the party the next morning when he found himself, of all places, on a paintball range. He was there with his father, Calvin Eckert, who looked like a slightly older, even chubbier version of himself. Sam had heard him described by several people as a "boy-man" or a "man-child." And as he got older, he was starting to see why. Calvin was the one who had shown Sam the "Star Wars," "Superman," James Bond, and "Indiana Jones" movies umpteen times. He was the one who took him to see R-rated flicks like "Blade Runner," "The Thing," and "National Lampoon's Vacation," always taking the heat from Francine when he returned him to her Sunday evenings.

Under the terms of his parents' divorce years earlier, Sam spent every other weekend with his dad. It was always a thrill when Sam was younger, as it usually meant a weekend of going to the movies, eating bad food at places like Little Tavern Hamburgers and Jerry's Sub Shop, and watching mindless TV like "The Love Boat" and "Fantasy Island" on Saturday nights.

But as Sam went from an adolescent to a teen, seeing his dad every other weekend was still fun. But Calvin was a much better father to him when he was a little kid than he had been the past couple of years as Sam developed real teenager issues and real teenager problems. Calvin missed his little boy, his little buddy, his little partner in crime.

But this weekend was different. Why were they on a paintball range at 10 o'clock on a Friday morning? As it turns out, it was to be Sam's first bachelor party. Frank Vallone, one of the mechanics who worked with

Calvin at the Lube Job, was getting married that weekend. His wife had ordered him to not have any strippers or hookers at his bachelor party. Also, there was to be no gambling or drinking, as Frank was a recovering alcoholic. So, that left paintball. And because there was to be no hanky-panky, booze, or games of chance, he could only round up three other guys from the shop. Calvin asked if his son could tag along, and Vallone gave a resounding "Yes! The more, the merrier!"

The other three guys were what you would describe as "grease monkeys." There was DeFao, the oldest of the mechanics. He was a tall, strapping man who had such big feet that his footwear was often described as "clown's shoes." There was Alejandro, the handsome, young ladies man of the shop. Single women and even a few married ones would pull their little Chevettes, VW bugs, and other cute cars into his bay, requesting his personal service. They'd even drive around and get in line again if they picked the wrong bay. And there was Mr. Liepens, the franchise owner of the Lube Job who gave his employees the morning off as long as he could tag along, too.

Sam was excited. Paintball had only been around for a few years and was completely new to Maryland. He had heard that this was the closest thing to real war you'd ever want to experience. The range was in a densely wooded area in rural Howard County. As Vallone and the others checked in at the front desk, Sam peeked through the office's lone window that overlooked the range. Mixed in with the various trees, the large, fenced-in area was filled with barricades and boulders for the various "paintballers" to hide behind while taking aim at each other. There was a slightly raised, wooden fort in the middle; a couple of dug-out foxholes; and even what looked like a makeshift command bunker on the far side. Everything was covered with splashes of bright blue, orange, green, and yellow paint.

Sam's visions of zipping around the range like John Rambo shooting everything in sight and not getting shot himself were interrupted by Vallone's booming voice. "Listen up, everyone!" he called out. "Jedediah here has a proposition for us."

Jedediah was the bearded, gap-toothed operator of the range. He wore jeans and a ratty old red plaid flannel shirt that had stains on it from at least the last couple of meals the man had eaten. He was a big man, who certainly commanded attention. "Alright y'alls," he said. "Now you can certainly go out there and shoot each other up. And that would be some big fun, that's for sure. But since y'alls got such a small number of ballers, and this is a slow mornin' here, my staff and I can show you boys a much better time. I think it'd be more fun if y'alls worked together and took us on out there on that there range. What do ya say?"

Vallone had such a look of joy and anticipation on his face, that the others couldn't say "No." After all, paintball really was meant for a group of 10 or more, not six. Taking on some real paintballers suddenly seemed like a great idea. Sam's dad playfully slapped his son on the shoulder. "You ready for this, Private?" he asked, in a mock Army guy voice. Then, turning to the group and imitating Jedediah, Calvin asked aloud, "Y'alls ready for some big fun? Y'alls ready to get it on out there on that there range, y'alls?!"

Sam was the only one of the group who noticed that Jedediah heard the whole thing, peering out from behind a curtain where he and his staff had started changing into their range outfits. Sam sensed immediately a mistake had possibly been made.

The first thing Vallone's group noticed was how old and scuffed up their rifles were. A couple of the guns, you had to squeeze the trigger three or four times before one paintball would discharge. The fatigues Jedediah gave them to change into were covered in splotches of paint from previous failed paintballers. And the goggles were ratty and old. Their straps had to be manually tied like shoelaces in order for the protective glasses to stay on their heads.

But it was still an exciting time, walking out on that range, going to the one end dressed head to toe like the Rebel commandoes on Endor. Vallone was the most excited. "This is gonna be so bad-ass!" he kept repeating, putting increasingly greater emphasis on the word "so" each time he uttered it.

DeFao was already uncomfortable and tripping over his own feet on the uneven, wooded ground. He couldn't even find a good tree to hide behind that would cover his full body. Each barricade and boulder always left some part of him exposed to enemy fire. "Look at me," he lamented, "I'm gonna be out in, like, 30 seconds. We should have gone to a titty bar."

Liepens was just happy to be with his employees. "I think this is going to be a marvelous team-building exercise," he stated. "This is the kind of thing corporate has been asking us to do with staff for some time now. Good choice, Frank. Good choice!"

Sam was about to say something when his Casio calculator watch that his dad gave him for his last birthday beeped. It beeped every hour on the hour, and he didn't know how to turn it off. DeFao jumped on the beep immediately. "Turn that shit off!" he barked. "If you're hiding out on the range, it's just gonna get you shot!"

"It only beeps on the hour, sir."

"Turn it off, or leave it in office!" Sam looked to his father for help, but the man shrunk from conflict and didn't come to his defense. That was kind of his dad's M.O. over the years, especially around guys like DeFao who intimidated him with either size or force of personality. Sam took the watch off and left it behind.

Alejandro, by contrast, was a much more quiet man. Sam looked at him, preparing for battle, and thought a number of clichéd phrases he had heard over the years -- phrases like "He has his game face on" and "He's got the eye of the tiger." Sam didn't know Alejandro as well as the other men, but he liked him a lot. The guy could easily be a male model or an actor. He was that good-looking. He spoke very little English, which leant him a bit of mystery. Instead, he smiled a lot. But he wasn't smiling that morning. He was squinting, peering out across the range at the first sign of activity on the other side. Roughly 100 yards away, Jedediah's forces began to amass. And under his breath, Alejandro muttered a few choice profanities in his native language.

Sam followed the man's gaze across the way. When he saw what Alejandro was seeing, he also let out a quiet "Oh, shit."

Jedediah and his five staffers had appeared on the other side of the paintball range in complete, head-to-toe battle fatigues and camouflage. "What the hell are they wearing?" Sam asked aloud. "And what's that on their heads?"

"Looks like military-style ski masks," Sam's dad replied.

"I can't tell them apart," Vallone added.

"And look at those ... those ... hand cannons!" DeFao marveled. Jedediah and his staffers' firearms were the latest in professional paintball weaponry. They were indeed souped-up, brand-new, tricked-out, top-of-the line "hand cannons," each fitted with long-range sniper scopes.

"Oh, man," DeFao lamented. "What are we doing here? What are we doing here?!"

Calvin was similarly concerned. "Yeah, we're just six schmoes out to have a good time on a Friday morning."

Then, a loud horn sounded, and Jedediah and the five other Yahoos immediately sprang into action. Their first move was to fan out and rush forward about 35 yards, taking cover behind the first few barricades all before Vallone and his men could squeeze off even a single shot. Frank, Sam, Calvin, DeFao, Liepens, and Alejandro were slow to follow suit, scrambling to get to their initial barricades as paintballs whizzed by them. DeFao was stuck in the left arm and right knee by separate shooters. But otherwise, he was still in the game. The others had yet to be hit.

Alejandro managed to fire the first shots of the bachelor party team, but his paintballs landed well short of their targets. DeFao noticed this and bellowed, "These cheap-ass guns have NO range! I doubt I could even shoot myself with them."

Sam, already out of breath from the first gallant rush, agreed, "We're gonna have to practically be on top of them to hit 'em!"

The six guys then started hearing strange sounds. They sounded like rhythmic bird tweets. The bachelor partiers looked at each other puzzled, then peered out across the range at their adversaries. "What in the hell are they doing?" Vallone asked, straining to see through his smudged-up goggles that were catching each of his frantic breaths and fogging up as a result.

DeFao, an experienced hunter, was the first to realize. "Oh my God!" he exclaimed, before clueing the others in. He recognized that the professional paintballers had begun using military hand signals to coordinate their attack. One of them indeed had a bird call-like thing he was doing with his lips that would prompt each of his team members' movements.

Sam and Calvin fired off a few rounds of paintballs that didn't come close to hitting their sprinting targets. Within three seconds of father and son rising up, the lead paintballer -- the one who had been sending out the bird calls and coordinating the assault -- provided rapid-fire cover hitting both Calvin and Sam several times in the arms, shoulders, and torso.

Back in a crouched position behind his barricade, Sam looked at his dad and almost laughed at how splattered with paint he was. Then, he looked over towards Alejandro, who was suddenly nowhere to be found. Liepens remained behind his barricade about 10 feet to Sam's left, rubbing one of his knees which he had apparently banged against the hard ground when taking cover. Meanwhile, DeFao and Vallone were trying to locate a target to fire at, but couldn't find one.

Sam locked eyes with DeFao, who was starting to breathe heavier and heavier the more he heard enemy footsteps drawing closer. "Uh, guys!" DeFao exclaimed, starting to freak out. "These dudes are some serious dudes! I don't want this!"

Then, all of a sudden, they seemed to be surrounded on all sides. Paintball fire erupted from every direction. "I don't want this!" DeFao kept screaming as paintballs rat-tat-tatted his back, chest, groin, and leg. "I told you we should have gone to a titty bar!!!"

Vallone started hollering, too. "This hurts SO bad! I'm sorry, guys! I am so, so sorry!"

The paintballers shot up Calvin the most, in obvious retribution for his earlier impression of Jedediah. As they fired, the heavily armed group of Jethros yelled things like "BOO-YAH!" and "Fire on the mountain, run boy run!" After what seemed like five minutes of this, but was only about 30 or 45 seconds, Sam and the others looked like they had been attacked by a platoon of demented impressionist painters. They were covered in so many colors.

"I guess we win this round!" Jedediah said from behind his mask.

"This round?!" Vallone and the guys answered in unison.

Jedediah started cackling. He took off his mask, looked at Sam's dad, and asked mockingly, "Aw, what's the matter? Ain't y'alls havin' fun?" His cackle continued for a few more seconds until he suddenly realized something. "Hey," he said, looking around. "Where's that I-talian guy who was with 'em?

The paintballer standing closest to his boss also pulled off his mask, gazed about, and said, "I dunno. But I thought he was Mexican."

The next one also pulled off his mask and added, "No, no. He was one of them A-rabs. A right pretty one, too. I was really looking forward to lightin' him up!"

Then, from about 10 feet behind them and from up above, Alejandro revealed his position. Without anyone noticing, he had somehow climbed one of the trees on the range, got a foothold, and stayed there until the paintballers had let down their guard. In one motion, he dropped down, landed square on his feet, took aim, and shot each of the Jethros in rapid-fire succession, squeezing his trigger as fast and as hard as he could. As he did so, he mockingly cried out, "BONZAI!"

When it was all over, Jedediah threw down his weapon, kicked it a few feet in front of him, and lamented, "Bonzai?! That sumbitch is Asian?!"

———

The bachelor party broke up soon after the paintball debacle. Their team was technically triumphant. But when only one man is left standing out of a total of 12, it's a pretty empty victory. At any rate, Vallone left by himself bitter and dejected that his "last hurrah" wasn't more fun. Liepens, DeFao, and Alejandro returned to the shop to put in a full shift. And Calvin had the day off, which he intended to spend with his son.

They set off in Calvin's car for one of their favorite eating spots: the lunch counter at Woolworth's. The old timers at the mall called Woolworth's the "dime store." More accurately, it was more like today's "dollar stores." It wasn't the store where you went and got back-to-school supplies or cold medicine or Halloween candy. That was the drug stores in town like Peoples Drug, Dart Drug, and Drug Fair.

Woolworth's was a bargain-priced, odds-and-ends store. It had toys and hardware supplies, yarn and knitting materials, books and a small music section. And it had the vaunted lunch counter that had been there since the 1950s where you could get a turkey club or a tuna melt or a grilled cheese sandwich. Two waitresses, usually quite old, worked the counter at all times even when it was empty. But for lunch on a weekday, it was rarely empty.

Sam and his dad were thrilled that their favorite waitress was there that day. Her name was Miss Lucy. She was an elderly African-American lady, who had worked the lunch counter for the past 15 years. Miss Lucy made the absolute best burger and chocolate milkshake combo in town. She was old, but she wasn't the kind of old that made you want to jump over the counter and give her help. Miss Lucy could still handle her business. She ruled that lunch counter. It was her domain. And she knew most of her regulars by name and lunch order.

"The usual?" she asked, with a slight giggle as Sam and Calvin approached.

"You bet, Miss Lucy!" Calvin replied.

Miss Lucy's laugh was that of a "Ah tee hee!" That morning, she felt compelled to turn to the customer sitting three stools down from where Calvin and Sam parked themselves to say. "Ah, tee, hee! These two boys have been coming in here since that one was knee-high and his daddy had no gray. And they order the same thing every single time. Burger and a chocolate shake, burger and a chocolate shake!"

Lucy got to work, and the customer she was talking to turned to Calvin and Sam and seemed to look down at both their pudgy frames. "Yeah, yeah, I know," Calvin said. "The last thing my son and I need are more burgers and shakes."

The customer, who could have easily passed for a barfly if this had been a tavern or drafthouse, took a cigarette from his ear, lit it, and said to them, "Eat away, brothers. Eat away, drink away, and smoke away. We're only on this rock once and for a short time. Just ask Len Bias."

"Bias?" Calvin asked aloud.

Len Bias had been in the news all week. He had been a star on the University of Maryland men's basketball team and was the second overall pick in the NBA Draft that had been held just three days earlier in New York City. He was due to make millions with the Boston Celtics. Most agreed that he was going to be the "next Michael Jordan," who had just been drafted two seasons earlier but was already making nightly highlight reels with his amazing dunks and clutch shooting.

When the stranger didn't answer right away, both Calvin and Sam sensed a certain heaviness come over the man. "What's happened to Bias?" Calvin asked.

The customer wasn't much for conversation. He reached into his pocket, pulled out a $10 bill, slapped it down on the counter, and said with as little tact as possible, "He's dead."

Both Eckerts were stunned. "What?!" they asked in unison.

"How?!"

"When?"

"When?" the man answered, leaving the counter. "Overnight. How? Radio and the TV says it was too much nose candy. Cocaine overdose."

"Oh my God," Calvin said softly.

He had just watched the NBA Draft on cable Tuesday night. Len Bias was practically a basketball God in those parts back then. He was on the same level as Patrick Ewing, Eric "Sleepy" Floyd, Albert King, and Buck Williams. He was going to be bigger than all of those local Maryland and Georgetown stars. A can't-miss, sure-fire future All-Star who was going to play with and get schooled in the ways of the pro game by Larry Bird, Kevin McHale, and Robert Parrish. The vaunted Celtics trio had just won another NBA Championship two weeks earlier over the Houston Rockets.

"I can't believe it," Sam said. "First Muffy and now Len Bias?!"

"Believe it, boy," the stranger said, wrapping a newspaper under his arm and heading towards the store's exit. "And like I said. Eat away, my brothers. Eat away, drink away, smoke away. Just don't snort away!"

Father and son listened to the man as he walked away cackling at his own bad joke. They then sat in stunned silence, taking in the loss of the young superstar. Calvin had taken Sam to a couple of Maryland Terrapins basketball games in the Len Bias era. Both times, the Terps won and Bias was brilliant, making clutch shots and throwing down rim-shaking dunks that got the students, fans, and alumni out of their seats and into a frenzy. He was like a Superman to many.

"Remember that 'helicopter dunk' we saw Bias throw down against Carolina?" Calvin asked, thinking about a play he saw in person, but didn't get to see the replay of until he got home that night and watched Channel 9 sportscaster Glenn Brenner repeat it three times on his 11 o'clock sportscast.

"Do I ever?" Sam replied, wide-eyed at the memory. "The way he gripped the ball with both hands and circled it around his head before he dunked. I think that was the most totally awesome play I've ever seen in person. Must be only three or four guys tops who could get the hang time to pull that dunk off."

Sam "talked with his hands," as his mother called his gestures, raving on about other great plays Bias became famous for during his college career. The alley oop in transition against Navy when he dueled David Robinson all afternoon. The turnaround jump shot he made against Duke late in their ACC Tournament match-up. Mostly, Sam just remembered the guy's big, kid-like smiles and excitement for being out there on the court, competing.

Sam was starting to feel profoundly sad at the loss. In the moment, he felt sadder over the passing of a man he never knew and had never actually met than for his classmate, Muffy. And part of him felt ashamed about that. "I've never been around this much death, Dad," he said quietly. "I hear Mel and the other old-timers at the mall talk about it all of the time. But I'm 15 and they're, like, a hundred."

Calvin put his hand on his son's arm and just held it gently. His boy was growing up. His forearm was meaty and big like his, like a man's forearm. And hairy, too. He hadn't noticed how mannish his boy was becoming until he was sitting there at that lunch counter, watching him process loss.

"I actually know how you're feeling," he said to him. "My decade growing up was the '60s, and it seemed like every six months or so we lost somebody big. JFK, RFK, MLK. There was Jim Morrison and Jimi Hendrix, Mama Cass and Janis Joplin, Judy Garland and Marilyn Monroe. God, I remember finding out about Jim Morrison. It was also at a restaurant. Pizza parlor actually. A bunch of hippies two tables over were crying and singing, 'This Is the End.' They sang the whole damn song. I asked the waitress what the deal was. And, obviously on drugs herself, she looked at me with this stoned look on her face and she said, 'Between what is known and unknown lie ... the Doors.' I said, 'Huh? What?' And she said, 'Jimmy's on the other side of the doors now, man.' She actually said all that. Real slow, too, just like I just said it. And I actually knew exactly what she meant! I just knew he was dead."

"Well, this is all new to me," Sam lamented. "And it's all happening in one year. First the Challenger back in January. Then, Muffy earlier this week. And now Len Bias?!"

By that point, Miss Lucy had milkshakes ready and in front of them. Sam started sipping his shake right away, seeking some comfort in the chocolaty delight. Calvin, though, could only stare at his shake. Sam's sadness was starting to wash over him now. "This is embarrassing to say, but..."

Sam was instantly curious. "What? What's embarrassing."

"It's silly, but I'm feeling a bit guilty here."

"Why?"

"Well, you know what a big Bullets fan I am, right? That's my team. I've been bleeding red, white, and blue ever since Unseld, Grevey, and Bobby D won the title eight years ago. When Bias got drafted by the freakin' Celtics of all teams this week, I got real mad watching it on TV. I hate Boston. Bird, McHale, Dennis Johnson. They're so damn arrogant. They win everything. And they're all ugly as sin. Ugliest damn champions ever! And then they were getting Len Freakin' Bias because of some stupid trade for draft picks years ago?! They were going to go from Bird to Bias and be set for another decade. Washington's been mediocre year in and year out ever since '79, and who do we get in the Draft? Freak shows like Kenny Green and Manute Bol. I loved Bias, but I could never have rooted for him in Celtics green. I was so bitter, sitting there on my couch and begrudging this kid his dream."

"Yeah, but you didn't wish death on him, Dad!" Sam said, with a slight chuckle. Calvin's pause to reply caused Sam to inquire, "You didn't, did you?"

"No, of course not. But I came close. And I'm really kind of ashamed of myself, you know?"

His father rarely opened up to him about anything serious. They spent most of their weekends together talking about trivial stuff -- sports and movies and TV. But Calvin seemed to be really making an effort here to go a little deeper. The little Chip voice inside Sam's head kept saying, "Don't share back! Don't tell him about the newspaper! Don't tell him anything!" But Calvin was his dad. He wanted to share with him. It was as basic a biological craving as he could have.

"Not half as ashamed as I am about what I've been doing and thinking lately," Sam said, knowing full well that it wouldn't take much coaxing to say more.

"Oh?" Calvin said simply.

Sam took a long sip from his milkshake, almost like it was some kind of alcoholic beverage that would give him "liquid courage." Taking a deep breath, he keyed his father in on all that had happened in the wake of Muffy's death. Calvin took it all in. At first, when he told him about the newspaper photo, his initial inclination was to laugh. It was actually a funny story. But it would probably be even funnier telling it years from now to people not involved.

Then, Sam got to the part that was a little "dicey," as he termed it. "So, I feel really guilty about all this, Dad. I shouldn't suddenly be friends with jocks like Brent and his buddies. I shouldn't be going to parties at the house of the star quarterback. But it's really been awesome! I just can't quite enjoy it, though. I know. It's that Catholic guilt thing being churned up. Always thinking of my next confession. So, I'm trying to be proactive. To make up for it -- and this is the part that's dicey, that you're probably not gonna like -- I've teamed up with Mr. Rabinowitz to help him catch the killer."

"You what?!"

"Rabinowitz? You know, that sad-sack P.I. who's always at the mall, trying to catch people having affairs. The McGregor family's hired him to find out who killed Muffy. Since he despises kids, and teenagers specifically, I'm helping him work the school angle."

Calvin adjusted himself on his lunch counter stool. The cushioned seat rotated with a slight creak. What Sam was proposing sounded extremely dangerous to him. Then, he thought about it for a few more moments, and he was sure of it. This *was* dangerous! Calvin's sense of parental protection instantly kicked in ... but not before his fear of his ex-wife. "Does your mother know about this?"

"No! And don't tell her ... please! She'd never allow it."

"Son, I'm not sure I'm allowing it! This nutjob's already killed once. What happens if you find out who it is. Then, *your* life could be in danger!"

Sam's little Chip voice suddenly started screaming "I told you so!" in his head. But Sam was determined. "Oh come on, Dad. I'm trusting you here. We've always been buddies first, right?"

"Yeah, about that--"

"Look, it's like Rabinowitz said. The police will probably catch this guy before we will. And, come on, you know I go to school with a bunch of silver-spoon-sucking, rich kids. The only thing they know about cars is how to let their parents pay for them. I really will be fine. Please don't tell Mom. Please?!"

The rest of the lunch was awkward. Miss Lucy brought the Eckert boys their burgers. The two sat there and ate them, slurping down their shakes. And when they did speak, they retreated back into their comfort zone. They remembered more great Len Bias plays. They talked about their food and the hot, humid June weather outside. They debated whether or not they should see the new "Karate Kid" movie opening that day or wait for their next weekend together. Calvin, though, couldn't help but feel a vague sense of dread where his boy was concerned.

————

When the two had finished with lunch, they were surprised to walk outside and find the June humidity had broke. A slight and steady breeze rushed through the parking lot of the open-air Laurel Shopping Center where Woolworth's was based alongside People's Drug, Albee's Shoes, Bart's Barber Shop, a Giant Food grocery store, and Buddy's family's cinema.

Calvin felt like driving, so he suggested they go visit Sam's grandfather's grave over at Fort Lincoln Cemetery. Sam hadn't been there since he and his dad put a Christmas wreath on the man's tombstone back in December. He could see that it was important to his dad, so he agreed without argument.

It was about a 30-minute drive out to Fort Lincoln, and the two flipped radio channels the whole way, alternating between the two Top 40 stations Sam liked and DC 101 rock radio that Calvin favored that played everything from Metallica to Judas Priest to Black Sabbath. It was a good mix of songs. Not a dud in the bunch. And it kept father and son from talking still.

Fort Lincoln had been voted one of the 10 Most Scenic Cemeteries in the United States for several years running. It was a massive grave-yard, separated into gardens each with a Biblical theme. There was the Garden of the Apostles, the Garden of the Meditation, the Garden of the Commandments, and so forth. Sam's grandfather was buried in the

Garden of the Crucifixion. It sat at the highest point of the cemetery on top of a hill that overlooked much of that part of Maryland's Prince George's County and on into D.C. At its center was a massive stone cross, 20 feet tall, with a chiseled figure of Jesus Christ hanging on it.

Graveside, Sam and his father were still largely quiet with each other. They had bought a small bouquet of flowers from one of the vendors positioned just outside the cemetery's entrance. Calvin placed the mix of roses and carnations in a vase that came out of the ground from just in front of his father's tombstone. He knelt and said a quick, silent prayer. And just as quickly as he had bent down, he got back up into a standing position until he was shoulder to shoulder with Sam.

"Losing my dad," he said, clearing his throat after his voice slightly cracked, "that was a really big turning point in my life, Sam. I wasn't much older than you are now. Suddenly, everything was different. I knew my future was going to be so different, and it scared the heck out of me. I don't think that I've not been scared since. It's why your mom and me didn't last. Not because we didn't love each other or because we fought and argued. Neither one of us cheated or fell out of love. It was all me and my dumb fears."

Sam put his hand on his dad's shoulders. He really didn't expect this, and he really didn't know far this was going to go. He'd seen movies with people blubbering at gravesides. And this whole scene felt like something out of a film. Except it wasn't a movie. It was real. Sam wasn't bitter towards his father at all. As divorces go, his mom and dad got along pretty well once apart. And Sam never went through a period where he blamed either parent. It was just his "normal." In his mind, there really wasn't any cause for his father to be contrite or remorseful at all.

"It's OK, Dad. It is what it is," he said.

Calvin had yet to shed a tear. He seemed to be going out of his way to not cry. "I know," he said. "I know it's all OK. It's surprisingly OK, all things considered, huh? Look at you. You're awesome. You're an awesome kid. But whenever I come here and I look down at my dad's name and his birth date and his death date, I just know..."

Calvin's voice trailed off. But Sam wanted him to complete his thought. "What, Dad? What do you just know?"

Calvin didn't look at him. He just kept looking down at the stone. Finally, he said, "I just know I would have been a better man had he lived. I look at you, and I listen to you. And you got no fear. I mean, you want to go after a killer! And, of course, that scares the crap out of me. But, you know, we all have turning points in our life, and it sounds like this girl's death is going to be one of yours. Just answer me one thing."

"What, Dad? Anything."

"You don't want to do this to get more popular at school, do you? Because if that's so, that's a real bullshit reason, son. Popularity isn't a real thing. Not really. Those kids aren't having any more fun than you and Chip and Buddy. And it's just a trap you'll fall right back into if you go to college or wherever you end up working. Jeez, just look at the Lube Job. You think I like DeFao bullying me and everyone else around? I hate it. You think I like that Alejandro is Mr. Popular, Mr. Ladies Man, Mr. Let Me Change This Tire Using Only My Penis? Heck, no. But, like you said, it is what it is. High school is temporary, man. But death? When you're dead, Sam, you're a long-time dead. You hear what I'm saying?"

Sam circled around his grandfather's grave until he was looking right at his father. He felt like Calvin was leading up to something big. "Yeah, I hear you. But I'm not sure I'm following you. Where are you going with this, Dad?"

"Where am I going with this? I'll tell you where I am going with this. I can't imagine what those McGregors are feeling right now. You know Muffy came into the Lube Job a couple of times with that Fiero of hers. Man, could she turn heads. She was special. And you're special, too. If I forbid you to help Rabinowitz, you're gonna help him anyway. Even if I rat you out to your mom, you're still gonna do this. Aren't you, son?"

Sam shook his head. He was indeed that committed. "Yeah," he answered his dad softly.

Calvin stepped towards his son and put his arm around him. Then, leading him away from the elder Eckert's grave, he declared, "Fine. Then, I'm gonna help you!"

"What?!"

"I'm gonna help you!"

"Dad, you don't have to--"

"You never could put together a jigsaw puzzle without me, and I could never finish a crossword puzzle without you. And this is, like ... the ultimate puzzle! And, so, I'm gonna help you, Sam. I don't know how I'm gonna help you. But I'm gonna help you!"

CHAPTER 7

"Sir, you get the HELL out of here right now!"

Chet Robitaille, the manager of Harmony Hut, was always very polite. It came from a Southern upbringing and years of top-notch, mall-based retail management, a career that had seen him move from lowly stock boy at Herman's Sporting Goods to sales clerk and eventually assistant manager at Commander Salamander in D.C.'s Georgetown neighborhood to manager of the best, most visible, most happening store at the Laurel Centre Mall ... the record store.

But his politeness had its limits. An annoying, little private investigator had been hanging around his store for the better part of the last two days. Mervyn Rabinowitz stuck out like a proverbial sore thumb on that side of the mall, at least three decades older than the teens and young twenty-somethings who made up Chet's core customers, along with the core clientele of the stores nearest Harmony Hut -- Spencer's, Chess King, and Friendly's. And Chet had heard that the detective had been asking questions about him, specifically about a recent argument he had in public.

Rabinowitz looked a bit scared, but more exasperated than anything. Chet's voice boomed over the very loud music playing over the store's speakers. Rabinowitz knew he shouldn't have ventured into Harmony Hut a second time in as many days. He should have stayed near the store, close to it, on the fringes. But he wasn't getting anywhere talking to random patrons and mall employees as they passed by. No one was answering his questions fully. Several people had seen parts of Chet and Muffy's altercation. But no one had seen the whole thing from beginning to end. Others had heard about it, but no consistent story had developed. No one knew how the fight started. Most knew how it ended ... with Chet storming off.

"I'm just doing my job," Rabinowitz replied. "But I get it. Your shop. I'm going, I'm going."

He turned to leave and got almost out of the store when he heard Chet call out, "You know, sir. If you want actual answers about something I did or did not do, did you ever think of asking me?"

Charles "Chet" Robitaille was from Louisiana, and you could still hear his accent from that part of the country in his voice. But he looked very much like he could have been an extra on "Miami Vice." Not Don Johnson, specifically. But incredibly good-looking, with a perpetual tan and a thick mane of hair combed straight back that always seemed to look like it was flowing in a slight breeze.

Rabinowitz could see why he had garnered the reputation of a ladies' man. But usually the ladies men he had come in contact with over the years were on the receiving end of anger ... from their girlfriends, from their girlfriends' boyfriends, from cheated-on spouses. By all accounts, though, it was Chet who had been the aggressor in the argument with Muffy.

Still, Rabinowitz proceeded with caution. "That's not usually how I work. I'm conducting a private investigation, after all."

Chet laugh-scoffed. "For a private investigation, you haven't been very private, Mister ... Lipschitz, is it?"

"Rabinowitz."

"Mr. Rabinowitz, I have already been questioned by the police for that very unfortunate scene Miss McGregor and I caused before she was taken way too soon from us. It's now a matter of public record, and I no longer have anything to hide, sir."

"So, you did indeed have a relationship with the deceased?"

The Icicle Works' percussion-heavy "Birds Fly (Whisper to a Scream)" had been playing over the store's speakers as they spoke, causing both men to talk a bit louder than they normally would have. But the song ended just as Rabinowitz asked his question, and the next tune that started immediately playing was the quieter "Taken In" off Mike + The Mechanics' recently released debut album. Chet liked to play three bouncy, aggressive songs in a row, then follow those with a slower selection to give customers a pace to their shopping experience. "Taken In" allowed him to lower his voice and once again make his embarrassing admission to another human being.

"Indeed, I did, sir," he said, obvious guilt in his voice. "I did, and I fear it is going to cost me my position here with the Harmony Hut corporation, a position I am more than suited for that I have spent my entire adult life working towards. I'd like to tell you that I was unaware that she was underage. But the truth of the matter is, I've been working malls off and on for some time now. I am just a man of 28, sir, and teenage young ladies are in my orbit all of the time. This is not ego talking, Mr. Rabinowitz. I want you to understand that. This is truth as I would tell it to Christ the Carpenter Himself. The girls like me. They're drawn to me. Fortunately, a lot of women of legal age are drawn to me, as well, and so I try and subsist on a steady diet of them. You understand?"

"It must be difficult for you."

"It is the cross I bear, sir. Just look throughout this store. Look at all of the underage gash ... I'm sorry ... the young teenage ladies who come in here for their Duran Duran, their George Michael. They come into this store, my store, day in and day out, night in and night out with their big hair and their short skirts. Their perfume. Many of them linger a long time in one's memory after leaving, I'm here to tell you. The restraint I have shown over the years has been darn near heroic, sir. They are a sweet, sweet nectar I had not tasted since ... well, since I was their age. Until, that is, I saw Miss McGregor one very slow Thursday afternoon, oh, about a month ago now. She was browsing my soundtracks section. And every 30 or 40 seconds, she'd look up and over my way. Just for a second. But it was enough. Enough to put the hook in me, sir. If there had just been one customer in that store that afternoon, I would've stayed away. I swear I would have. At least, I like to think I would have."

To Rabinowitz, the man seemed genuinely shamed. Maybe it was his Southern drawl, but he also seemed honest, too. Mervyn often bragged that he had a "built-in B.S. detector." Normally, a man under suspicion who talked this much was a man who was trying to deflect, a man who had something much darker he was trying to conceal. But Chet's whole confession sounded more like therapy than anything.

"So, you two started -- what -- dating?"

"Oh, no, no, sir. We started having sex. I have a lovely, pull-out couch in my back office that I use for such intimacies. But she was the adventurous type. I had to convince her several times that discretion was almost certainly the wiser course of action. She especially came to love the dressing rooms of our fine mall's department-store anchor tenants. There was this one time in Montgomery Ward's right before--"

"Alright, alright. I get the picture. So, what went wrong?"

"Taken In" was almost finished, and Chet knew the next song in the cue was going to be a loud, extended 12-inch remix of A-ha's "The Sun Always Shines on T.V." The song would begin slow, then kick in with the Norwegian pop group's signature drum beats and over-dramatic orchestrations. He wanted to get the next part of his admission out before he had to yell it. So, he spoke fast and direct.

"I found out that our initial meeting was not a chance meeting at all. You see, I do have -- or, at least, I did have -- the reputation among these kids of being the big fish one tries to reel into the boat. I had been propositioned many, many times by young ladies every bit as attractive as Miss McGregor. But I had never cracked. Never. Well, I learned that a couple of her friends were gum-smacking one day, and Miss Muffy said that she could have any man that she wanted. And so they made a little wager. She said, 'Pick any man, any man in this mall, and I can have him in my bed by the end of the week.' It already being a Thursday, they thought they had it in the bag."

"And by picking you, huh?"

"Yes, sir. Needless to say, Miss McGregor sprang into action. And to answer your next question, I have no idea what made me succumb to her charms and not any of the others over the years. There was just something about her. You see, I very quickly developed real feelings for her. It surprised even me. And when I found out about the bet, when I found out I was nothing more to her than a prize pony, I didn't handle it very well. I just saw her over by that Friendly's, and I'm afraid my family's old famous Robitaille Rage came out. But that was truly the end of it, Mr. Rabinowitz. I am not a killer, sir. And I would have no idea whatsoever how to rig up an automobile to explode in that fashion. You must believe me on that, sir. I think the authorities do. At this time, they have said they will not inform her lawyer-father of my shameful behavior with his daughter. I am hoping you won't, as well. It would only cause all concerned more misery."

Rabinowitz told him that he believed him, too, and that he would likely no longer pursue this angle. But the spat had been very public and known to even people who didn't know either Chet or Muffy. There was no guarantee it would not get back to the McGregor family. Nevertheless, Sam had called him earlier and asked to meet in the food court on his lunch break. He said he had some new information to share. A school angle, after all? The boyfriend? Rabinowitz thanked Chet for his time and his honesty and exited the store.

Chip saw the whole intense conversation from across the shop, but was unable to hear any of the specifics. As innocently as he could, he walked over and asked his boss, "So, what was that all about?"

Chet didn't look at him. He held his stare on Rabinowitz as he made his way from Harmony Hut to the nearby escalator leading up to the mall's second level. "Nothing to worry about," he finally answered. "That gentleman just had a few questions only I could answer."

"Did you?"

Chet gave his young employee a sly smile and answered, "More or less."

———

"So, whattaya got for me, kid?"

Sam was 15 minutes into his lunch break and deep into a Roy Roger's roast beef sandwich when Rabinowitz finally showed up at his table at the food court. The detective munched on a few of his French fries while Sam chewed enough of his last bite in order to answer him. Rabinowitz seemed annoyed at the kid's slow chomping. Sighing, he said, "Oh, please. By all means, take your time."

"It may be nothing," Sam finally replied, "but I think we may need to explore the Brent Fitzpatrick angle. My friend, Chip, and I were at a party the other night, Brent was drunk, and he was acting really weird."

Rabinowitz rolled his eyes. "Weird? What does that mean? You're all weird at your age, especially with some cheap swill in you. Did he actually say he killed his girlfriend?"

"Well, no. But when Chip mentioned his boss's name, that Chet guy who Muffy argued with, Brent got real, real dark. Like creepy dark. He grabbed Chip and started yelling, 'You work for Chet Robitaille?! You work for Chet Freaking Robitaille?!' By the way, what kind of name is Robe-ah-tie?"

"French."

"Well then that's the guy we should be focusing on."

Rabinowitz briefly chuckled at the boy's distaste for the French. Still, he immediately felt the need to rein him back in. "Not so fast. I just had a heart-to-heart with Mr. Robitaille. As it turns out, he may have murdered the girl's virginity -- although I highly doubt that -- but he didn't murder the girl. I have a sneaking suspicion that Brent may have thought he was Muffy's one and only, and then found out he wasn't. So, let me follow up on that angle. If this kid turns out to have a loose screw, I don't want you anywhere near him."

Sam nodded his head. As seductive as it was to have the most popular guy in school be his newfound buddy, the fact that he could be capable of murder -- even it if was a crime of passion or simple, targeted revenge -- was not worth invitations to a few more parties or car rides around town in his cool, classic Mustang.

Sam felt a strange rush of adrenaline the more he thought about the prospect of Brent being their man. "Oh, wow, Rabinowitz," he said. "Is this how it feels? Is this what's it like to be hot on the trail? Can you imagine if we're the ones who catch Muffy's killer before even the cops do? It would be a miracle!"

"Oh please, Sam. That wouldn't be a miracle. A miracle would be a shih tzu that can sing 'Figaro.' You and I solving this case would be just dumb luck."

Sam crinkled his eyebrows. He was taken aback by the P.I.'s pessimistic attitude. What happened to turn a man like Rabinowitz into such a negative curmudgeon. He rarely saw the guy smile. "Dumb luck? How so?"

"Two things, kid. First, like I told you before, these kinds of cases are almost always solved by the cops. They're probably already zeroing in on their prime suspect right now. But, if somehow, some way, we beat them to the punch, it will likely be because we stumbled over some small, tiny clue they missed because they were looking somewhere totally different. And, second, don't throw around the word 'miracle,' OK? Just don't. Whoever did this, when they get caught, it's not going to be some glowing moment of victory for you or me. It's going to be sad, especially if it's someone you know. One human being felt compelled to take another human being's life, for whatever reason. Believe me, Sam, there is no joy to be derived here. None whatsoever."

Sam only had a couple of minutes left on his lunch break before he had to go back to 16 Plus. Collette seemed like the kind of boss to stand by the store's entrance with her index finger on her watch, waiting for him. And he had the feeling that she had not been pleased with his work so far. But, still, Rabinowitz and his attitude made him curious. He knew very few adults who were actually happy with their lives. But this man didn't seem to get joy from anything.

"Rabinowitz," he questioned, "why do you do what you do? I mean, I know I'm young. But I can't imagine going through life working at a job that doesn't give me any joy whatsoever. Why didn't you become a ... a--"

"What? A doctor? A lawyer? An accountant? Why didn't I get my-self a nice 'Jewish job?'"

"Well ... yeah."

Rabinowitz shook his head in disapproval. It was the same question his mother had asked him many times over the years. And he had always been a disappointment to his father, a federal judge, while the man was alive. Now, he had the daily disapproval of his wife and children. The very last thing he needed was this pudgy, red-headed punk kid busting his balls about his chosen vocation.

"The truth is, it WAS exciting in the beginning," he said. "But that was when I wanted to do the job. Now with a mortgage and a car payment and three ... I don't know ... four kids, now I *have* to do the job. I can't quit. I can't turn down work. I gotta make the money. And, believe me, now I wish it was doctor or lawyer money. The kids, the Mrs., I love them to my core. But they're always wanting or needing something. I hear you and your friends riffing on movies and TV shows. Well, I quote from my favorite flick, 'Ben Hur.' They keep me alive to serve this ship."

"Jesus, Rabinowitz."

"No, really. Most days I walk around the house with the permanent expression of Han Solo in carbonite on my face. The only joy in this job is it gets me out of the house. And at odd times, too. Sometimes late at night, sometimes in the middle of the afternoon. She Who Must Be Obeyed doesn't like it. But it's necessary. I don't care how good your marriage is, Sam. And I really do have a good one. You need breathers from each other."

"Even lovers need a holiday?"

Rabinowitz didn't even get the Chicago song reference. He just kept rambling. "Oh, not even a holiday. A beach, an umbrella, and a rum drink is a friggin' dream at this point. Just a couple of hours apart is sometimes all you need to keep things going, to keep the romance alive. And it's sometimes all you get. For months. And when you get those couple of hours, you gotta make 'em count. And I'm not talking about going down to the local fuck, suck, and feel either. Nudie bars and massage parlors are rip-offs. I've seen enough cheating to know I'm no cheater. I'm talking about a fine meal at a good restaurant. I'm talking about having the extra scratch to order an appetizer. Telling the wait-ress, 'No rush,' when she asks if you're ready for the check. Asking for the dessert tray and-- "

"Rabinowitz!" a voice boomed from behind. The private eye knew immediately who it was. Beauregard Knox, the police homicide detective assigned to Muffy's case. The man was a towering presence, a naturally big guy with broad shoulders and meaty forearms, who made everyone around him seem smaller. With his bulging, bullfrog-like eyes and severe widow's peak, his physicality intimidated Sam immediately.

"Oh, hello, Lieutenant Detective Knox," Rabinowitz said, smiling nervously. "Beauregard, is it?"

"You know my name, Rabinowitz. It's easy to remember. They call me Beau, and I have no regard for pesky, little, bottom-feeding private eyes like you who insinuate themselves into my investigations."

The man was leaning his full body against the sitting Rabinowitz's, making him feel quite uncomfortable. Knox's crotch grinded into Rabinowitz's shoulder, as he seemed to be applying the full weight of his mid-section against the private eye. "You're out of your league here," he said, more than a hint of menace in his voice. "But if, by chance, you come up with a lead in this case -- any lead at all -- you best share it with me. Understood?"

Rabinowitz didn't like the pressure tactics. He knew that Knox was a guy who could take away his freedom on a whim. But he also knew that a lot of eyes were on this case. There was a local sensationalism sur-rounding it. He himself was the third person to ask certain mall denizens questions about the murder, after Knox and the various news reporters lingering around. For whatever reason, in the moment, Rabinowitz felt compelled to rattle sabers with the cop.

"Oh, I understand loud and clear," he replied, looking up at the man. "Giving it the old college try on this one, are we, Knox? But I guess in your case, it's the old community college try."

Knox glared at him. "I have no idea why the McGregors hired a small-timer like you. But then again, I've stopped trying to figure out why people do some of the things they do, especially the wealthy."

"Hmm, isn't figuring things out your job, *Detective*?"

"You just stay the hell out of my way! Understand?"

"Sure thing, Detective."

And with that, Knox was gone. And he was gone fast. He hadn't even looked at Sam once during the whole encounter or wondered why he was sitting at that table. His focus was entirely on Rabinowitz. As big and as powerful he was, though, he did seem a bit nervous to Sam.

"Shit," Rabinowitz said under his breath.

"Yeah, looks like you made an enemy."

Sam could see worry in Rabinowitz's eyes now, too. "It's not that," the older man said. "If I'm reading Knox right, the police have NO clue who killed Muffy!"

———

Collette wasn't by the entrance of her store waiting for Sam to return. But she was at the counter with a look of extreme disapproval on her face. "Sam, can I see you in the back?" she asked, upon her young employee's arrival.

Sam didn't like being called to the mat for anything. He hated the tone in his mother's voice whenever she would say, "Sam, we need to have a talk." He hated it whenever a teacher would say, "Sam, will you see me after class." And now, with Collette being his first-ever boss, he was getting that same ominous tone from her.

Once they were behind closed doors in her back office, he thought it best to head her off before she could lay into him. "Miss Stephenson, I know I'm a few minutes late coming back from my lunch. And I know I haven't had the best first week or two of work. I'm sorry. It's just been a REALLY stressful time. I promise I'll--"

"Sam!" she interrupted. "How do you know I've called you back here to chastise you?"

Collette sat as Sam remained standing. The office was cramped and tiny, and the only other thing to sit on besides her office chair was a small stool that typically had three or four dresses and blouses draped over it to the point where it was always on the verge of falling over from being top-heavy. Sam was surprised to see Collette smiling warmly. Maybe he was way off base. Maybe she was calling him in to give him words of praise or even a small raise.

"Really?!" he said, in his best "golly-gee-whiz" voice. "You mean, I've been doing a good job?"

Collette's smile disappeared. "No, you've pretty much sucked from the get-go. What is up with you these past few days? It can't all be the Muffler getting char-broiled."

Once again, Sam was surprised at how callous Collette was towards his recently deceased classmate. She really didn't like her, and he briefly wondered if maybe his boss was an investigation angle worth pursuing. He made a mental note to bring her up to Rabinowitz at their next meeting. "Miss Stephenson, I--"

"Call me Collette, OK?"

"OK. Well, there's just been a lot going on since Muffy died. Because of that stupid photo in the paper, I can't go anywhere without people recognizing me as 'The Crying Boy.' Suddenly, I'm friends with kids I was never friends with before. Cool kids like Brent and his buddies and--"

"Barbara?"

Sam shrugged. "I don't know," he said. "We did have a nice moment the other night at a party, I guess. And that's another thing. I'm suddenly being invited to parties. Like, real parties with booze and cheerleaders and people making out on the floor. But it's all because Muffy died and some idiot photographer caught me at not my finest moment. Now I know how Sean Penn and Madonna feel. The paparazzi are shameless, I tell ya! Just shameless and--"

"What's up with you and that guy Rabinowitz?"

Sam hadn't realized anyone had taken notice of his few encounters with the detective. Certainly not Collette, who seemed to always be at her store and not out on the mall. He fumbled for a response. "Nothing's up," he stammered. "He's, uh, just an interesting guy to talk to. Did you know he's a private eye?"

"Uh huh," she replied, holding her gaze at Sam, making him feel increasingly uncomfortable. Because of that gaze, he felt compelled to tell her a bit more. "Did you also know he's looking into Muffy's death?"

"Has he found anything out yet?"

Sam was feeling increasingly off-balance with Collette's demeanor and quick, direct questions. He thought he was being called into the back to get reamed out for his work performance. But, now, he was getting asked about Rabinowitz's investigation. He wasn't prepared for that. Collette didn't seem to realize he was helping the man. And he wasn't about to give her any details, because he didn't have any. But, still, she was his boss. And lying to her would probably get him fired immediately if she ever found out. So, he continued to fumble his replies.

"Not yet," he said, then quickly added. "I mean, I don't know. It's not like he's going to tell me anything. He's, you know, just a cool guy to talk to. And as you know, I'm a talker. I also like talking to those old timers' on the benches and at the food court. Did you know that one dude, Mel, fought in World War II with General Patton? He said the soldiers would call Patton 'Old Blood and Guts' ... our blood and his guts. Mel and his friend, Rodney, also--"

Collette cut him off again. "Don't change the subject," she said. "I want to hear more about this investigation. So, what's this Rabinowitz been asking you?"

Sam stiffened. It was clear she wasn't letting go of this. "Not much really. Just if I thought any of my classmates were capable of murder, and if Muffy had any enemies at school."

"What did you tell him?"

"I told him Muffy was rich, she was popular, she was hot, and she was a cheerleader. Of course, she had enemies. Heck, even someone like you obviously hated her."

"Did you tell him that?" Collette asked, leaning forward in her chair.

"No, of course not. Your name hasn't come up."

Collette quickly checked herself. "It better not have."

"What are you worried about?"

"I'm not worried," she replied, choosing her next words carefully. "Let's just say that I have certain ... ambitions. And if 16 Plus gets pulled into this mess, even peripherally, my chances for career advancement and getting to where I want to go in the company could be impacted. But, what you're saying is, Rabinowitz has only wanted to know about school so far?"

Sam nodded. "Yeah, I don't think he's particularly comfortable around teenagers. He's looking for any 'in' he can get. Mostly, though, he just bitches about his life."

"Oh?"

"Yeah, he can be a real sad-sack. He doesn't like his job or his life. According to him, his kids are just a bunch of money-sucking vampires. What is it with you adults? No grown up I know seems to be happy. My dad has all these fears and regrets. My mother is only up and happy when she's got her sewing circle together, talking about nighttime soaps, and sucking down Chardonnay. Mel and those other oldies, but goodies are always talking about their aches and pains. And you--"

"Careful, Sam."

"Look, all I'm saying is you were a Big Beautiful Woman model. You rocked! And, yeah, now you're working retail. But that isn't so bad, is it?"

A certain regret appeared in Collette's eyes for the first time. Her next words were measured. "Let's just say that sometimes the thing that gets your foot in the door is the same thing that won't allow you to leave." This vague answer sounded almost vulnerable to Sam, even though the boy didn't quite know what it meant.

"Hey, you wouldn't happen to have a spare back issue of yours lying around that I could take off your hands?" he asked, trying to lighten the mood.

Collette smiled warmly at her young employee. "You're sweet, Sam," she said.

"Thanks. But I was kind of being serious. Our apartment building is starting a recycling program next month, and I'm afraid Mom's back issues are going to be among the first things to go."

Collette ignored the request altogether. She liked Sam. There wasn't a sinister bone in his body, at least not yet. "That's your problem, you know? You're too sweet. I think a girl like Barbara, a big girl, is going to want more of a take-charge kind of guy. Someone with a bit of an edge. To her, you're too soft, too cuddly. She probably sees you as some big, red-headed Muppet."

"Yeah, a Muppet that likes to bone!" a defensive Sam immediately retorted.

Collette laughed hard. "See, you're just so darn cute. Not even that sounded remotely sexual. But maybe I'm wrong. We working adults may not have our dreams come true very often, but apparently you might."

"What do you mean?"

"I mean while you were on your excessively long lunch break, Barbara did finally come into the store. And she wasn't looking to shop. She was looking for you."

A big, goofy, and yes Muppet-like grin came over Sam's face. It was a smile that conveyed surprise, joy, and intense anticipation all at once. "Me?!" he exclaimed. "She actually asked for me?!"

Collette pulled a folded piece of paper from the breast pocket of her flowered summer blouse. Dangling it in front of Sam, she said, "She was busy and couldn't wait for you to return, so she left you her phone number."

Sam grabbed the number so fast, it almost left a paper cut on Collette's finger. He un-folded it, read the numbers, and immediately wondered when a good time to call would be. "Did she say what she wanted?" he asked.

Collette rose from her chair. Opening the door to her office to return to work, she was back on the storeroom floor before she answered, "Yeah, Sam. She did. Something about Rabinowitz."

CHAPTER 8

Sam was surprisingly not nervous when he phoned Barbara to see what she wanted. She immediately answered, too. And she was still pleasant to him. They chatted for a good minute or two about the summer, about different classmates, about nothing really before Sam asked why she had come around looking for him.

Barbara didn't mention Rabinowitz. She simply and rather cryptically invited him down to the high school the next afternoon at 3 p.m. if he didn't have work. Fortunately, Sam did not. He did ask, "What's this all about?" And her only reply was a teasing "You'll see when you get there."

Our Lady of Sorrows was within walking distance of his apartment, so Sam made the short stroll. He didn't want to seem too eager, so he left his home at 3 o'clock exactly so he would get there at about 3:15. He was puzzled by what he saw the second he rounded the corner and the old, Gothic-looking, brick-and-stone school building came into full view.

There was a mass of people gathered; students and adults he recognized, many he did not. There were parents and teachers, administrators and alumni, nuns and Father Henry. It felt very much like approaching a town festival, with blue and white balloons denoting the school's colors bopping in the summer breeze; the local Top 40 station, WAVA 105.1, blaring over several large outdoor speakers; and about a dozen booths set up. Dominating the spectacle was a large banner strewn across the front entrance of the school that read: "A Celebration of Muffy McGregor's Life."

Sam slumped at the sight. "It just doesn't end, does it?" he muttered to himself.

He briefly wondered if he would have to give a speech again, and he suddenly started to become a bit nervous. At least, he didn't have to maintain a look of sadness and grief on his face. This was much more of a party atmosphere, with smiles, laughs, and people talking in loud voices over the music. As he got closer, the smell of food wafted up his nostrils. Somewhat fittingly, Steve Winwood's "Higher Love" started playing on the radio. Sam even heard a few random people sprinkled throughout the gathering start to sing its opening lines.

"Think about it ... there must be higher love."

Even Sam started humming as he began mingling amongst the people. Some of his newfound friends like head cheerleader Elena Eveler and Jimmy Whitehouse, the class president, either said "Hi" or gave him a quick nod of acknowledgement. One of Brent's offensive linemen had broken away from his pack and yelled out a hearty "Sam! Sam the Man!"

Then he heard a more sarcastic version of the same greeting. "Sam," someone spat from the boy's left. "Sam the Man."

It was Chip. He had somehow been roped into working the booth where there were cupcakes, pies, and pastries for sale. And he didn't look happy.

"What's all this?" Sam asked.

Chip, obvious disdain in his voice, answered, "I tried calling you, but I guess you've been too busy playing amateur private eye. Barbara and her friends put all this together. They're trying to raise funds to start a scholarship in Muffy's honor. They--"

Just as he was about to go on, one of the older mothers interrupted. Placing her hand on Chip's forearm, she said to him, "Young man, that was such a wonderful little speech you gave earlier. You are SO articulate!" The lady then bought a half-dozen cupcakes and paid Chip a dollar more than was required. "Now, that's not a tip for you to pocket, young man," she said. "That's for the Muffy Fund."

When the woman was out of earshot, Sam marveled, "Holy shit, dude! You gave a speech?"

Chip scowled. "Oh yeah. I thought I was here for just the baked goods and bigotry. But then Father Henry and Brent tag-teamed me and brought me up on stage. Hey, too bad you couldn't have arrived 15 minutes earlier, huh? Barbara told you 3. I thought you'd get here at 2:45. Silly me!"

The sarcasm just dripped out of Chip's mouth. He had a weird, intense way about him, like he'd been smiling too long. "So where were you?" he asked.

Sam didn't want to tell him he had purposefully decided to be fashionably late. So, he thought about the last thing he did do before heading out. "I got into an old 'Good Times' rerun on Channel 20, and the time must have gotten away from me."

"An old 'Good Times' rerun!" Chip repeated in his mock-crazed voice, drawing out the word "old." He then fake-chuckled and exclaimed "Dy-no-mite! Which one was it?"

Sam took a step back from him. Chip was getting a bit too weird. "I don't know," he mumble-answered.

"Oh, you know!"

"It was the one where Willona needed to pay for ice-skating lessons for Penny. So she took an extra job watching women change clothes at her store through two-way mirrors in the dressing room to catch shoplifters. But she--"

"What an absorbing episode," Chip shot back. "Hey, right now, I sure wish I could change MY clothes!"

Sam took another step back, as Chip grabbed the front shoulders of the shirt he was wearing and pointed his index fingers downward at the image displayed on its front. To Sam's horror, it was a perfect reproduction of the front page of that fateful edition of the *Laurel Times* with him and Chip "crying." Sam looked around the crowd and noticed a number of people wearing the same shirt. He then saw the booth, manned by Brent and Barbara, where they were being sold.

"What the?!"

"Oh yeah!" Chip said, absolutely punch-drunk at this point. "They're sellin' 'em for ten bucks a pop. A bona fide, limited-edition, collector's shirt to commemorate this memorable time in all our young lives. Get 'em while they're hot, Sam. It's all for a good cause."

Sam looked at his friend, whose facial expressions were starting to return to normal the more he ranted. "This is bad, huh?"

"Do ya think?!"

"What can we do?"

"What can *we* do?" he said, lowering his voice. "YOU can take your 16 Plus paycheck and buy every single one of these shirts! And then WE can go have a nice bonfire way, way out of town somewhere. I would imagine these shirts would make for some damn fine kindling, wouldn't you say?"

At that, both Brent and Barbara noticed Sam and excitedly motioned him over. Brent held up one of the shirts excitedly, pointing to it with a big goofy grin on his face. Sam looked back at Chip, who was busy with another customer. Once again, it was a mother with money in her hand. "Don't take this the wrong way," she said. "But do you have anything left that's NOT chocolate?"

As Sam walked over towards the T-shirt booth, he could hear Chip pleading, "Don't leave me, Sam. Don't leave me!"

The walk over to Barbara and Brent was a slow one, as Sam had to wind through a thickening crowd. Little kids half his size, the younger brothers and sisters of his classmates, ran by him with their cookies and cupcakes, almost tripping him. One woman just walked in front of him and stopped, and he had to politely maneuver around her. The whole way, he tried to keep his gaze on Barbara without seeming too creepy. A small pang of jealousy tugged at his heart when he saw how familiar she was with Brent. They couldn't be a couple this fast, Sam told himself. Besides, Brent went for the thin, gorgeous cheerleader type, and there would be plenty of those to choose from in the days to come.

Sam was relieved when Barbara turned her full attention to him when he finally got to the booth. "You finally made it!" she exclaimed.

"Yeah, sorry I'm late."

Brent immediately interjected. Thrusting a shirt into Sam's chest, he commanded, "Put it on, bro! You're comped, by the way."

Sam looked down at the shirt. He still couldn't believe the quality of the reproduction. It wasn't an iron-on or some cheap decal. It was the front page embedded into the garment. And there he and Chip were, plain as day, next to the angelic picture of Muffy. Even now, after looking at the image so many times, Sam could hardly believe his eyes.

"Quite a shirt, huh?" Barbara asked.

"Quite," Sam answered quietly.

"Bro!" Brent exclaimed. "Don't you start cryin' again! 'Cause if you start cryin', I'll start cryin'! This is a celebration. Now, put that shirt on, get back behind here, and help us move some merchandise. It's for Muffy, man. Muffy!"

Sam suddenly realized that he had been roped in to being the shirt's model. Brent was nice enough to not call attention to the shirt being a 2XL. On most kids, it would have been the size of a nightgown. But putting it on over his Izod shirt now, it fit perfectly and came down right past his belt.

Once he had it on, he immediately heard murmurs from those passing by. "Look, it's him!" and "Hey, there he is ... the Crying Boy!" were the two most common whispers. A few people, classmates mostly, knew him by name as they passed by and commented. Some gave him the "thumbs up" sign. Others just told him he looked good in the shirt.

"It really does look good on you, Sam," Barbara complimented.

Sam looked down again at the image. "Thanks," he said. "How did you make these?"

"The newspaper made them. Apparently, it's a new thing they can do on the computer as a way of drumming up revenue. They can transfer any front page from the last couple of years onto a shirt or a pillow or a coffee mug."

Sam looked over at Chip, whose booth was about 50 yards directly in front of him. Almost on cue, he held up a large thermos with the infamous front page imprinted on it. He pointed to it intensely and mouthed the words, "Oh yeah. This, too"

Brent noticed that Chip was displaying the drink container. "Yeah, see! Our boy Chip has one of the thermoses. His drink will stay cold while it's hot out, or he can put some hot soup in there or maybe some cocoa when it gets cold again. I hope he always thinks of Muffy when he uses it."

Sam nodded. "I am 100 percent certain he will, Brent."

"We just made up those and the shirts. Muffy's parents thought if we did the whole line of merchandise, it would be too tacky."

"They were probably right, Brent" Sam said. Then, after a slight pause in which it seemed they didn't have anything more to say on the subject, Sam asked, "So, tell me, are they selling well?"

"Like rubbers during Beach Week, bro!"

With that bit of eloquence, Brent turned back to his line of customers inquiring about different sizes. He was almost out of the larges and the XLs. But he had plenty of the other variations. Sam noticed that the jock seemed in much better and more sober spirits than he was at the party the other night.

In the time that Sam watched Brent work the customers, Barbara had joined them in slipping a commemorative shirt on over her blouse. Her hair was slightly mussed after, and Sam made a move to brush her bangs back from her forehead.

"Thanks," she bristled slightly. "I got it."

"Sorry," he replied.

Sam was hoping Barbara had stopped into the store to ask him to go for coffee or a lunch at the food court. She really didn't give him much on the phone, instead preferring to keep the Muffy celebration a surprise for whatever reason. Then, he remembered the reason Collette said she had stopped by.

"Hey, Barbara. Why didn't you tell me about all this over the phone."

"Oh, Sam. I've seen you at pep rallies and assemblies. You always look like you want to be anywhere but there. But everybody really wanted you here, and they figured if I asked."

"Yeah, they figured right. But I'm curious. My boss said you came by to ask me something about that guy Rabinowitz."

At that, Brent broke off his customer service. "Rabinowitz?!" he raged. "That private eye, Rabinowitz?!"

Sam pivoted and backed up, and Barbara also sidestepped away from the football player and his sudden intensity. Brent's hair-trigger temper was quite frightening in the moment, and it made both of them recoil in reaction. But just as quickly as his rage bubbled to the surface, he took a deep breath, and said calmly. "Why are you mentioning that dude's name?"

Barbara answered before Sam could. "He came to my house yesterday and asked my mom some questions about Muffy's dad. She's a paralegal in his law office."

"Mr. McGregor?! Shit, did he mention me?" Brent asked.

"I don't know what he asked. She wouldn't tell me specifically. But I've seen Sam hanging out with Rabinowitz at the mall from time to time. So, I thought maybe he knew."

Brent's glare turned back to Sam, and it unnerved him. Both he and Rabinowitz had hoped to keep their connection quiet for as long as possible. But in a relatively small town like Laurel where so many people knew each other, word was sure to get around sooner or later.

"So, what do you know, Sam?" Brent asked. "And why are you hanging around with that old Jewish guy?"

Sam immediately tried to deflect. "I hang around with a lot of different people at the mall. Rabinowitz is always there, following somebody about something. Usually, it's someone cheating on their wife or husband. Hey, do you think Mr. McGregor's having an affair?"

"What?! No!" Barbara and Brent answered, almost in unison. They then proceeded to tell Sam what he already knew. That the McGregors were impatient with the police investigation, that they wanted to be proactive in finding their daughter's killer, and so they hired Rabinowitz to investigate. Sam feigned like this was all the first time he'd heard any of it.

"Oh," he said. "That must have been why he was at the funeral then."

"So, he hasn't hit you up about me?" Brent asked intensely.

Sam shook his head. Fibbing, he came back with, "Uh, no. No, he hasn't. What's going on, Brent?"

Brent started rubbing his knuckles. Sam noticed they were quite red and swollen. Whatever made them that way had just recently happened. "Nothing's going on," Brent muttered, not looking at either of them. "Other than I think that damn P.I. thinks I did it. He thinks I might have killed Muffy! My coach called last night and said he'd been asking around the weight room about me. Coach said he had also talked to Father Henry. And you'll never guess what he was doing this morning?"

Both Sam and Barbara shrugged.

"My boys and I caught him going through my parents' trash cans! Can you believe that?!"

"Your boys?" Sam asked.

"My boys! My offensive line! My protection!"

Sam was almost afraid to ask the next questions. "What was he looking for? And what did you do?"

Brent took a swig from whatever was in his commemorative, collector's edition Muffy thermos. Wiping his mouth, he said, "What do you think he was looking for? Some kind of evidence. I don't know. Matches. TNT. Whatever it is that makes a car bomb, I guess."

Sam was very curious about what Brent did next. "So, Brent," he said, slowing his words. "What did you do?"

Brent stood tall. Proudly, he answered, "We beat his ass!"

"What?!"

"Not bad. He's fine. My boys just held him while I punched him in the stomach until he threw up. Then, he crawled back into his candy-ass Oldsmobuick or whatever the hell it was he was driving and sped off."

Sam was horrified. "Poor Rabinowitz," he said under his breath.

He was glad Brent returned to selling shirts and thermoses to customers so he didn't have to do too much more pretending. The more he was coming to know the jock, the more he was coming to see his extremes. He could be a violent, boastful bully one moment, with negative emotions that went up and down like a bad EKG reading. But in the next moment, he was all about love and loyalty and friendship. He seemed to feel every-thing intensely. And maybe that intensity could be channeled into jealous, vindictive rage.

But a murder like Muffy's wasn't just something that happened in the moment. It had to have been planned and pre-meditated, requiring a cer-tain level of skill. Did Brent possess such skill? Was he that sinister and patient? Matches? TNT? Sam didn't know much about car bombs. But he was pretty sure it was more elaborate than that. Still, Brent being the killer just didn't feel right to Sam, and it had nothing to do with wanting the star quarterback to like him.

And then he thought of Rabinowitz. He knew he had to go to him. He would stay at the celebration for a respectable amount of time. But Rabinowitz's office was also within walking distance, and Sam knew he had to go there next.

———

After waiting a respectable amount of time, Chip was all-too-willing to leave the celebration and go with Sam to the P.I.'s office. Chip didn't even care all that much for Rabinowitz. He just wanted to get away from the spectacle.

The office was in the "old part of town," as the locals called it. The various doctor's and law offices, small stores and cafes, filling stations and homes had been there for decades. Rabinowitz's place of business was in a small, one-story office complex that also had a pawn shop, a bail bonds-man, and a Chinese take-out eatery. Across the street was a funeral home and on the next corner down was the Valencia roadside motel. They were in a part of Laurel that Sam and Chip usually drove through to get to the mall or the movie theater or the entrance to Interstate 95.

Sam immediately noticed that the door to the private eye's office was ajar, so he and Chip walked right in. The smell of Chinese food from next door permeated the air. Chip was also sensitive to cigarette smoke, and he definitely caught a whiff of that, too, even though Rabinowitz was not a smoker. He surmised that a number of his clients were, as there was a large ashtray full of butts just inside the door on an end table.

The office was two rooms with a doorway in between. Old wood paneling was on the walls. The ashtray was the only thing in disarray in the office. Rabinowitz kept a respectably clean business environment, with new carpeting under foot and ceiling fans that helped circulate the air and took strain off the window-unit air conditioners that were working overtime in the June heat and humidity.

They found Rabinowitz sacked out on his office couch, a cold compress on his head, a hand on his stomach. He was staring blankly up at the ceiling. He barely even acknowledged the boys' presence, grunting upon their entrance. Or, maybe it was more than a grunt. It could have been a strained "Hi" or "Hey" greeting. Sam and Chip couldn't tell. Whatever it was, he didn't sit up or get up.

"We heard what happened," Sam said. "Are you OK?"

Rabinowitz flipped the compress to the cooler side and moved it down over his eyes. That was his answer. But it told Sam and Chip all he wanted them to know. He was clearly in a lot of discomfort and not wanting to talk. He'd been beaten up worse before by angry husbands and other disgruntled surveillance targets. But it had been a long time since he got his butt kicked by kids. That was what he was most bitter about.

"Is there anything we can get you?" Chip asked.

Even with his eyes covered, the two boys could sense that Rabinowitz was actually contemplating Chip's question. Maybe it was the slight cock of his head. Maybe it was the raising of one finger in the air, as if to say, "Gimme a moment, I'm thinking." Finally, he spoke. "It's days like today that really make me contemplate a new career. It's the thought that ran through my head seconds before I knew I was going to get my ass so completely kicked. So, that guy, Brent ... he's coming at me with the muscles and the sweat and those garden-hose-size veins running down his biceps. And all I kept thinking while he's pummeling my stomach was, 'I could go get a job at my cousin's delicatessen.' It wouldn't be that much of a pay cut. Five ... six grand a year tops. This is really just not worth it anymore."

"Rabinowitz," Sam said, kneeling at the foot of the man's sofa. "I'm sorry. I should've warned you about Brent's temper. He's really all over the map these days with his emotions. And I guess I'm coming to accept that he really could have gotten angry enough to kill Muffy and--"

"It's the 'roids."

"The what?"

Rabinowitz removed the washcloth to look the boy in the eye. "Steroids, Sam. Brent and half the football team are shooting up. It's why he's all 'Raging Bull' one minute and weepy 'Love Story' the next. It's also why you guys were 10-0 last season. Apparently, there's nothing more important than beating DeMatha and Riverdale Baptist. It's one of the things I found out, poking around, and asking questions."

"So," Chip interjected, "he was mad because you found out about his steroid use and not because you think he killed Muffy?"

"He's mad about everything. It's kind of impressive actually."

Rabinowitz slowly pulled himself up to a sitting position, wincing as he did so. His movements were awkward, like a pregnant woman in her third trimester trying to suddenly go from a bed to a chair. He winced and even let out a brief whine as his bruised stomach tightened and contracted. "Look," he said, exhaling loudly until the pain dulled. "Brent may have been voted Most Likely to Monger Wars in the high school yearbook, but he's not our guy. He's too front and center in all this. He'd be confessing all over the place if he did this. If I had to guess, all those steroids he's been taking have probably also been taking the lead out of his No. 2 pencil, if you know what I mean."

Looking at Chip, he continued, "Probably sent her right into the arms of your boss. If Brent was going to kill anyone, it would have been our man, Robitaille. Ugh. This is so screwed up, I can't see straight. And I really don't know what kind of progress report I'm going to give the McGregors the next time I see them. I was even considering giving them their deposit back and walking away. But, of course, how's this for timing? I just got--"

Rabinowitz stopped himself before completing his sentence. Unfortunately, he had both boys' full attention, and they weren't about to let him trail off and keep a secret. "You just got what?" Sam asked.

Rabinowitz got to his feet. Standing under his office's overhead light, Sam noticed more bruising on his jaw and neck. "I just got my first potentially big break in this case," he said with a sigh.

The P.I. pushed a button on his telephone answering machine. All three listened to the high-pitched, chipmunk-like gibberish of a phone message being rewound to its beginning. The machine briefly beeped, then kicked in with its saved message: "Rabinowitz," a breathy, muffled voice was heard saying, " I know who killed the girl. You're lookin' in all the wrong places. All the answers you seek are in the files of Pedro Machado Francisco."

To Sam and Chip, it sounded like a prank call, like someone using a fake voice to have a little fun with their detective-friend. But to Rabinowitz, it clearly meant something. Chip was the first to bite. "Pedro Machado Fran-who-sco?"

Rabinowitz let out another sigh. He draped the washcloth over his left shoulder and leaned against his desk for support. "This was one of the things I was afraid of when taking this case," he said to the boys. Briefly adopting a grandiose Spanish accent, he sang, "Pedro Machado Francisco!" before dialing it back down to his regular voice. "He's the closest our little burg has to an organized criminal. Officially, he's an 'import-export man.' Unofficially, he brings in dope, girls, hot merchandise, you name it. He's everywhere in Laurel, and that includes on the board of the local hospital, the Chamber of Commerce, the Rotary Club. I think he's even in the Kiwanis."

"He's got girls?" Chip asked, hoping for a few more details on that front.

Rabinowitz didn't acknowledge him. He simply went on. "If Muffy somehow ran afoul of him, there's certainly people in his orbit or employ who could rig up a car."

"Dy-no-mite," Chip muttered softly.

Sam pondered this. Then, instinctively, he raised his hand with a question.

Rabinowitz scoffed. "Seriously?"

Sam immediately lowered his hand, then said, "Question. How would Muffy even know someone like this San Francisco dude. She was a pom-pom."

"Answer. Poppa McGregor is Francisco's long-time lawyer. And on that note, maybe it wasn't Muffy who ran afoul of him. Maybe it was her daddy."

"Oof!" Chip replied.

"Oof, indeed," Mervyn said. "I guess I have to go check this out. And there's no time like the present. From what I hear, Francisco is at a celebration down at the school in Muffy's honor. Why aren't you two there? Never mind, I don't care. It's also a Sunday, so his offices are almost certainly closed and empty right now."

The second Rabinowitz stopped using his desk for support, he stumbled forward and almost fell on his face. Sam and Chip both rushed to steady him. He probably had a concussion, they figured. He wasn't dizzy, but his equilibrium was certainly off. The drive from the Fitzpatrick house to his office was arduous, to say the least. But, now, he wasn't going to get a better opportunity to do a little professional sleuthing at Francisco's office. If only he could stay upright for more than a minute or two at a time.

"You're not in any condition to go anywhere," Sam said. "So, we're all going to go together."

"We're all going to do what?!" Chip exclaimed.

CHAPTER 9

Rabinowitz and Chip bickered with Sam the whole way to Francisco's office, but he had an answer for everything. He was almost punch-drunk with excitement as he countered their increasing nervousness with flip and wise-cracking answers of his own. Probably the most annoying thing he did was begin referring to the alleged gangster by his initials. As in "Aw, come on. PMF is a pussycat. He won't mind us dropping by."

Nevertheless, the two continued to pepper Sam with protests all the way to Francisco's building, which was in a much better part of town. Chip parked Rabinowitz's car two blocks from Francisco's office, in the lot of a small rundown motel that was one of the few remnants of the redevelopment that had taken place in that part of town. As they made their way to their destination on foot, all three kept looking about at their surroundings to see if anyone was around. But this little section of Laurel was eerily deserted.

"I can't put you two in harm's way," Rabinowitz said, upon arriving. The detective was quite nervous.

"Rabinowitz, we're coming with you," Sam replied. "You've been wincing every time Chip makes a turn."

"That's because he's been driving like a real jerk-off."

"And why exactly am I here?" Chip questioned, after putting the detective's car in park.

"Because Rabinowitz is in no condition to drive," Sam answered, "and you have your permit."

Rabinowitz and Chip's protests continued as they started to make their way to Francisco's front door. And Sam remained dismissive the whole way.

"I really thought you two would stay in the car." Rabinowitz grumbled, unable to control the two kids.

"I thought you said things might get bad, and you wanted some back-up."

"I never said that. You know I never said that. "

"I'm just the Black Guy," Chip groused. "I should stay in the car."

"You're not just the Black Guy," Sam reassured.

"I don't even know what that means," Mervyn muttered.

The one aspect of this whole little misadventure that all three agreed they were uncomfortable with was the "breaking and entering" part. Rabinowitz had certainly picked locks before and had gained access to any number of homes, apartments, and offices. But he always worked alone. And he never picked the lock of someone with the notorious reputation of Francisco.

It wasn't a terribly uncommon sight for that part of town to be largely empty on a Sunday. It was mostly professional offices and support services, like a Kinko's Copy shop and a deli that was only open during weekdays for breakfast and lunch serving those who worked in that part of town. Even the motel didn't have anyone mulling about outside. In fact, there was only one other car in the whole parking lot, likely an employee's.

They each noticed a different, single strange thing, though. For Chip, it was that the traffic lights kept changing from green to yellow to red at regular intervals even though there were no cars around. For Sam, it was the fact that more small animals were out on the sidewalks and streets than would normally be seen in such a developed part of town. Several squirrels and one stray cat were visible just from his vantage point near Francisco's office door. It was almost post-apocalyptic, he thought. Like a cheesy end-of-the-world movie he saw a couple of weeks back on VHS called "Night of the Comet."

For Rabinowitz, the one really strange thing was that the front door to Francisco's office was not only unlocked, it was slightly ajar. Sam found it amusing. He joked and cracked wise partly to needle Chip, but mostly to keep from being nervous himself. "I just gotta say it, guys. This is SO much like an episode of 'Magnum!' Rabinowitz, it's like you're Magnum, I'm Rick, and Chip is TC."

Chip scoffed. "Oh please. I can accept you as Rick and me as TC. But there's no way this man is Magnum P.I. Rabinowitz is Higgins!"

"Dude, you're so right!" Sam exclaimed. "Well, then where's Magnum?"

Chip thought for a couple of seconds before coming up with an answer. "He's like in a hospital somewhere. This is one of those episodes where Magnum has gotten hurt in the first few minutes, and he's laid up in bed while his friends try and find out who did it. But really it's just Tom Selleck taking time off the show to film 'High Road to China' or 'Lassiter' or something."

"'High Road to China' was a 'Raiders' rip-off. But 'Lassiter' was awesome. WAY underrated. The women in that flick--"

"Oh, hell yes!" Chip exclaimed. "Jane Seymour, Lauren Hutton..."

"And Selleck makes himself look good by surrounding himself with nothing but ugly guys like Ed Lauter and Bob Hoskins and Joe Regalbuto."

"Those are some ugly-ass dudes."

"Those are some WAY ugly-ass dudes!"

"You know, after this, we should call up Buddy and rent--"

"Guys, guys!" Rabinowitz barked, boiling mad. "You shut your mouths! Shut up!" He quickly got himself back under control and dropped his voice back down to a hushed whisper. "Either you two shut your traps and follow my lead, or we're just going to forget this whole thing, OK?"

Sam and Chip both nodded in agreement, with Sam making a zipping motion across his lips to signal he would be especially quiet and behaved from then on. Rabinowitz nudged the office door open, and it moved inward with a slight creak.

"Just like on 'Magnum!'" Sam excitedly whispered.

Rabinowitz shot him a dirty look, and Sam instantly knew he had to change his tone and tenor. The office was nicer than Rabinowitz's, as it was a much newer building with central air conditioning and not window units, painted walls and not wood paneling, and fancy recessed lighting. It wasn't a terribly large office space. There was a desk for a receptionist, a nice couch and two chairs for visitors to sit on, and some fine art with Spanish and Portuguese influences hanging on the walls. Francisco had the end-unit office, so there were two windows on one wall and two on an adjoining wall that illuminated the interior without any need to turn on lights or even open the closed blinds.

The three made their way through the reception area and opened a door that led into Francisco's private office. Every 10 or 15 seconds, they would call out a faint "Hello?" or a "Is anybody there?" His office was quite large with more fine art on the walls, metal filing cabinets catty-cornered to the left and right as they walked in, and two desks. One was quite large and centered in the middle of the room towards the back wall. Clearly, it was the desk of a boss, an executive. It was Francisco's.

The other desk, a clean and almost empty one, was off to the right. Rabinowitz deduced that it belonged to Francisco's son, who he had heard wanted no part of his father's business. But Francisco kept a desk for him anyway, hoping that one day the young man would come to his senses and join him at his side. It was a smaller piece of furniture, but newer than the father's. Rabinowitz bypassed it altogether and immediately started snooping around the notes and folders left out in the open on Francisco's desk. He then started carefully sifting and rifling through the drawers, making sure to leave the contents and everything inside exactly the way he found it.

Sam and Chip stood awkwardly in the middle of the office. "What should we be doing?" Chip asked.

Rabinowitz barely looked up from his sleuthing. "Don't just stand there playing pocket pool," he answered. "Be my lookouts."

Rabinowitz didn't think he'd find anything on or in the man's desk. But he started there regardless. As expected, he found nothing of any value or consequence in his initial sweep. Just a bunch of papers and receipts and ledgers that all looked legitimate.

He turned his attention to the file cabinet closest to him, the one in the left corner of the room. Rabinowitz wore gloves, and that always impeded his searches as he paged through files, folders, and binders. But he sifted at a hurried pace, never once turning his gaze over to Sam and Chip pacing about with virtually nothing to do.

No sooner had Rabinowitz gotten halfway through the second drawer when he started to hear voices from outside. They came from the parking lot. "What's going on out there?" he asked, motioning the boys to go take a look.

Chip and Sam raced to the reception area to peer through a narrow strip where one of the blinds didn't quite cover the entire pane of glass. Two men had pulled up in separate cars and had gotten out of their vehicles. They were chatting loudly, saying things like "It doesn't look like a break-in from the outside" and "Let's be careful. They may still be in there." Chip didn't recognize either man, but Sam knew one of them.

"Shit!" he exclaimed, loud enough for Rabinowitz to hear in the other room. "It's that Lieutenant Detective Knox guy from the mall!"

"What?!" Rabinowitz instinctively slammed the file cabinet door shut, then winced at the loud sound it made. Immediately dropping his voice to an urgent whisper, he started calling out, "Oh crap. Crap, crap, crap! Hide. Hide!"

Chip and Sam retreated back into Francisco's office and closed the door. All three knew immediately there was no back exit. Sam quickly ran over to the room's lone side window, but it was locked. And he didn't have time to figure out the double clasp to get it to open so they could climb out. He could hear the two men coming in through the office's front door.

"Hide!" Rabinowitz implored, repositioning Francisco's chair and diving hard under his desk. There was room enough under there for Sam between the set of three drawers on either side. Chip took their cue and hid under Francisco's son's desk. The three immediately fell silent, hoping against hope that Knox and what was likely Francisco would stay out in the reception area.

The quiet lingered for a good 10 or 15 seconds before Chip pierced it with a whimpering, "Sam, there's a LOT of dry boogers under here!"

Rabinowitz and Sam both shushed him back into silence. They looked at each other with a mix of fear and frustration. Rabinowitz's eyes clearly communicated what he was thinking. "We should never have come!" And Sam's eyes responded with, "I know, I know." They strained to hear what the two men were saying in the other room. Their voices were muffled through the closed, connecting door. From the tone, it sounded like Knox was asking questions and the other man was answering them with short replies.

Rabinowitz's concentration was broken by a sudden, persistent beeping that seemed to be coming from Sam's wrist. It was the boy's Casio calculator watch. And it wasn't just doing its two brief beeps on the hour. Its alarm was going off. "What the hell?! Shut that off. Shut it off!" he scream-whispered.

Sam tried frantically to deactivate the alarm. It wasn't very loud. But to the three frightened people in the room, it might as well have been the Red Alert klaxon on "Star Trek." Sam hit every combination of buttons he could think of, but nothing worked. He really loved that watch. It was the best gift his dad had ever given him, and it was the one expensive thing he owned that the rich kids at school really seemed to take notice of and covet. But he had to make it stop. Somehow. Some way.

In a panic, he ripped it off his wrist and beat it incessantly into the floor until it was thoroughly broke. There was a lot of emotion in Sam's face at the watch's demise. "Oh God," he muttered. "This was just like Hawkeye and the chicken."

"What?!" Rabinowitz questioned.

"It wasn't a chicken, Rabinowitz. It was a baby. A baby!"

From across the room, both heard Chip through gritted teeth rasp, "The 'M*A*S*H' finale, Sam? Really? Really?!"

Both he and Rabinowitz were about to thoroughly rebuke the boy, but they each realized the voices in the other room had stopped chattering altogether. And then there was several seconds of agonizing nothing. Had Knox and the man left? Were they still out there? Had they heard Sam's watch? Rabinowitz was about to rise up and peer around the desk when -- BAM! -- the door to the room jolted open, swinging all the way from the frame to the wall and back again. Knox must have kicked it open to see if he could surprise whoever may have been inside.

"Hmmm, guess there's nobody in here either, Mr. Francisco," Knox was heard saying. "False alarm, I guess. But you did the right thing, calling the authorities. Does everything seem in order to you?"

Sam and Rabinowitz could hear Francisco slowly walking around the space in front of the two desks they were hiding under. They heard a few papers rustle overhead. The man made a small tapping sound with what must have been a pen or a pencil or possibly one of his fingers. "Yes," he finally replied, "everything appears to be in order."

"What about the file cabinets?"

Francisco walked over to the one Rabinowitz had been rifling through. Because it was at an angle, it was just out of view of the underneath portion of the desk. So, Sam and Rabinowitz couldn't see him, and he couldn't see them. But they could hear him opening and shutting each of the drawers.

"Uh huh, uh huh," he said, as he checked each one. "Yes, all good, Lieutenant. All good."

Knox was very close to the desk when Sam and Rabinowitz heard him let out a loud, dramatic sigh. "Good," the cop said. "There's enough in those files to bury you, me, and the whole department."

Francisco laughed. "I tell you to relax, my friend. There is no one file that will bury any of us. It is a combination of files that have to be connected with an eye trained to know what to look for. It's like a fine explosive device. Lots of parts that only work when working together. Do you know how many moving parts went into making just that little girl's car bomb alone? I didn't just purchase the materials altogether in one place. Six places, maybe seven. A receipt here, a charge slip there. Relax."

Sam and Rabinowitz looked at each other, eyes big. They both had stumbled onto the proverbial mother load. They wanted Knox and Francisco to leave, of course. But they also wanted them to keep talking.

Knox spoke next. "You know that little, piss-ant P.I. Rabinowitz is poking his hook nose into all this. I tried to scare him off the scent at the mall the other day, but no luck."

"We will kill him, too," Francisco said, matter-of-factly. "Not a problem."

Rabinowitz sat up so fast underneath that desk, he almost hit his head. Adrenaline rushed through him, and his antsy movements alarmed Sam who had just crushed his beloved watch and was doing everything he could to barely breathe. Sam put his hand on the older man's wrist to try and calm him. Slowly, he brought his other hand, index finger extended, to his lips to give him the universal "Shhhh!" sign. Rabinowitz slowly brought his hand up to his lips, too, but made the middle finger gesture.

"Yes, but, how?" Knox asked. "I'll probably catch that case, too. So, any head's up would be greatly appreciated, boss."

"Make sure you do catch the case, my friend. In fact, I am counting on it. Hmmm, yes. How shall we kill Rabinowitz? Not another explosive. I am only that humane to pretty, young girls who know too much. Perhaps a bullet to the back of the head when the wee man isn't looking. Lights out, good night, yes? Or maybe poison his matzo ball soup? Sprinkle some kill dust on his potato latkes?"

Rabinowitz looked absolutely petrified. He kept mouthing the "F" word without making a sound. If their lives weren't in mortal jeopardy, Sam might have chuckled at how big and exaggerated the man's quiet panic was. Sam then briefly thought of what Chip was thinking and feeling at that moment. He imagined his friend across the room, under the desk, peeking out, and looking for an opportunity to bolt out of the room when the two standing men weren't looking. Maybe he had done so already. Chip was so much closer to the door than he and Rabinowitz were.

Knox picked up the conversation. Laughing, he said, "Poison his matzo ball soup? Ha! Good one, Mr. Francisco! But I think we should stick with the automotive theme, especially if we're gonna pin it all on that pimple-faced, red-headed kid he hangs around with. You know, the one who looks like the kid from 'Mask,' but without all the ugly."

It was Sam who suddenly stiffened, straightened, and almost hit his head on the underside of the desk. Sam started mouthing obscenities, too, as he and Rabinowitz clasped and squeezed each other's hands hard.

"After all," Knox continued, "his pop works down at the Lube Job. It'll be an easy tie-in. We'll let it be known he was beating off to the McGregor chick for months and finally flipped his noodle when he couldn't have her. Then, he sticks close to Rabinowitz to keep track of his investigation, then offs him when he saw he was getting too close."

"You're right, of course," Francisco said. "I'll get one of my people to cut Rabinowitz's brake lines. And if that doesn't work ... yeah, what the hell? Another car bomb. Instead of one in the ignition, we'll just have it go off when he opens the driver's side door."

"Boom!" they both sang with cackling glee.

"And speaking of boom..." said Knox, his voice trailing off.

"Ah yes," said Francisco. Sam and Rabinowitz were both relieved that the two men started to move now away from their desk and towards the door back to the reception area. But what Francisco had to say next was anything but relieving. "Well, I guess it is time to say farewell to this place, too."

"You're really gonna torch it, huh?"

"Absolutely. It's time, Lieutenant. We're going to do this the Portuguese way. I've got kegs of dynamite stashed under this building. It's a Sunday. No one's around. Let's you and I get a block or two away, and then I'll blow this whole thing to Hell. Collect the insurance money and rebuild bigger and better than ever."

And with that, they were gone and out the door.

"Fuck!" Rabinowitz finally verbalized when he was fairly certain Knox and Francisco were out of earshot. He then repeated the obscenity at least three more times aloud, before stating, "I'm out! I am oh-ficially out!"

"Chip, are you still here?" Sam called out, stumbling to get to his feet.

Chip was already upright. "Of course, I'm still here! Couldn't you smell me pissing myself from across the room? Oh, man, did they ever sing!"

Rabinowitz let out a cough that hurt his insides from where he had been pummeled earlier by Brent and his gang. Rasping, he said, "Lord, have mercy, they sang like a couple of hysterical macaws on steroids!"

"And most importantly, they never mentioned me," Chip said. "They know nothing of the Black Guy. So, let's keep it that way! What did one library card say to the other library card?"

"What?" replied Sam.

"Let's book!"

With Rabinowitz in the lead, the three tore out of Francisco's workplace like it was already on fire. They weren't more than five steps into the daylight when they realized they had been duped. Once outside, Knox and Francisco had assembled a myriad of cops and employees who were waiting with cameras, flash bulbs, party horns, and confetti. Some yelled "Surprise!" Others just pointed and laughed. Knox, the ringleader, was the loudest and most animated of them all. "Pussies!" he hollered, pointing and guffawing from the hood of his squad car. "You pussy asses!" His open-mouthed laugh coupled with his widow's peak hairline gave him a weirdly skeletal look.

It didn't help that when Rabinowitz put his brakes on in mid-sprint that Sam and Chip crashed into the back of him, sending the P.I. to the pavement. The two boys helped the older man to his feet, and he came up livid. "Wait! Are you telling me all that inside was a put-up job?!"

Flash bulbs continued to pop, and now someone was throwing popcorn. Knox turned his left hand into a mock phone receiver, with his thumb as the earpiece and his pinkie as the mouthpiece. Then, in a breathy tone, he repeated the voice message he left on Mervyn's answering machine, adding a few choice words. "Rabinowitz, you dope. I know who killed the girl. As usual, you're lookin' in all the wrong places. All the answers you seek are in the files of Pedro Machado Francisco. Also ... you're a retard!"

Then, Francisco stepped forward. "Rabinowitz!" he grinned. "I have three questions for you, sir. One, do you really think that if I killed that girl, I'd keep proof of it in my place of business?" He then turned to those staff members of his gathered and said, "He really thinks that!" This prompted even louder laughter.

"Two, sir, do you think if I had some disagreement with my attorney, I would discipline him by murdering his daughter ... and in such a public fashion?!" Even more chuckles and guffaws followed.

Rabinowitz sighed. Hanging his head, he spat, "And three?"

"Three? I am a legitimate businessman." This prompted several of his workers to laugh the loudest, which immediately drew a stern look from their boss. They shut up immediately. He let his disapproving glare linger on each of them as he continued, "I am a very legitimate business-man from the great country of Portugal. Do you really think your time and resources are best served investigating me, such a pillar of this fine community?"

Rabinowitz didn't answer him. Instead, he turned his attention to Knox. The smug look on the cop's face was almost too much to bear. "Knox, you are the scum of the Earth. You and this despicable criminal wasted an entire afternoon setting up this bit of theater for your own amusements. And, meanwhile, you could have been out there tracking Muffy's killer!"

Knox climbed down off his car's hood. The vehicle bobbed up and down a couple of times after being freed of the large man's weight. The homicide detective towered over Rabinowitz, causing him to back up a few steps and draw even with Sam and Chip. Both boys knees were shaking, which Knox noticed. He decided to address them rather than his P.I. adversary. "A word of advice, you two. Go home, take off your soiled Underoos, and thank God you're not in my jail tonight for breaking into Mr. Francisco's office. This ends here, gentlemen. Muffy McGregor's murder is a police matter, and we are close. Very close. And we don't need you three screwing it all up."

Both boys nodded in agreement. Knox scanned and measured both of them. He immediately believed Chip. That kid looked completely ready to give up and move on. It was clear in his face and eyes. But there was something about his portly, red-headed friend, a certain distant resolve, that prompted Knox to get in his face.

"I mean it, boy," Knox said in a low, threatening grumble. "This ain't Scooby-Doo. We're putting that dog down right here, right now."

The cartoon reference elicited a few snickers from those gathered. One of the cops even let out a Scooby-like "Ruh roh!" to further mock Sam. The vibe was definitely hostile. Sam hated that he couldn't stop his knees from shaking and that he couldn't stand very steady. There was a real darkness to Knox, one that Sam had not experienced in another human being before. In that moment, he was absolutely frightened of him.

But Sam's resolve was strong. He wanted an answer to one question, and he wasn't afraid to ask it. "I know you were just having your way with us back there in the office, Detective, but how did you know all that stuff about me? I'm nobody important."

Knox's smugness turned into a self-satisfied, Bill Paxton-like smirk. "You're nobody at all. But you've been hanging around with ol' Mervyn here so much, I had to find out who you were. And what a waste of time that was. A stock boy at 16 Plus?! At this point, your virginity is bordering on terminal, kid."

"Yeah, yeah, but there's one thing I want to make clear, sir. I never had a crush on Muffy McGregor. I'm in love with--"

Sam caught sight of something behind Knox, off in the distant background, that caused him to leave the rest of his thought hanging in the air. It was a car, a familiar car, that pulled into the parking lot of that old fleabag motel where Chip had parked Rabinowitz's vehicle.

Knox, though, seized on the boy's words. "Oh, smoochy, smoochy," he mocked. Then, motioning over to Chip, he added, "Yeah, despite his and your blubbering in the newspaper, word is you only have eyes for ... what's her name? Friend of Muffy's. Big girl. Ha! Very big girl. Christ, she's a beast. Help me out here, Fruit Loop. What's her name?"

Sam didn't look at him. He was still fixated on the distant automobile. The driver's side door opened, and a single individual exited. She was instantly familiar to Sam. Could it be her? It was. It was her! It was Barbara. She looked all about at her surroundings, then hurried over to one of the motel room doors and knocked on it. From Sam's distance and angle, he couldn't see who opened it. But he could hear a clear and excited squeal. And he could see Barbara enter into some kind of embrace as the door closed.

"Hey," Knox barked, "I'm asking you a question, boy. What's her name?"

Sam kept looking at the motel room, its window, its closed curtains. His heart sank as he answered softly, regretfully, "Barbara."

CHAPTER 10

Maybe it was the humiliation he had just suffered at the hands of Knox, Francisco, and their cronies. Maybe it was just the shock of seeing his longtime crush get out of a car, go to a seedy motel, and squeal with delight at the sight of whomever opened the guest room door she knocked on. Or, maybe it was just the kind of false bravado young teenage boys are able to summon when they have no fear of going up to such a door, knocking on it, and demanding to know who and what's on the other side. Whatever the case, Sam strode past Rabinowitz's car in that motel parking lot and went right towards the room in question, which was on the bottom floor of the two-story lodging.

"Where are you going?" Chip called after him, as his friend's pace seemed to quicken. Chip just wanted to get out of that part of town. He was done. But being a good friend, he followed Sam and repeated his question, this time a bit louder.

About 20 feet from the room, Sam turned on his heel. In a low, angry whisper, he pointed to his destination and answered, "Barbara's behind that door, right there. I just saw her go in."

Chip glanced at the motel room door, then back at his buddy. "So, what are you gonna do? Sam, you're not her boyfriend. And she's not your--"

"She may be in trouble."

Sam knew what he had just said was a lie. He didn't even try and make it sound convincing. Nevertheless, he turned back towards the room she had gone in and continued his determined march towards it. Chip skipped ahead and got in front of him just before he could knock. "Sam," he said, making sure to keep his voice down so whoever was inside didn't hear him. "If she drove here, was all by herself, knocked on that door, and went inside ... you don't wanna do this."

"I have to do this," he replied, lunging past Chip to rap hard with his knuckles just below the room's crooked number.

Sam and Chip immediately heard a fair amount of rustling from inside. The muffled sounds of a TV got lower. Someone coughed. No answer. Sam knocked again. He could clearly hear Barbara mutter a profanity. "Damn!"

She was close to the door. Sam could feel her approach. The door opened just a crack, and their eyes met. Clearly, she didn't expect it to be him on the other side. "Sam?!" she exclaimed, a mix of emotions in her voice. Surprise. Embarrassment. Anger. "What the hell are you doing here? Did you follow me?!"

Rabinowitz, who had been trailing at a distance and was unaware of everything, had almost made it to his car. He'd been looking down at the pavement the whole way back from Francisco's office, muttering to himself and making future alternative plans to leave the P.I. profession. This time, he was serious. When he saw Chip and Sam talking to some girl at the door of a motel room, he first assumed she was a hooker.

"No time for that!" he called out.

"Oh my God!" Barbara raged. "You brought Chip? You brought the detective?!"

Sam was immediately on the defensive. But, as he was with Knox, he didn't shrink from the questioning. "It's not like that. We were tracking down a lead on Muffy's killer, and I saw you get out of your car. What are you doing here?"

Chip leaned in. With a sly smile, he added, "What he means to ask is, '*Who* are you doing here?'"

Barbara made a move to slam the door, but Sam blocked her. His sudden physicality surprised the girl. A certain panic started to set in on her face and in her voice. Sam scanned the small motel room, which was disheveled and quite messy as if it hadn't received maid service in several days. But he didn't see anybody else. A couple of seconds later, he heard a flush and took notice that a rickety bathroom fan was whirring quite loudly from behind a closed door to Barbara's left. "Sam," Barbara pleaded. "You have to leave now. Please!"

To Sam, it suddenly sounded like Barbara really was in trouble. Something was definitely not right, which compelled him to soften his tone. "Why? What's going on here?"

The bathroom door then opened. Before Sam and Chip could see who it was, the person called out not knowing there was more than Barbara on the other side. "Barbie, I ordered us a pizza. Is it here?"

The boys were surprised to hear that it was a soft voice. A female voice. A familiar voice. The next sight caused them both to gasp. Her hair had changed. It was no longer blonde, but brown. She didn't look stylish in any way. No designer labels. No Jordache jeans. And no make-up whatsoever. But Sam and Chip recognized her immediately.

Muffy McGregor was alive!

All four teenagers just stared at each other for several seconds in stunned silence. Sam and Chip looked at Muffy. Muffy looked at Barbara. Barbara looked at Sam. Sam looked at Chip. There was shock. There was disbelief. There was hesitancy. And then there was a steady stream of profanity for a good half-minute, mostly variations of "Shit," "Oh shit," and "Holy shit!"

A dozen questions immediately came to Sam's mind. To Chip's, too. They almost stumbled over each other in getting the first barrage out.

"You're alive?!"

"Did you fake your own death?!"

"Have you been hiding out here the whole time?"

"Do you know what this has done to your family?

"Your friends?!"

"Why would you do this?!"

"If it wasn't you, then who blew up in your car?"

Muffy responded only to the last question. She seemed almost pleased with herself when she answered, "Bag Lady Betty. And I bet she hasn't been missed." Muffy then shot one more look over at Barbara and posed the question: "Did you bring them here?"

Barbara was almost frantic in her defensive answer. "I swear Muffy! I had NO idea they were at the door when I answered. I thought--"

"You didn't think!" she chastised. "Oh God! This is the last thing he and I need!"

Sam stepped forward. "He? Who he? Muffy, what the frig is going on?!"

"None of your damn business!" she yelled. The ferocity of her response caused Sam to step back and away from her. A look of disgust came over Muffy's face when he was once again shoulder to shoulder with Chip. "And I've got a question for you two thumb-dicks. Why the Hell were you bawling over me in the newspaper?! We were in home-room together. That's it!"

Sam and Chip sheepishly looked at each other and fumbled for a response. Neither one of them really got a coherent sentence out beyond "Uh, well, you know ... the moment ... it was ... all sad ... and--"

Sam then called out, "Rabinowitz! Get in here! Get in here now!" He looked over at Barbara, who was now sitting on the motel room's one double bed. Tears were streaming down her face. As Muffy started throwing clothes in a large purse that was close to the room's TV set, Sam turned to Barbara and asked, "Did you know about this the whole time? Was all that stuff at the funeral and the wake and the celebration today just an act?"

Barbara didn't answer. She could only look at Muffy and plead, "Don't go! I just got you back! I'm sorry. I'm SO sorry!"

Chip, on the other hand, was drawn more to the TV in the room and what was on. "Oh my god, Sam!" he exclaimed. "Look! It's 'Lassiter!' What are the odds?!"

Sam was incredulous. "'Lassiter?! Who the hell cares about 'Lassiter?!'"

"I think this is HBO!" he stated excitedly, sitting down at the foot of the bed. Then, turning to Muffy, he asked, "Is this HBO? Because if it is, we're only, like, two scenes away from Jane Seymour naked. Buns and side boobage!"

Sam shook his head. Turning to Muffy who was just about finished putting her bare essentials in a large handbag, he said, "Muffy, Barbara's right. You can't leave. Not without telling us what this is all about." Sam called out for Rabinowitz again.

Muffy flung her bag, which was now heaving with clothes, over her left shoulder. She then gave Sam the middle finger gesture and replied, "Sit on this and spin! I'm out of here!"

She made for the open door at the exact same time Rabinowitz entered the motel room. They both froze, and it took the P.I. only a couple of seconds to realize just who it was he was looking at. When he did, his reaction was pretty much the same as Sam and Chip's. He couldn't get a coherent sentence out. He could only whisper "Oh shit."

Muffy didn't hesitate. She balled up her fist and hit Rabinowitz square in the stomach. The blow landed right where he had been hit repeatedly by Brent earlier in the day. It knocked the wind out of him, and he crumpled to his knees, dropping his car keys as he fell. Muffy scooped them up and made her way to the parking lot. She heard a bus in the distant background, its air brakes exhaling at a stop that sounded at least three or four blocks away. She didn't even consider waiting for it. There were only three vehicles in the entire lot, and she was reasonably sure the one parked furthest from the motel was the detective's.

Back inside the room, Sam rushed to Rabinowitz's aid as the older man gasped for air and cursed all teenagers worldwide. But his laments were brief. He knew they couldn't lose Muffy. Looking up at Sam, his voice strained, he ordered, "Forget me! Go after the girl!"

Sam complied immediately. But no sooner had he set one foot out the motel room door when--

Kaboom!!! Rabinowitz's car exploded with a fury that lifted the boy off his feet and propelled him backwards in the air. His head actually hit the motel room's bed, and he bounced awkwardly back forward and to the side. Barbara screamed and fell off the mattress the opposite way, her feet kicking Chip in the head. They both rolled off and landed hard on the floor.

Rabinowitz who was still in a kneeling position and recovering from Muffy's punch, instinctively flung himself forward at the first sound of the blast. He was lying flat, face down on the floor, as the room filled almost immediately with smoke and bits of flaming glass and metal. A bit of the shrapnel landed on the back of his neck, and he quickly brushed it off before it could sear him too badly.

"Holy God!" Rabinowitz yelled.

Once it seemed the brief rain of debris had stopped both inside and outside the room, he rolled over onto his back to see what had happened. At first, the smoke billowing towards him was too thick to make anything out. He started to cough as it swiftly became hard to breathe. But the thickness of the haze didn't last long. In a matter of seconds, he could see that his obliterated car was now a fiery shell of its former self.

Rabinowitz looked for Muffy. Any sign of her. But there was none. He turned back to the three young people in the room. "Is everybody OK?" he called out.

Sam was closest to him. His coughing kept him from being in a state of complete shock. The boy was on his back, rubbing his neck, but he appeared to be unharmed for the most part. Chip was already helping Barbara back to the bed. The girl seemed almost catatonic. "What just happened?" she asked.

Chip looked at Rabinowitz for an answer. All he could see in the man's eyes was horror and tragedy. "OK, seriously," Chip said. "For real, did what just happen really happen?"

Rabinowitz nodded. "Yeah," he answered. Then, looking back at the burning remnants of his vehicle, he added, "Oh, we really shit the bed on this one."

Sam finally was able to muster a question. "What *did* just happen?" Finally, he was able to pull himself up to a sitting position and look out the door. His heart sank when he saw the destruction. "Oh, no," he first said quietly before adding, "Are you kidding me?! How can someone want someone dead this much?! Poor Muffy!"

Rabinowitz sidled over to his young friend. A small trickle of blood was starting to flow from what looked like a glass cut above Sam's right eye. Rabinowitz pulled out a napkin that he had in his pants pocket, crouched down, and dabbed at the fresh wound. Holding pressure on it, he looked at his young friend and at Chip and said, "That blast wasn't meant for Muffy. That was MY car! It was meant for me! Maybe even for us. Whoever rigged it to blow must have done so while we were futzing around in Francisco's office."

Chip joined the two men on the floor, taking up a catcher's stance. He took the napkin from Rabinowitz and worked on his friend for him. The only sounds they heard in the moment were the flickering flames of the car fire outside and the mournful, whimpering sobs of Barbara, whose face was buried in two pillows.

Rabinowitz shook his head. One thought came to his head that he felt like vocalizing, "Oh, God. I wonder if Knox heard that thing go off?"

Not a second later, they all heard the first police sirens.

————

Detective Knox and several of his fellow officers were still at Francisco's office a couple blocks away when the car bomb went off. As a result, it may have been the fastest police response to a crime in Laurel's history. Rabinowitz never gave the local cops much credit for anything really. But even he was impressed with how fast they cordoned off the area and isolated the crime scene. It helped that the Chief of Police was called to the scene and took command immediately upon arriving. And Laurel's Fire Department also responded swiftly, putting the vehicle fire out even faster than the first one not two weeks earlier.

Rabinowitz's first thoughts were that Knox was somehow involved. But he found the man's immediate bewilderment, especially in the initial moments on the scene, to be genuine. He didn't even show any disappointment that it was not Rabinowitz who was torched in the car. And Knox didn't keep him out of the loop either. He needed information quick with his boss there.

In the chaos, one of the first things Knox and his men did upon realizing Muffy had been killed for real this time was take Sam, Chip, and Barbara and place them in one of the motel rooms farthest from the blast. He stationed an officer inside with them and told the cop to report anything that was said between the three. He then took Rabinowitz to another room to get his statement. What Rabinowitz told him was unbelievable.

"You saw her?!" he questioned. "You are absolutely certain it was Muffy McGregor?"

"Yes, yes. Her hair was a different color. She wasn't gussied up like the store-bought princess we've seen in all the pictures. But it was her."

"Alright, Rabinowitz. Tell me all you know."

By this point, they were joined by two other cops, one of whom was taking down everything that was said in a notebook. The other was there just to look tough, Rabinowitz surmised. A third cop then walked in with what looked to be the motel's manager. Rabinowitz didn't pay any of them any attention. He didn't know any of them. He only knew Knox.

"Know? All I know is the redheaded kid saw a girl he knew from his school -- that one you were asking him about, Barbara. He saw her go into that motel room. Room 3A. He went and knocked on the door. She answered, he must've pushed his way in -- you know how teen boys get -- and inside he found Muffy. I didn't get there 'til late. I'm about to get into my car and slink the Hell out of here after the day I've had. Thank God, I didn't! Thank God, the kid called out to me. 'Rabinowitz! Rabinowitz! Get in here!' I walk in. I see the girl. I can't believe it. She sucker-punches me in the gut, takes my keys, and moments later--"

"Kaboom."

"Kablooey."

Knox paced the room. None of this made sense to him. Turning to the manager, he ordered, "OK, now you. Talk."

The manager was an older man. Scuzzy was probably the word that best described him. In a couple or three years, he would probably qualify as "elderly." His hair was still black, though. It was probably a dye job. He sort of looked liked a skinnier, less nourished Ronald Reagan, albeit not in a suit, but in a soiled undershirt and denim shorts. He was a nasty man with an old military tattoo on his left bicep and chest hair that stretched from each shoulder on up to his Adam's apple.

"What do ya wanna know?" he asked in a gravelly voice.

"The girl in 3A. Tell me everything you know about her."

"Jailbait probably. But good cans. Kept hopin' she'd use the pool. Pouty lips, too. I'm a lips man. And when I saw her--"

"Fool, I know what she looked like!" Knox said, practically launching himself across the room at the man. The manager's eyes never widened above a squint, though. "What I don't know is, when did she check in? How did she pay? Was she here with anyone else?"

"OK, that's a lot of questions. And I only got the second one. She paid with cash. Paid for the first week with a wad of bills. Paid for the second week with an envelope of money she slid under my office door."

"Was she staying here with anyone else? Did you ever see anyone go into 3A other than her?"

The manager pulled a cigarette that he had resting above his right ear and was about to light it when Knox flicked it out of his hand. The cop didn't need to restate his last two questions. The scowl on his face was enough to prompt the manager to answer. "Yeah, someone was there with her. But never during the day. Only at night. And maybe not every night either. But several nights this week and several nights last. At least I think so."

"Male? Female?"

"Definitely a dude. He'd come off the bus and go right for 3A."

"Description?"

"Oh, man. He was thin, I can tell ya that much. Thin and kind of tall."

"Kind of tall or tall?" Knox sought to clarify.

"Well, not Len Bias tall. But, you know, tall. Look, it was always dark, and he was always like a shadow when I'd see him out my office window. You know, like one of those ... what do you call 'ems? Somersets?"

"Silhouettes."

"Yeah. Sil-oh-ettes. That's what he was. One of them. He'd always show up just before the 10 O'Clock News. And, hey, he and she ... if they were together-together, they sure kept quiet. What can I say? Cash money on time and no noise complaints? Best I can ask for in this gig. They never even called for housekeeping."

Knox sighed. Still nothing made sense. He turned to Rabinowitz. "Anything you wanna ask him?"

Rabinowitz shook his head. " I got nothing," he lamented. "But I know someone who I would dearly love to ask a few questions of right now."

"Barbara Jensen?"

"You bet."

———

Barbara was motionless, lying on the one lone queen-sized bed in the guest room Knox had put her, Sam, and Chip in. She still couldn't believe Muffy had "died" again. Her ears still rung from the explosion. She felt antsy. She felt completely out of sorts. And it didn't help that Sam's love-sick face was just a few feet from her own, staring at her with the utmost concern. She couldn't look at him. She just couldn't look at him.

"Was it all an act?" he asked, hurt very much in his voice. "How long did you know? The whole time?"

"Yes, Miss Jensen," Knox said in a booming voice as he entered the small, sparsely decorated room. "How long indeed?"

Barbara jumped at his quick and sudden appearance, and she scurried across the bed away from him into the corner where the mattress met the room's far wall. She was very aware that she was trembling, and she wondered if the others could see it.

Rabinowitz entered just behind Knox and closed the door. There were now six people in the small room, including the one officer who Knox stationed with them. Barbara had seen enough cop shows on TV to know she was at a distinct disadvantage. "Shouldn't I have an attorney present for this?" she sobbed. Then, turning to Rabinowitz, she asked, "You're probably also a lawyer, right?"

Rabinowitz frowned at her. "Oh yeah," he replied, sarcasm thick in his tone. "I'm a P.I. AND a lawyer. And Chip here plays in the NBA, and Sam's the bastard son of Burger King."

Knox immediately cut him off. "Give it a rest, why don't you." He then became surprisingly soothing. He grabbed the room's lone chair and dragged it over to the foot of Barbara's bed. Before he sat, he ran water from a nearby sink into a glass and gave it to the girl to sip. "You don't need a lawyer, Miss," he said. "Not if you haven't done anything wrong. If you have? Then, yes. My officer here will give you a ride down to the station, and we'll get an attorney and your parents and whoever else we have to get involved. Or we can just have our conversation right here."

Barbara took a drink from the glass and thought for a moment. The whole room waited for her response, and she very much felt the pressure. She knew she had done nothing wrong or illegal. At least, she didn't think she had. And she really didn't want to go to a police station. So, she decided to answer Knox's questions.

"I just found out a little over an hour ago. Two hours ago now, I guess. I swear it. Muffy called me out of the blue. Someone had been calling my house for the last couple of days. Each time, my mom or my dad or my little brother would answer, and the person on the other end would hang up. Finally, I answered. And it was her. I couldn't believe it was her, but it was. I'd just gotten home from the celebration of her life. And I was really lucky no one else was home, because I just lost it over the phone. I was so happy."

By the time Barbara had gotten to that last sentence, she had worked herself back up into a good cry. Sam wanted to comfort her. He wanted to get on the bed, pull the covers over the both of them, and just hold her.

But she just wasn't giving him anything. She still hadn't looked at him since the explosion.

"Miss Jensen, I am sorry for your loss ... again," Knox said, trying to calm her just a bit. "But there are questions that need to be answered. The law needs to know everything Muffy shared with you. Anything less would indeed be a crime."

"I really don't know all that much. That's why I came here. To get answers."

"Let's take this one at a time then. Did Muffy indeed fake her own death?"

"Yes. She did tell me that much over the phone."

"OK. Do you know who helped her? Because whoever helped her set the first bomb almost certainly set the second one."

"I don't know, sir. I truly don't. I'd tell you if I knew."

"I believe you. The motel manager spoke of a man who would get off the bus outside here most evenings, and he'd spend the night. Was it her boyfriend from school? Was it Brent Fitzpatrick?"

Barbara started rocking back and forth from a balled-up position on the bed. She hoped the motion would stop her shaking, but it didn't. It was embarrassing. She could feel the room tensing up as she didn't answer immediately. Finally, she did. "I told you. I don't know who it was. Muffy always had several guys on the string who were way into her. It wasn't just Brent. And before you ask, I don't think he had any clue she was still alive either. But I don't know 100 percent, OK? So, if it ends up being him..."

Knox jotted down a few notes of his own as she talked. "Uh huh," he said after every other sentence of hers. It was a little trick he picked up over the years as part of his interrogation training. If you kept muttering "Uh huh," most interviewees will continue to talk more than they want. He also used another tactic on Barbara when he kept saying, "I believe you. I believe you." After that last one, he then said, "One more question, Miss Jensen, but a big one. With the first car explosion, we found Muffy's purse, her car keys, and her charred ID in the wreckage. We found all that stuff burned up with her. But, obviously, it wasn't her. So, who was it?"

All three of the teens answered in unison. "Bag Lady Betty!"

Both Knox and Rabinowitz were immediately horrified. Everyone who knew the mall, knew Bag Lady Betty. She was what they called "local color." "That's terrible!" the private eye said. "Are you saying ... do you mean to tell me? Oh, that poor homeless woman!"

"So, Muffy and some mystery guy set Betty up to roast?" the cop asked. "Damn, that's cold."

Rabinowitz nodded in agreement. "What kind of a messed-up school are you kids going to? I mean, I .... I--"

Knox finished his sentence. "I don't remember pom-poms ever being this cutthroat. You?"

"I went to Hebrew school. There wasn't much cheer. So, how did all three of you know?"

Sam was quick to answer. "Muffy just told us. In fact, it was the only thing she told us before..."

Sam's voice dropped off for two reasons. One, because he still couldn't quite vocalize all that had just transpired. And, two, there was a knock at the motel room door. Knox went to answer it and was surprised to see his boss, Police Chief Everett Greenslade. Not surprisingly, the tall, intense looking, African-American man appeared glum.

Knox slumped, immediately sensing his day was about to get even worse. "What now, sir?"

"Muffy McGregor's father just arrived," the commander answered. "And you're gonna tell him."

CHAPTER 11

Sam couldn't remember the last time he woke up in his own bed and had both of his parents there with him. But there they were, Calvin and Francine, back together again and sitting at the foot of his mattress with worried looks on their faces. It was almost as if he had a bad case of the flu, and they had stayed up all night with him like when he was a little kid. This was not the case, of course.

Neither parent woke Sam up. It was the TV in his room that was playing at a low volume that beckoned him back to consciousness. CBS's Washington affiliate, Channel 9, was carrying a live early morning press conference. Sam immediately recognized three of the faces on camera: Police Chief Greenslade, Detective Knox, and Rabinowitz.

"Turn it up," Sam said, woozily, sitting up in bed.

Calvin complied. Greenslade was front and center. "Thank you for your thoughtful questions and your sensitivity in this matter," he said. "To sum up, Muffy McGregor was most definitely not killed in the June 16 car bomb. But she DID perish in a second car bombing yesterday in the early evening. The blast was not meant for her, but for the operator of the vehicle, private investigator Mervyn Rabinowitz. Mr. Rabinowitz had tracked a lead to the Safari Inn. He exited his automobile and placed this lodging under surveillance from a nearby location so as not to be seen. When he discovered Miss McGregor alive and well and in temporary residency at the lodging, he went to her guest room door -- Room 3A -- and confronted her. An argument ensued where Miss McGregor was able to get Mr. Rabinowitz's car keys from him, and she attempted to flee in his vehicle. However, someone had rigged the vehicle to blow, and that's what it did when Miss McGregor opened the driver side door. We believe Miss McGregor and an accomplice staged the first explosion for reasons unknown. We believe her accomplice set the second bomb, not targeting Miss McGregor but Mr. Rabinowitz. We are now actively hunting this suspect. Thank you."

All three men exited to the right and out of camera range. Reporter Phyllis Armstrong then appeared on camera, summing up what Greenslade had just said.

"Unbelievable," Sam muttered.

"Unbelievable indeed," Francine quietly said, anger simmering just underneath her calm, cool cadence. She spoke calmly, slowly, almost sweetly as if she were telling her once-little boy a bedtime story. "Unbelievable that you could have been killed. Unbelievable that the authorities are keeping yours and Chip's name out of all this. And unbelievable that this man, your father, knew about all of this and didn't share with me, your mother."

Francine didn't look at "this man," her ex-husband, as she spoke. She had barely said two words to him since they were both called to the motel the evening before to pick up their son, who had decided to play amateur private investigator for reasons she still didn't quite understand. Calvin palmed her shoulder, and she immediately tensed. "Franny, I'm sorry. I thought--"

"Off me."

Calvin immediately removed his hand.

"Sam," she continued, "you were literally a car door away from getting yourself killed. I am so incredibly grateful that didn't happen. But I'm also so incredibly furious at you for putting yourself in that kind of danger in the first place. Please don't ramble on about penance and Catholic guilt and all that nonsensical manure you were shoveling last night. I want you to tell me the whole story ... the real story!"

Sam was straining to hear the information that Armstrong was relaying back to the Channel 9 news studio. Calvin had turned the volume down so they could talk. "Could you turn that back up?" Sam asked.

"Oh my God!" Francine raged. "Are you kidding me? Sam, I'm talking to you."

"I know, Mom. But I need to know what's being said about all this."

"What's being said?! Nothing is being said to you about any of this anymore. Chief Greenslade and that officer, that Detective Knox, made that very clear last night when your father and I picked you up. Thank God, they want to keep you and your friend out of this. You're lucky your faces aren't on the front page of every local newspaper this morning ... crying for real!"

Calvin agreed. "Your mother is right. And I should never have--"

"Silence, you," Francine calmly seethed.

"But, Mom, Chief Greenslade isn't telling the whole truth. He's barely telling half of it. I'm the one who found Muffy."

"By sheer, dumb luck!" his mother exclaimed, pointing her index finger in a way that only a mother can do.

"Yeah," Sam agreed, "and he's leaving that part out, too. He and Detective Knox and Rabinowitz, they huddled for a long time before they talked to Mr. and Mrs. McGregor. And they kept Chip and Barbara and me in that motel room for a long, long time, too, then slipped us out the side before anybody could see us. And then--"

"Sam," Francine interrupted, her voice having gone from storybook soothing to concerned parent exasperated. "You're letting this go. This isn't about a murder anymore. This is about bureaucracy."

"Bureaucracy?"

Sam had heard the word. They threw it around a lot on those political talk shows that would air Sunday mornings on TV. "Meet the Press," "The McLaughlin Group." But he never really thought about what it meant.

"The police, the city, probably the McGregor family. Everyone's covering their asses now," Calvin simplified.

"Shut up," Francine ordered, finally locking eyes with him.

Calvin launched himself out of his chair. "No, I won't shut up, Franny! I'm agreeing with you. Sam, I think I was so eager to be your friend and not your parent that I made a bone-headed decision. I was even going to help you somehow. I really don't know how I was gonna help you. But I was gonna try. And I ... I could have lost you! We all got lucky on this one. Real lucky! So, yeah, just let this go, Sam, OK? Go to work. You got work today, right? Go to your job. Go back to being a kid, a regular ordinary kid. Would you please do that?"

Sam's head fell back to his pillow. He let out a loud, adolescent sigh and came close to a pout. He knew there was more to this. He could feel it. He didn't know what. But it taunted him.

"A regular, ordinary kid," he lamented in his mind. The regular and the ordinary were all he had ever been surrounded by, he thought. Maybe that's why he had always felt the music of Billy Joel more deeply than other artists. Here was an ordinary looking dude who had scored the extraordinary supermodel Christie Brinkley. Just for that, his songs had to mean something. Sam must have heard Joel's classic hit, "Piano Man," a couple hundred times over the years. It was a song he had grown up with. And he always -- always -- felt the lyric, "Well, I'm sure I could be a movie star, if I could get out of this place."

He had gotten close to the extraordinary with the Muffy McGregor case. Everything that was now transpiring and would be transpiring in the days to come was a direct result of him just having his eyes open and seeing Barbara get out of her car at that particular time and place. Sam wanted to believe it was because of his instinct or his dogged determination. He was even willing to believe it was God's will that put him there at that exact instant. He was willing to believe anything other than it was "sheer, dumb luck."

His mother could see the conflict and defiance in Sam's eyes. Once again, she said sternly, "Let this go, Sam."

Surprising to Sam, he started to tear up. It was the one thing he hadn't done throughout all of this. He didn't really cry that day his picture was snapped for the paper. He didn't cry at Muffy's funeral. And he couldn't bring himself to cry with Barbara at the real loss of her friend the day before. Now, it was all catching up to him. The emotions, the magnitude of it all. He started crying. Hard. Both his parents tried to console him, but he slapped both their hands away.

"It's hard to let this go, Mom!" he exclaimed. "I mean, they're not even saying anything about Betty!"

"Betty?" Francine and Calvin asked at the same time.

"Bag Lady Betty," he replied. "Yeah, I know it's wrong. But that's what the kids and most of the people who work at the mall called that homeless woman who would prowl the mall's parking lot and ask people for change as they got out of their cars. She'd always rage about the evils of the shopping center and how life in Laurel was so much better before the mall was put up. She was the one that Muffy and whoever coaxed to take Muffy's car that day. They must have given her Muffy's purse and keys. Poor woman. She must have thought she hit the jackpot. Shows you how thin Muffy was that she had the same body type as a dope fiend."

Sam's tears fell hard and fast as he related the story. He didn't expect much insight or even empathy from his parents. One thing the two had in common was their complete unwillingness to give any homeless person even a dime or a nickel from their pocket, whether it was the homeless Vietnam vet who had been outside of the Safeway supermarket for years or Bag Lady Betty herself. But he really didn't expect his mom's response. "Poor Cindy!" she said.

"Poor Cindy?" Sam repeated.

Francine seemed lost in a memory. Her eyes darted from side to side, and she didn't blink. "Yeah, poor Cindy. She always felt guilty for Betty's downward spiral. That woman was no dope fiend. She was just a down-on-her-luck poor soul who Cindy caught shoplifting at Hecht's a couple of years ago. She tried to stuff all sorts of merchandise under her coat in one of the dressing rooms. Cindy had no choice. She had to turn her over to the authorities. It was her job. Betty was high on something, she resisted arrest, and the whole thing just tore her life to smithereens. Lost her husband, her kid, and eventually her dignity. Cindy would park on the other side of the mall just to avoid Betty."

Sam felt as emotional as Brent. Even Betty's story caused him to weep. "Just gimme a second, OK?" he bawled, covering his eyes with his hands. Then, in a mocking voice directed at his dad, he added, "Gimme a second to get ready for my job."

Calvin was not to be mocked. "Hey, now you be thankful for that job. Work's important, son. Work can give you a purpose when you can't find purpose in anything else. Do you know how many times my life has turned to crap, and I just threw myself into my oil changes and my tune-ups? Maybe I'm not living my dream of changing oil and tires for Bobby Unser or Cale Yarborough. But I'm changing 'em for my friends and neighbors. I'm even still changing 'em for this one." Calvin pointed over to Francine and let out a nervous chuckle.

Sam couldn't quite join Calvin in his laugh, but at least he was calming down. He even accepted a supportive hug from his mother. "I'm sorry, Mom," he told her. But it was a doubled-edged apology. He was sorry that he didn't tell her the truth about all that had been going on. And he was also sorry that he still wouldn't be leaving Muffy McGregor's murder alone.

———

Vernon Roundtree wasn't quite so gentle with his son when he woke up that morning. "Good morning, dumb ass!" he exclaimed. "Guess what? You're still alive!"

Chip immediately rolled his eyes. From the get-go, he felt like he had been pulled into all of this tragic ridiculousness against his will. But he often felt like he didn't have many choices. He never wanted to go to a nearly all-white Catholic school. He wanted to go to the local public school. But his dad had made his mom a promise. It was very important to her that he have a Christian-based education, and there were no decent Lutheran or Baptist high schools anywhere near Laurel.

Similarly, Chip had told Sam time and again, he didn't wanted to be a part of his "crazy Goonies adventure" or his "damn, fool idealistic crusade," trying to use pop culture references to convince his friend to just leave everything be. And he really didn't want to keep things from his father. He never had before. He knew the man would find out. The man always found things out.

"I don't know how many times I can say 'I'm sorry, Dad,'" Chip replied, fighting back a yawn. He held it in so as to not irritate Vernon further.

Vernon had been watching the morning press conference on Channel 9, too. He was irked that he had the sound up, and his son wasn't even stirring to listen. Only when Chief Greenslade had left the podium did Chip even start to rouse. "Where did I go wrong?" Vernon asked thin air. "Everyone used to call you 'Chip Off the 'Ol Block,' 'cause you and I have always been so much alike. But now? Who are you? 'Let the Chips Fall Where They May?' Will that be your Indian name now?"

"Oh come on, Dad--"

"I tell you who you almost were yesterday. 'Chips and Pieces All Over the Place!'"

"Is this prepared material, Dad? I was expecting a lecture when I woke up this morning, not shtick."

"Don't smart-mouth me, boy! Or I'll shtick your little narrow behind in the--"

Chip cut him off. "Hey, move over just a bit! You're blocking the screen. It's Rabinowitz!" From over his father's shoulder, Chip could see the private investigator on TV trying to make his way out of the police station while being followed and questioned by reporters. At first, Rabinowitz tried to walk hurriedly ahead of them while refusing to answer questions. He definitely looked tired, like he had been up all night. Suddenly, one of the questions must have got to the P.I., because he stopped and decided to answer.

"Yes, let me repeat that again," he said, looking right into the camera. "To any and all hearing this or watching at home on television, especially any mad bombers out there, Mervyn Rabinowitz is no longer a private investigator. I am permanently closing my practice, effective immediately."

"But, sir," one journalist interrupted, shoving a tape recorder in Rabinowitz's face. "Why quit now when you could be so close to cracking this case?"

Rabinowitz looked about as scared as a grown man could be. He corrected the reporter immediately. "I am not close to solving this case. I never was, and now I never will be. If you have a tip or any information on the murder of Muffy McGregor, please contact Detective Beauregard Knox of the County Police. The P.I. practice of Mervyn Rabinowitz is officially closed."

The next questions came in rapid-fire succession as Rabinowitz resumed his hurried gait.

"What about your other cases?"

"How will your other clients react?"

"Is there anything you want to say to those clients who are relying on you?"

Rabinowitz stopped again. To Chip, he looked like Kermit the Frog flailing at the beginning of each "Muppet Show" episode. "How will they react? How will they react?! I don't know! How does anyone react to anything anymore? It always comes down to the same thing, doesn't it? How does this affect ME?"

Vernon turned to Chip and said, "Wow, your man is losin' it!"

Rabinowitz raged on, the shaky TV camera zeroing in on his face. "Well, for once, I am going to think about how something affects Rabinowitz! What do I say to my other clients? I say ... yes, your husband is likely cheating on you! Yes, you wife is very likely cheating on you! No, that old lost love from high school does NOT want you to find her! That old lost love is very likely married, a couple of kids, house in the 'burbs. I know, I know. Refunds! Once the Bomb Squad has completed its sweep of my home and office, I will be issuing full refunds to all of my clients with outstanding cases. And then I will be pulling up stakes and leaving the state with my loving family."

One male reporter off-camera then had the gall to note aloud: "But, sir, you don't have a car."

Rabinowitz shot eye daggers at the man. "What? Is that supposed to be funny? I mean, is this Weekend Update? I'm Chevy Chase, and you're not? I know I don't have a car. I'll rent one. I'll borrow one. I'll steal the fucker if I have to! Where's YOUR car?!"

Seconds after Rabinowitz uttered his profanity, Channel 9 cut back to the studio and the on-air host apologized for anyone watching who was just offended. Vernon turned the set off, disappointed that he wasn't going to see how far the scene was going to play out. "Rabinowitz ain't exactly what they call 'media-savvy,' is he?"

Chip shook his head "no." Falling back to his pillow, he said with a groan, "What a fuster cluck." He never could curse in front of his father.

Vernon could see his son was deeply troubled and decided to soften his tone a bit. It had been a tense, confusing night, picking his son up from police custody, seeing Sam's mother and father there also and them being just as in the dark about what the two boys had been up to as he was. "You know what the surprising thing in all this is?" Vernon asked.

"No, what?"

"That Sam -- SAM! -- got you into this much trouble. I always thought of him as this Pillsbury Doughboy kind of kid. Every time you've ever asked, 'Dad can I go over to Sam's place?' or 'Dad, I'm going to the movies with Sam,' I never worried. You were with Sam. Pudgy-ass, Muppet-faced Sam. So, what's the deal? Hormones? Did he have a thing for this Muffy? I thought he was all into the chunky asses?"

Chip had forgotten that his father knew nothing of the newspaper photo that put this whole series of events into motion. He briefly debated telling his dad everything, but he really was just tired of the whole thing. He didn't want to keep lying, or at least not telling him the whole truth. But his desire to move on was greater. So he said simply, "Oh, he still likes 'em large. I guess he was trying to impress this girl, Barbara, who was Muffy's best friend. Be the hero and all."

"Then, that boy's crazy. But, man, looking back now, I guess he always was at least a little crazy, huh? I remember when I took you two ice skating last year at Supplee, and he saw that big girl out on the ice in that tight sweater with the POW! and the POW!" Vernon motioned to his chest area and buttocks area with each "Pow!"

Chip chuckled at the memory. "Yeah, I remember."

"What was that chick's name? She had a sister's name?"

"Yvette."

"Yeah, Yvette. Man, what was that pick-up line he used on her? I remember thinking at the time: 'Worst pick-up line ever!'"

Chip's chuckle turned into a laugh. Vernon poked him in the ribs. "You remember what it was, don't you? What was it?"

Through his laughing, Chip said, "Hey, baby. I'm Dorothy Hamill on the streets, Mark Hamill in the sheets."

Both Roundtree men shared a good laugh at the memory, and both agreed that Sam was probably always a little crazy. Harmless, for the most part ... but definitely crazy. And eventually Vernon nudged his son from bed to get ready for his mall job. Vernon was also a dedicated working man like Calvin. And he wasn't going to let his son's responsibilities go by the wayside. It was time to get past this.

———

As fate would have it, Sam and Chip reported for work right at the same time that morning. They had come in different doors of the mall. But they crossed paths just as Sam was heading towards 16 Plus and Chip was making his way to Harmony Hut. It was 9:55 a.m., and the mall was minutes from opening.

There was an immediate tension between the two boys. Fears and feelings and tensions had been churned up that hadn't been there before. They spent several hours together after Muffy's death -- her real death -- but they hadn't talked much. At first, it was pure shock. But as the minutes became hours and little was said, a certain awkwardness began to set in that had never been there before.

They made small talk there in the middle of the mall that morning. "You OK?" asked Sam.

"Yeah," Chip answered. "You?"

Sam nodded in the affirmative. "So, did you see Rabinowitz on the news?"

"Yeah, he's really freaked out. But who can blame him?"

"I can't believe he's just quitting on us," Sam lamented. "We're so damn close."

Chip glared at his friend. "What are you talking about? Are you, like, still thinking you're on some big P.I. case?! Jeez, Sam! You must have a death wish or something? We really gotta let this go. We almost friggin' died yesterday!"

Sam resumed his walk towards 16 Plus. No Rabinowitz. No Chip. No problem. He'd go it alone. Maybe it was better this way. "Fine," he muttered. "Just fine."

Against his better judgment, Chip hurried after him. "Look, before, there at least was Rabinowitz. And we were just sniffing around our class. But, yesterday, it got real. Dude, I am not even processing yesterday. I'm flipping out. But you and I can't just leave town. I mean, we can. But I ain't runnin' away. I'm delicate, dude. Fragile. I wouldn't last on the run."

Sam kept up his stride. He was almost at 16 Plus, and he knew Chip wouldn't follow him into the store. "We're not running away," Sam said in a very determined voice, "and we're not going to pretend like we're not a part of this. The cops and Rabinowitz may have kept our names out of everything to save face, but whoever rigged that car knows we're involved. Aren't you even the least bit pissed that someone tried to kill us? I know you're scared. I'm scared, too. But I'm seeing this through."

Chip was dumbfounded. He truly had never seen his friend like this. He didn't know what to make of him. He could only muster one word. "Why?"

Sam hadn't even noticed that the two of them had drifted inside of 16 Plus. They were within earshot of Collette when he replied, "Why? I'll tell you why. Because I don't wanna be like every other sad-sack grown-up punching a time clock and living for the weekend. At least not yet. I know I'm only a couple of years away from it ... from working here at the mall full-time or down at the Lube Job with my dad. My folks got no money saved up for college. I'm not even college material. And I ain't going in the military! So, I'm two years away from this drudgery. But this murder and playing P.I. and trying to find out who killed Muffy. It's done something to me, Chip. It's horrible to say, but ... man, I've never felt more alive!"

It was at that point, both boys realized that Collette had heard the whole thing. Sam couldn't read her emotion. If ever a woman could clean up at poker, it was Collette Stephenson. Was she pissed that he had unwittingly lumped her in as a sad-sack grown-up punching a time clock? Was she disappointed that he had lied to her about "playing P.I." Was it both? Regardless, her demeanor was stoic, even icy. Her voice was authoritative. "Thank you for being on time this morning, Sam. Could you please go tend to the stockroom."

CHAPTER 12

That morning, Sam stayed in the back stockroom and out of sight for longer than normal. Even though he had enough work back there with summer inventory and other responsibilities to keep him legitimately busy, he was purposefully avoiding Collette. After a while, though, Collette had to go to her office in the back room to take a call. Sam stayed busy, sorting through hangers and cataloging merchandise as she kept her door open.

She wasn't long on the phone. And instead of getting up and returning to the front of the store, she decided to linger in her office just to see how long Sam could find new things to do to avoid speaking to her. After a while, she decided to make small talk. "It's too bad you didn't work yesterday, Sam. Lots of pretty big gals came in, trying on lots of sexy blouses and swimsuits."

"Oh yeah?" Sam replied, not looking up from his hangers.

"Yeah, I think we set some kind of store record for exposed back fat."

"You don't say."

Collette let out a loud sigh. "OK. I think we should discuss the elephant in the room," she said, wryly adding. "And I don't mean me."

"Collette, I didn't mean that stuff I said out there to my friend. I--"

"Oh, yes you did. You most certainly did, Sam. And, believe me, I don't disagree with you. You don't have to be a deep thinker or a Philosophy major to wonder, 'Is this all there is? Is there nothing more to life than working, getting paid, getting laid, and watching TV?' And you know what the answer to that is?"

"What?"

Collette leaned back in her seat, a bit self-satisfied that she had an answer. "In all honestly, the answer is ... 'I don't know!' It's all drudgery. Even if you find a job you love, it's still ends up being routine eventually. That's why TV stars leave hit shows. That's why ball players become free agents. We all think they're crazy. But they're no different from us. I've worked for three different clothing chains in my life. I bet your dad's worked for umpteen car places. But it all ends up being the same mouthwash. It just gets swished from cheek to cheek."

Sam considered this. He remembered an old saying his mom used to utter whenever she'd bitch about her job to her "Dallas" friends. "Same shit, different day, huh?"

"Basically."

Sam stopped fiddling with the hangers and went and sat down in Collette's office. There really was no point in not discussing with her what she overheard. "Look, I'm pretty sure you heard just about everything I said to Chip. So, you know I have indeed been helping out Rabinowitz, and you know that ever since that damn photo ran in the paper, things have been ... well ... pretty dang awesome for me at least socially. But it's all because of tragedy. Or what I thought was tragedy. But now it's really tragedy again."

"Yeah, I woke up to all this shit this morning. What do you know?"

"I was there, Collette! I found Muffy in that motel, not Rabinowitz. OK, I stumbled onto her. But sometimes that's how things go down, right? Right place, right time."

"Almost the wrong time, though, right?"

"Yeah, the second car blast. That wasn't meant for Muffy. It was meant for Rabinowitz. And, I guess, by extension for me and Chip, too. Somebody set it while we were away from the car. It's freaked out Rabinowitz. He's quitting and leaving town. And Chip doesn't want anything to do with this anymore either, not that he ever really did. But, Collette, I can't help it. I know I should be freaked out. And, yeah, I *am* scared. But, at the same time, I'm ... like ... jazzed! This is, like, real living on the edge type stuff. I must be close, don't you think? I mean, I must be real, real close."

It was then that Sam realized that Collette had been hanging on his every word. It was like he was telling a story in front of a campfire, and she had both her hands on either side of her face, listening intently. Her mouth was even slightly agape.

"What do you think, Collette?" he inquired. "You're the straightest shooter I know. Do you think I should give up and leave well enough alone? Or, for once in my life, should I see something through?"

Collette processed his words for a few more seconds, then measured what she had to say next. "Sam, I think you've gotten yourself in way over your head. You've heard the expression, 'Curiosity killed the cat.' Well, curiosity is gonna fry this pussy sooner or later. If you think you're close, you're probably not. Or maybe you're too close, and you're missing something right in front of your eyes that you're never going to see. I'll tell you what. I think you're missing something very obvious for sure."

"Oh yeah. What?"

Collette briefly looked past him, as if her next words were going to travel further than the room they were in. In a hushed tone, she said, "This bomber, obviously he's a bastard. According to the news, he torched someone else to make it look like Muffy, right? Well, if what you're telling me is indeed the truth, he didn't intend to kill Muffy with the first bomb OR the second one. So, not only are you dealing with a pretty cold bastard. You're now dealing with a pretty cold bastard who could very well be full of grief and, possibly, full of--"

Sam gulped. He literally gulped, as he had not considered the concern Collette was raising. "Revenge?" he said, finishing her thought for her.

Collette nodded. She let the realization wash over the boy for a few moments. Then, she offered a bit of consolation. "Look, this guy would be a fool to set a third bomb. A damn fool actually. He's got the whole town on high alert now. Like East Coast blizzard alert. The little brains are probably out there right now buying milk, bread, and toilet paper and preparing to hole up in their homes. But that'll all fade in a couple of days.

It always does. And that's just another thing you'll come to learn, Sam. As much as life is about routine and drudgery, it's also about change. It doesn't always seem like it, but life is always changing. And when you look back in years to come on things that you thought were big in the moment, they're really just blips on a radar screen. Like me and my time at this store. Like me at the Columbia store. Like me when I was a BBW model. And before that, when I was in the ... well, it doesn't matter. It's all just blips. Life is always changing. And life, for me, is about to change again."

Sam didn't like the sound of that. He couldn't take any more change right now. There had already been so much of it. "What do you mean?" he asked.

Collette's eyes lit up. She'd been holding so much information in for so long, she felt positively giddy she could finally share. "Well," she said, "I want you to be the first to know -- I'm lying, of course. You're not the first -- I got my dream re-assignment! I'm going to be managing the company's brand-new store in ... Aruba!"

Sam was stunned. "Aruba?! You mean, like, the island Aruba?"

"The island paradise Aruba! 16 Plus on the Beach, they're calling it. You know, if you're gonna submit to drudgery, you might as well do it with island drinks and plenty of swarthy men around you, right?"

"Yeah, I guess. That's ... uh ... that's incredible, Collette. So, when's your last day here?"

Collette broke into the first few words of Frank Sinatra's "New York, New York." Swaying back and forth, she crooned, "Start spreading the news."

Sam was incredulous. "What, today? You're leaving today?!"

"Today's my last day on the job. I'm flying out tonight."

"So, you've known about this for a while?"

"What can I say? I hate goodbyes, long or otherwise. Julianna's more than ready to step in for me, so the store will be fine. And she likes you a lot. So no worries about the job. But, seriously, Sam. If you really are going to end up as a mechanic or a mailman or in retail, do it in Hawaii. Do it in Key West. Islanders need their oil changed, too, right? They need their bills and their TV Guides delivered. 'Aloha, sir. Here's your mail.'"

She even made a point of grabbing a few bits of actual mail from her desk and handing it to him. Then, getting up and heading back towards the register, she declared, "That's all I have for you, Sam. Now, if you can just get out of this summer without being blown to bits, you might just have a good life. But remember what I told you about blips on the radar screen of life. Just don't be one of those blips that disappears never to be seen again, OK? You're too good a kid."

———

Chip could barely concentrate on his job at Harmony Hut, and his boss could see it. Stocking the cassette tapes, he had put Luther Vandross in with Van Halen and a-Ha in with Alabama. It might have been alphabetically correct, but definitely not category correct. Chip had never made such mistakes before, and he wondered if it was a good idea that he even came in to work at all that day.

"It's all getting to you this morning, isn't it?" Chet Robitaille asked.

Chip jumped at the question. He wasn't even aware that his boss was as close to him as he was. "Huh?" he said, practically jumping to military attention. "Oh, no, I'm fine. Really. Just having a few brain farts."

Robitaille chuckled. "The Fat Boys and the Beach Boys together on the same rack? That's some serious mind flatulence, young sir. Tell me what's on your mind. Or, do I even have to ask?"

"I can't believe she was still alive.".

"Miss McGregor was indeed full of surprises, wasn't she?" Robitaille's tone was one of admiration, with a slight hint of sadness.

Chip found his boss an enigma at times. He had heard all of the rumors about him and Muffy, but Chet always kept it close to the vest with his employees and customers. Coy was the word that best described his attitude at times. Coy and very Southern. Chip thought often of that day when Rabinowitz was in the store questioning him. He wished he was in closer earshot of that conversation.

There was no doubt that Chet and Muffy had been involved. And Chip was also sure that Chet hadn't been completely truthful with Rabinowitz. "More or less" were the words that kept echoing in his mind over and over again ever since that day. Chip hated himself for still being intrigued on any level with Muffy's demise. But he just had to ask, "Sir, just how well did you know her?"

Chet immediately turned on that evasive charm he was known for. "Oh, now, Chip. I never took you for someone who went in for gossip and innuendo. Malls are like a bushel of your Maryland crabs. Even if you make it to the top, there's still dozens of arms trying to pull you back down."

"Chet, I didn't mean to--"

"It's alright, it's alright," Chet said, as he helped his young employee move his poorly placed cassettes to their proper categories throughout the store. "I did indeed have a dalliance with Miss McGregor. A brief and shameful one. It's gotten to the point where I can neither deny nor sidestep it any longer. And with that comes questions, as there should be. I would certainly have them if I were you. But, please, young man. I still like to think of myself as both a private person and a discreet person. If there is something you absolutely must know, go ahead and ask. But know that this is not the forum for any salacious details to be bandied about. And also please know that I feel like I have already spoken plenty ill of Miss McGregor to both law enforcement and Mr. Rabinowitz."

Chip felt like he may have the chance to ask just one question in the matter. So, he had better make it a good one. Fortunately, he only really had one. The one he wanted to know. "When you replied, 'More or less' when I asked you if you had answered all of Rabinowitz's questions, what did you mean by that?"

Chet let out a small laugh at the memory. "Yes, I could see where that reply would fire the imagination."

Robitaille's voice drifted out. He didn't know how much he wanted to tell his employee, and he really didn't have much more to confess anyway. He was still worried about his job with the company and was hoping this whole sad episode of his life would just pass. But with Muffy's "second death" and no word on if a suspect had even been identified, the story was going to stay front and center for at least a little while longer.

Chip grew impatient with the man's silence. Assertively, he inquired, "Well?!"

"My apologies, young sir. I was lost in thought there, wasn't I? You see, I'm from Louisiana originally. And we Louisianans really don't like 'dishing on the dead,' as my granny used to term it. I can only tell you that Muffy was a spirited, rebellious, young woman who liked to 'sample the cuisine,' as they say."

"Sample the cuisine?" Chip was unfamiliar with the phrase.

"Let's just say she liked herself a variety when it came to matters of the flesh and of the heart. In that way, she and I were a lot alike. She was well on her way to building up quite a collection. There was me, the older, experienced man who was the forbidden fruit. And there was her jock quarterback beau who helped solidify her social standing at school. But she once mentioned that one of her female friends also was quite fond of her -- and, yes, I do mean fond as in intimate fond. Muffy even teased her once with a kiss. In our passion and disagreements, she also mentioned to me a third man. Or maybe he was a fourth. Whoever he was, she didn't mean to tell me about him. And I know she didn't want her daddy to know."

"Oh yeah? Why is that?"

"She told me that this was a man of ... oh, how shall I put this ... he was a man of ethnicity."

"Black?"

"Maybe?"

"Maybe? What does that mean?"

"She called him 'Third World.' But to a girl of Muffy's age and inexperience with the actual real world, that could mean black, Hispanic. Who knows? I'm sure it was just a fling. She told me in complete confidence. Pillow talk, you understand? And, oh, call it honor among thieves or whatever. But it would have been mighty un-toward of me to continue speaking so ill of her to authorities and that private investigator."

Chip took in what Chet had just told him. Muffy had a third lover? Could this be the elusive bomber everybody had been hunting for? Chip looked at the clock on the wall shaped like the Rolling Stones' famous lips logo. It was almost his lunch break, and a part of him couldn't wait to tell Sam. At the same time, he wished he didn't have this knowledge at all. What he needed was food.

"Hey, do you mind if I take my lunch just a couple of minutes early, boss?" he asked.

Robitaille agreed without hesitation.

Chip rushed out of the store and nearly ran smack dab into Brent and what could only be described as a small harem. The jock was being consoled by three very attractive members of Our Lady of Sorrows' cheerleader team. Two were under each arm of the quarterback, while the third trailed just behind them.

"Brent!" Chip exclaimed. "Hey, man, I'm sorry. I was looking for you earlier. I guess you know, or, you've probably heard that--"

Brent kissed one the girls hard on her forehead and brought the second one closer to his body. His movements were hard and physical, and both young ladies winced at his tightening embrace but giggled and smiled regardless. "Don't mention her name, bro," he commanded. "Not today, and not ever again."

Chip agreed. He then observed, "Well, I see you're moving on quite nicely."

And move on he did. Brent didn't say another word to Chip. He just led his adoring, entourage in the opposite direction of where Chip was heading. And where Chip was headed was the mall food court.

———

"That's because everyone is too pansy to let Skynet call the shots!" exclaimed Buddy from his usual seat across from Sam.

Once again, Chip had come late to a pop-culture discussion in front of Orange Julius. Sam and Buddy were arguing passionately about the automated defense grid that was the real villain of the first "Terminator" movie. Sam wasn't having any of what Buddy was pushing. "Oh, come on! There's no way Reagan would let something like Skynet go active. Even he would know that it would learn at an exponential rate, deem humans a threat, and decide our fate in a micro-second. And you've seen enough flicks to know what that fate would be. Global thermonuclear war."

Buddy quickly retorted. "Skynet for real would be smarter than that, bro. Much smarter. It would know that even a single nuke air-burst over an American city would send out an electro-magnetic pulse so great, that it would cripple the entire network. Cripple Skynet itself! Central control, Sam. It's the only way to go in the future, you mark my words."

"I can't go with you on that," Sam retorted. "I won't go with you on that. Not Skynet. My big ass played paintball recently and got shot up. No way I'd survive a post-apocalyptic future, dodging hunter-killers and Austrian cyborgs in the rubble. But I will say, I agree with you on Reagan's 'Star Wars' defense system. Shooting down nukes from space with orbiting laser cannons? Now, that's bad-ass."

"Dude, that's totally bad-ass! That's some 'Real Genius'-'Spies Like Us' shit right there!"

Sam had missed these trivial discussions with Buddy, so many of which had taken place over greasy, bad mall food. He had also missed Chip's input. He could riff on movies and pop culture as well as anyone. And here he was looking unsure of whether to sit down with him and Buddy and discuss something -- anything -- other than Muffy McGregor's murder.

Chip stood a few feet away, waiting for any delay in the nerd jousting. Looking for an ally, Buddy said, "Take a load off, Chipper, and help me set Sam straight on a few things. Hey, you OK? You kind of look like someone's been shooting at you from geosynchronous orbit."

Sam was immediately concerned. "What's wrong?" he asked gravely. "What's happened?"

"Nothing's happened," Chip assured. "Everything is cool. And from the deep philosophical debate I just interrupted, I take it all's cool with you?"

Sam nodded affirmative.

"Good, good. Have you heard from Barbara at all? How's she doing?"

"Nothing. I've heard nothing. After yesterday, I'm sure any chance I ever had with her is out the window. I'm thinking of just becoming a monk after senior year. I'm not getting sex anyway. So why not get fed, clothed, and housed? I can follow my boss's advice. I'll become a monk in Bermuda or Maui. It really wouldn't be a bad life. The pressure would be off. That's for damn sure."

"I don't think I'd become a monk," Buddy interjected. "But I'd definitely become a priest so some hot chick in my congregation could seduce me. You know, forbidden fruit at all. That would be hot. HOT!"

Sam shook his head in disgust. "You know, Buddy, Chip and I only have to worry about car bombs. You, on the other hand, have bolts of lightning that are gonna be raining down on you sooner or later."

Buddy just chuckled confidently. "I don't think so," he said dismissively. "You know, I'm still a little miffed you two didn't include me in all your super-sleuthing. I've only seen every movie ever made. And mad bomber movies are my specialty."

"Really?" Chip challenged. "Your specialty? Name five."

Buddy didn't hesitate. "OK, obviously, there was 'The Mad Bomber,' 1973 Chuck Connors flick. Then there's 'Rollercoaster,' about a sick, twisted dodo who sets radio-controlled bombs in amusement parks nationwide, then blackmails the various companies involved. Partially filmed at our own Kings Dominion near Richmond, by the way. Third, there's my personal favorite, 'Black Sunday.' Bruce Dern is a Vietnam vet who flips his noodle and decides to strap a bomb to a Goodyear Blimp and detonate it over the Super Bowl. If you've seen it, it goes without saying that Robert Shaw is a god amongst men in that film. Number four, there's--"

"OK, OK!" Chip cut him off. "It's your specialty. So, tell us Mad Bomber Movie Guru, do you have any insight into our very real, deranged loon?"

"Not a clue," Buddy answered quickly. "And even if I did, I'm not putting myself in his crosshairs."

"Bombs don't have crosshairs, retard!" Chip shot back.

Buddy was surprised by the level of disdain in Chip's voice. "You're on the edge, man," he said, making a point of moving his chair a few feet away from his as if the foot or two of extra distance would be enough to save him from a third blast.

"Yeah, you are," Sam said. "And it's more than just Muffy. What's going on?"

Chip ducked the question. He didn't utter a single word in reply. His stomach grumbled, and he knew he should have ordered lunch first before rattling sabers with Sam and Buddy. His break time was dwindling, too, and he really needed food to stuff in his mouth. The French fries that he had been swiping one by one from Buddy's Roy Rogers meal without his knowledge were not enough, though.

Sam, nonetheless, pressed. "Chip, you've obviously got something you're not telling us. What is it?"

Chip broke down and told him what he knew, stopping before every couple of sentences to repeat, "But I'm not getting involved." He ended his recap by repeating one of the first things he told them. "So, Muffy had her jock quarterback. She had her hunky older man. And she was also apparently stepping out with a man of color."

"You mean, he was a brother?" Buddy asked.

Chip winced at the question, as if it had physically caused him discomfort. "OK, you're not allowed to use the word 'brother' ever, alright? Even when you're talking about your own actual flesh-and-blood brother. And, for the record, I don't know if this other guy was black. Like my boss put it. He was of 'Third World ethnicity.'"

Chip could see the wheels turning in Sam's head. This opened up a myriad of new possibilities. Since Chip was the only kid of color at Our

Lady of Sorrows, it was likely not a classmate. So, was it someone who went to the local public school? Someone who worked at the mall? Or just someone she met somewhere? Maybe in town? Maybe out of town? Did Brent know? He seemed to know about Chet Robitaille. Dare he even go and ask him? No, there was someone else, someone better, he needed to talk to first and most immediately.

"Sam," Chip said, wearily, "what are you thinking?"

Sam smiled slyly. "I think we better take this to Rabinowitz," he replied, "before he leaves town!"

CHAPTER 13

Sam was always surprised when he walked into a grown-up's home and it was worse than his. Of course, worse to an '80s teenager could mean many things. In Sam's case, he was surprised that Rabinowitz lived in an apartment that had just one more bedroom than the apartment he shared with his mom. The furniture was right out of the 1970s, too, with gaudy floral patterns and coarse fabrics. Even the living room television was a black-and-white model, one of those you turned on and it took a good half-minute or so to warm up and display a picture.

It didn't help that Rabinowitz really was in the process of frantically packing up and getting him and his family out of Laurel. The place was a mess, with multiple kids running all over screaming. Sam counted at least three young Rabinowitzs, maybe four. There might have been twins. He couldn't tell as the various youngsters, all boys who looked to be anywhere from age 4 to 11, ran in and out of rooms.

"Jeez, Rabinowitz. All these kids and you still live in an apartment?" Sam asked.

Partially out of breath from his hurried packing, Rabinowitz answered, "It's a condo, kid. A condo!"

"What's the difference?"

"A condominium you own ... like a house, y'know? An apartment, you rent. You pay a monthly rent."

"So, you own this?"

Sam clearly had a bit of a snobby, elitist tone to his voice. Too much of that ritzy, Catholic school, Rabinowitz surmised. "I *will* own it in about seven more years."

Sam was slightly confused. He never did understand things like real estate and bill paying, no matter how much he watched his mom and dad writing checks and working calculators at their different desks each month. "So, you don't really own this. I mean, what's the difference between paying a monthly mortgage and paying a monthly rent?"

"Christ on a pony, Sam! I don't have time to explain the intricacies of residential real estate to you. Why have you come here? To say 'so long?' Well, so long, farewell, Auf Weidersehen, good night!"

Sam sat down on Rabinowitz's couch, which was the only piece of furniture in the living room that had a tarp over it. It was an old, musty sheet, but Sam actually liked the smell of it. It reminded him of a cedar chest his grandma once had. "So, you're really out of here, huh?" he asked the older man, wistfully.

Chip took a seat next to him on the sofa. Watching Rabinowitz fumble around putting his and his family's belongings in boxes, Chip sarcastically answered for him. "Wow, Sam. Your detective skills are growing by leaps and bounds."

Sam ignored the taunt. He stayed focused on Rabinowitz. "You're really leaving before this is all settled? Before the case is solved?"

Rabinowitz looked up at him briefly from his work. "Look at all the fucks I don't give, kid," he spat, then returned to his boxing and labeling.

Sam briefly caught a glimpse of Mrs. Rabinowitz. She was a bit younger than her husband, but she had the same sort of hard, frazzled look to her as Mervyn did. They were a good compliment to each other, and people often referred to them as the "Danny DeVito and Rhea Perlman of Laurel" wherever they would go in town. Sam had heard her chatter from one of the bedrooms before he actually saw her. He instantly deduced that she was on the phone with someone. Sure enough, every once in a while, she would pace past the open bedroom door, phone in hand, and Sam and

Chip would catch a few words of what she was saying to the person on the other line.

"Yes, today," she said at one point, hoarse and more than a bit exasperated. "We're leaving today. Right now, in fact. So, if you have someone in mind, make the deal." Then, she yelled out to her husband. "Mervyn, are you sure you want to sublet?!"

Rabinowitz matched her tone and tenor. "Yes, yes! As soon as possible, and whatever we can get for it a month!"

Sam looked at him quizzically. "Sublet?" He was unfamiliar with the term.

"I don't have time!" Rabinowitz shot back.

Chip sprang up from the couch, almost banging into Rabinowitz's youngest son who was running by at that moment with two "Masters of the Universe" action figures in his hands. "Just ask this fool what you came here to ask him, and let's go," he ordered.

"Ah, Sam, are you here about the case? What's the matter with you? You make me wanna jump out of this third-story window. You really are going to get yourself killed. And for what? Seriously, boy. Why is this so flipping important to you?"

"Why does everybody keep asking me that?!"

Chip answered before Rabinowitz could. "Because you haven't given us or yourself a good enough answer! So, what is it?! Huh, huh, huh?!"

The "huh, huh, huh?!" sent Sam over the edge. It was in such a mocking tone. "Because I think I can do this!" he raged. "And I'm someone who has never done anything EVER!"

"What?" Chip said, still failing to understand his friend. "That's not true."

"It is true! I'm so friggin' ordinary. Sometimes I feel like I'm like an extra in my own movie. I haven't done shit in 15 years on this planet, and I don't think I'm going to do shit in 15 or 30 or 45 more."

"Well, you just did multiples of 15 in your head, kid," Rabinowitz said. "That's something."

"Great, I can make change. I can work at McDonald's and get the dimes and nickels right. I'm telling you two. I've never even gotten an 'A' on a report card. I almost got one once in second-grade Math, but I botched a pop quiz and it threw off my whole grade. It's been nothing but straight Bs and Cs since. My mom calls me 'Even Steven.' Even when my dad said he'd give me $5 for each A I got on a report card, I still couldn't do it. And that was years ago he made that offer. It's been so long, he's probably forgotten. He never even raised the offer to $10 or $15."

"See, Sam," Rabinowitz said in a reassuring tone. He really was starting to feel for the kid. "You just did multiples of five. You should think about being an accountant. I should have been an accountant."

"That's also my problem," Sam continued. " I don't know what I want to be. I have no clue. None. But for right now, I just want to see this one thing through. For once, I want to be the guy who got the answer, who solved the problem, who put together the puzzle. Until then, I'm pathetic. I've been pathetic since this furniture was new furniture."

"My furniture?" Rabinowitz asked, a bit hurt.

"Yeah, let me guess. You bought all this in the '70s, right? That was a fucked-up decade to grow up in, man. All those games and toys setting kids like me up to fail. I never could get that damn funny bone out of the Operation game."

"Who could?" Chip chimed in.

Sam continued, "I couldn't get the friggin' Slinky to walk down the steps either. I've never solved a jigsaw puzzle on my own. I used to swear the game makers weren't putting all the pieces in the box. That's how I would rationalize it and then just give up or get my dad to help me. And that Simon game? Five, maybe six colors and I was out. Every time!"

Chip chimed in again. "See, that's why you like the big bitches. They're attainable."

Sam smarted at the observation. He considered it for a second, then said, "No, I really do like big chicks, man. Leave it alone."

"Alright."

"The '80s haven't been any better. They're worse, in fact."

"What, the Rubik's Cube?" Chip asked.

"Yeah, there's that. I can't even solve one side of the freakin' thing. I almost did once. Once!"

"Then there was Intellivision."

Defensive, Sam replied, "I don't care what anyone says about that. I will always believe it's better than Atari."

"It had no joystick!"

"The dial and number pad were better, Chip! And the graphics killed the 2600. Killed it! But put all that aside. It's been more than that. It's every year now, more people asking, 'What do you want to do with your life, Sam?' They don't ask, 'What do you want to be when you grow up?' any more. That's something you ask a little kid. No, when you're a tubby bitch like me, you already look grown up at, like, 12. And a kid who looks grown up at 12 doesn't get talked to like he's a kid anymore. I found that out. I've also found--"

Rabinowitz cut him off right there. In his view, Sam's rant was getting too close to a whine. "Jesus, Sam. I got news for you. Growing up in any decade sucks. You think you've had it hard with Operation and jigsaw puzzles and the freakin' Rubik's Cube? My generation had none of those things. You wanna know what we had? We had bats and balls and toy guns. We had wars. Real wars. TV was in its infancy, and it sucked. The movies were worse. You couldn't see a tit. Now there's tits in every movie. Every movie that I see at least. And the music? Total snoozeville." Then, pointing at Chip, he added, "And it would have been worse for you!"

Chip nodded in agreement. "Hey, you won't be getting me in a DeLorean."

Sam wouldn't allow the brief moment of levity to improve his mood. "So, what are you saying, Rabinowitz? That 'things are tough all over.'"

"Yeah, pretty much."

"Easy for you to say," he shot back immediately. "You have freedom of movement. If something doesn't work out one place, you can just go to a different place and give it another try there. You're leaving. Collette's leaving. Maybe that's what Muffy was trying to do. Maybe she felt trapped, and this was her way of getting the heck out. The rest of us be damned."

Rabinowitz's living room then had a rare long moment of quiet. Even his kids, however many there were in that condo, weren't making a sound. Mrs. Rabinowitz was moving around in the other room, but she was off the phone now. It actually felt like a goodbye scene from a movie, Chip briefly thought.

Finally, Rabinowitz broke the silence. "So, what do you want, Sam? What did you come here for?"

Sam didn't hesitate. "We've found out that Muffy had been with a third dude. There was Brent, and there was Chet. But apparently there was someone else in the mix. A minority apparently. Someone who she saw as taboo, but someone she also may have truly cared about. Someone, at the very least, she was willing to run away with."

Rabinowitz pondered the information. He didn't want to. He was truly done with it all. But he had indeed heard rumors here and there in the course of his investigation, rumors that might have led to something if he were staying in town. But he was no longer interested, no longer curious. He needed to derail. Rabinowitz looked over to Chip and asked, "Did you know about this?"

Chip's face contorted in four different ways. "What? Through the Super-Secret Underground Negro Notification Network?! What do you think happens? Do you think we send out an All Black Alert? Attention, attention! White girl in suburbia ... willing!"

Sam didn't want the discussion to get too far off track. He steered it back to the question at hand. "Chip is the one who found this little nugget out just by talking to Chet. Apparently he got more out of him than you did."

Rabinowitz stiffened at the insult. Young Sam was definitely feeling his oats. "What is that supposed to mean? That I missed something? That I didn't do my job properly? A guy like Robataille isn't going to spill everything in one conversation, especially not to someone like me. He's a narcissist. You question him a second time only when he doesn't think you're coming back. That way, you catch him off-guard. Oh, and silly me. I figured we'd all get a bunch of information from a bunch of different people, coming at it from three different angles. And then it was going to be up to me, the trained professional, to put the pieces together. That's why we were working together, Sam, remember?"

"So, why give up?"

"Why give up?! Because all this ridiculousness ain't worth getting killed over! Look, Sam, I've been chased down alleys and streets and out of umpteen buildings by cheating husbands, by daddies dodging child support payments, by all sorts of angry dumb asses who didn't want me sniffing around their pathetic lives. You know what, though? I always outran 'em. Well, most of 'em. Rabinowitz doesn't look it, but he's quite spry. But nobody can outrun a bomb. And there ain't a one of you who is worth me getting incinerated, most especially Muffy who wasn't even dead in the first place!"

Sam could see there was no chance he was going to get Rabinowitz to stay. If he ever hoped to have his own personal Yoda or Mr. Miyagi or Doc Brown, this wasn't going to be the guy. Neither the Jedi Master nor the karate master nor the time-traveling scientist had the kind of personal responsibilities and obligations Mervyn had. And, certainly, none of them had the kind of fear he had either.

Rabinowitz was almost done with his packing. He kept handing boxes to his older sons, and they kept loading them into the family's rental station wagon three flights below. Even Mrs. Rabinowitz had left for the blue Ford Fairmont, ordering her husband on the way out to "Stop messing around with those kids. Come to the car, and take the highway, not the back roads. I have cramps, and I don't want any bumps!"

The one thing that was left was Rabinowitz's briefcase, the last remnant of his now former profession. It sat on the living room table, locked, and waiting for the ex-detective to scoop it up and take it with him. Rabinowitz had excused himself from the room briefly to use the toilet before his long drive south. He was headed to Charlotte where one of his brothers operated a dry cleaners. It would be temporary employment and temporary residence, but at least it was far away from Laurel.

When Rabinowitz did emerge from the hall bathroom, he noticed Sam running his fingers along his briefcase's frayed leather exterior. The teenager then began to thumb the circular dial numbers that would form a three-digit combination to unlock the case.

"Hey, get your hands off that," Rabinowitz ordered.

"Well," Sam razzed, "since you're giving up, turning tail, and running, can I have your files on Muffy? Will you give me your notes and anything else you have? Maybe I can spot something you missed."

Rabinowitz reached for his case. Snatching it away from the boy, he held it close to his chest and said, "No way. Those files are mine, and they're going to stay that way. I almost got you killed once. It's not going to be on me if it happens for real."

"So, there *is* something in that case that could be important!"

Rabinowitz bristled. In truth, the files inside were not on Muffy. A couple of days earlier, he had gathered everything he had on Francisco and stored it in the case. And he had a few photos and documents that might have actually led to something ... again, if he were staying in town, that is.

"Sam, I wrote down a bunch of stuff in my notes. They're my own thoughts and observations, and they would make no sense to anyone but me. And nothing about this has made much sense. Did I hear tell that Muffy was seeing some other dude? Yes. Had I heard he wasn't white? Eh, maybe. Who cares? And was she reckless and fond of fooling around in parked cars and all over the Laurel Centre Mall? Again, why couldn't I have lived in this decade?"

Sam didn't back down. He was desperate, and Mrs. Rabinowitz was now honking the horn from the parking lot below. "Come on, man!" he said. "Open the case and leave me just one of the files!"

Sam reached for the case, and the two started to wrestle over it. Rabinowitz had his hand firmly on the handle and was not giving it up. Sam threw his full weight into the struggle, and they each grabbed at each other's shoulders and necks in between back-and-forth pulls of the case.

Chip was a second or two late in joining the tussle. "Sam!" he yelled. "Have you lost your Vulcan mind?"

The three then started to pull each other all over the room, banging hard into the living room's walls and furniture. To an outside observer, the struggle would have looked quite comical, especially with the ridiculous grunts and other sounds the three were making. Between those noises, Sam and Rabinowitz were able to trade a few barbs.

"Give up, Rabinowitz! It's what you do best!"

"You're not getting this case, Sam! But you can tell yourself that you ALMOST got it!"

Chip tried with all his might to break the two of them up. But it seemed the more he insinuated himself into their scuffle, the harder the two fought. As the trio became intertwined, trying to pull the briefcase in three different directions, a funny thing happened. For a brief instant, all three shifted their weight and pull strategies and yanked the case in the same direction at the same time. The resulting force flung it out of their hands and through the open living room window. It quickly lost altitude and plunged towards the parking lot below, landing in the condo complex's dumpster where Rabinowitz and his family had hastily tossed a number of items that wouldn't fit into their increasingly packed rental vehicle. Sam, Chip, and Rabinowitz's momentum caused them to stumble towards the open window, which gave them each a perfect bird's eye view for when the case landed hard in the three-quarters-full dumpster ... and exploded!

It wasn't a big kaboom. But, once detonated, the explosion was powerful enough that it caused all three to instantaneously jump back. And they immediately went into the half-sentences that had become their trademark in the aftermath of such blasts.

"What the--"

"Was that another--"

"That couldn't have been--"

The first one who was able to get a full sentence out was actually Mrs. Rabinowitz three stories below. Thankfully, she and the kids were OK, parked several spaces to the left of the dumpster, which had absorbed near-ly all of the blast. "Mervyn, I thought you said the Bomb Squad swept the place?! What the hell was that?!"

Rabinowitz popped his head out the window to make sure his family was alright. He was pretty sure all of his kids were in the car and safe with the Mrs. "They did! But I've had my briefcase with me the whole time! Just stay there! Stay there, I'll be right down, and we'll get out of here!"

Sam suddenly snapped back into coherence. "What? You're not gon-na call this in? You're not gonna wait for the cops?"

"Kid, I'm not even gonna believe that just happened. Take care of yourself, have a good life. To quote my favorite SNL'er: 'That's the news, and I am out of here!'"

Sam turned to Chip for help in stopping Rabinowitz. But to his sur-prise, his friend was already out the door, too. Sam sprinted out of the condo and to the steps leading down from the third-story walk-up. He heard Chip on the metal stairs, already two flights below and about to emerge on ground level. He wasn't running. But he certainly had a good pace going. Sam called out to him, but Chip didn't look back. He didn't even acknowledge him.

———

Later that evening, Sam laid on his bed at home. He didn't play any mu-sic. He didn't have the TV on. He wasn't even under any illusion that the phone would ring and it would be Chip or Barbara or anyone else. He felt very alone. Abandoned. Was he done? Was there anywhere else to go on this?

The room had grown too quiet. The whole apartment was quiet. His mom was in the kitchen reading the latest Jackie Collins novel. There was always some sound to hone in on, whether it was the neighbors next door or others mulling about in the community's courtyard just outside his open bedroom window. But tonight, there was total stillness. The East

Coast humidity had broken once again earlier in the afternoon, and it had turned into a quite cool night for Maryland in late June.

Sam's restlessness finally prompted him to turn on the TV. He didn't have a remote controlled set back then, so he had to sit on the edge of his bed and reach for the dial to flip around. There wasn't much on, even though his antenna could get both the Washington, D.C., and Baltimore channels.

He flipped to Baltimore's Channel 13 and caught the tail end of his favorite weekend program, "At the Movies" with film critics Siskel and Ebert. That week they had reviewed "About Last Night," "Psycho III," "The Great Mouse Detective," and "Big Trouble in Little China." All four films looked like crap, Sam thought. And he still hadn't seen the three movies that hit theaters the previous week, "Running Scared," "Labyrinth," and the one Buddy beamed about earlier, "Ruthless People."

He wanted to see them all, plus "The Karate Kid, Part II" and "Back to School" that had been in theaters for a couple of weeks prior. And he wanted to screen "Top Gun" and "Ferris Bueller's Day Off" a second time before they left cinemas. But he knew he'd probably only make it out to three, maybe four of them at the most with his limited time and funds. He also doubted that his good movie buddy, Chip, would want to go anywhere with him anymore. So, he would be relying on weekends with his dad and the occasional invite from Buddy and his family.

But at least he had options. He also wanted more options on the TV. Sam flipped around the tube for another minute or two. It was the bottom half of the hour. Almost 7:30 p.m. And nearly every station was in commercial break. Finally, he arrived at the Baltimore UHF station, Channel 45, and the familiar theme song of one of his favorite sitcoms started.

"Good Times! Anytime you meet a payment! Good Times! Anytime you need a friend..."

Ah, comfort TV. A show about people who had it worse than he did. Temporary layoffs, easy credit rip-offs, scratchin' and survivin'. Maybe that really was all life was about. If it was, he had to get good with that.

He had to go back to being Sam, just Sam, keeping his head above water, making a wave when he could. At least he was alive.

To his mild surprise, the episode re-running that evening was the one he had just seen recently where little Penny wanted to learn to ice skate, and her adoptive mother Willona accepted a job as a store detective to make some extra money to afford the expensive lessons. Channel 45 was always several days behind D.C.'s Channel 20 in their reruns of the show, which was a comfort actually. If Sam missed one of his favorite episodes on 20, he didn't have to wait long for 45 to air it. Or, if it was one he really liked, he'd watch it again a few days later. And this was one of his favorite ones, mainly because it had Gordon Jump from "WKRP in Cincinnati" as the store's manager. And he loved "WKRP." D.C.'s Channel 5 aired reruns of that great sitcom every weeknight at 11 p.m., and Sam would keep the volume down real low on school nights if he couldn't fall asleep and didn't want his mom chastising him.

As he got into the episode, his anticipation for his favorite scene grew and grew. The Willona character was behind a two-way mirror in one of the store's dressing rooms to spy on female customers to see if they were stuffing merchandise into their purses and pocketbooks. She had a problem with that. She thought the invasion of privacy was going too far. But her boss kept reminding her that it was all for her daughter. Willona had remarked earlier in the episode that she "didn't do windows." Well, as it turns out, she did do windows and she spied through them, too.

Until she actually caught her first customer stealing, that is. The woman stuffed blouses and other garments into a bag, and Willona couldn't help herself. She couldn't turn her in. It would be going against her conscience. So, she started pounding on the wall from the other side of the two-way mirror, yelling, "Hey! Hey, fool! Put those back! Get out of there!" The studio audience howled with laughter. It was a very funny moment, especially because of the silly, over-the-top panicked reactions of the extra they hired to play the shoplifter.

And then it hit Sam. The moment of inspiration he'd been waiting for. Muffy used to fool around with guys throughout the mall, right? In back rooms ... in parked cars ... in ... in department-store dressing rooms! Cindy! Sam's mom's friend, Cindy. She was a store detective at The Hecht Co. department store. Did Hecht's dressing rooms have two-way mirrors? And, if so, had Cindy or any of her security staff observed Muffy with her mystery man?

Sam switched off the TV so hard, he almost brought it down off his dresser. "Mom!" he called out. "Mom!"

His tone was so intense that she leapt up from her seat at the kitchen table, dropping her book to the floor in the process. "What? What's wrong?"

The two met halfway between the kitchen and Sam's bedroom, in the hallway that was lined with many photos of Sam's life from his earliest baby photos to his sophomore year class picture. Their heavy footsteps to each other rattled several of the hanging frames. "Nothing's wrong, Mom. Do you know if Cindy is working security at the store tonight?"

"Yes, I think so. Why?"

Sam practically shook with excitement. "Can you call her on the phone?"

"I actually just tried to reach her at her office to see if she was still on for Merlot Monday. No answer. She must be on the storeroom floor or taking care of something. Sam, this isn't about--"

"We have to go there!"

CHAPTER 14

Francine drove Sam to the mall against her better judgment. On the one hand, he was doing exactly what she told him not to do. He was continuing to obsess over Muffy McGregor's death. On the other hand, she had never seen him so passionate about anything, so driven, so single-mindedly determined to see something through to the end.

She tried to get him in to sports as a young child. He didn't last a year in soccer, in Pop Warner football, or in Little League baseball. He wasn't coordinated enough to be good at any of them, so he rode the bench mostly and was miserable. He eventually got tired of the groans and grimaces his teammates would give him whenever he was put into games by the coaches. Similarly, his "two left feet" kept him off roller skates, ice skates, even bicycles.

He never showed interest in any of the usual activities boys growing up typically get into. He didn't want to be a Boy Scout. He had no musical or artistic talent, so he was never in a school play or a church choir. He did attend Sunday School, but never took part in their church's youth groups.

All he really loved to do was eat, watch TV, and go to movies. Francine was surprised he even wanted to get a summer job, as the months of June, July, and August had always been prime couch time for Sam. Yet, now, here she was driving her son to see her friend who worked store security, because he sincerely believed he had a "hunch" regarding a double murder. Where did she go wrong as a mother, she wondered.

They were almost to the mall. One traffic light to go. And, as they approached, the bulb went from green to yellow. When Sam sensed her foot slide from the gas to the brake, he ordered, "Run the light, Mom!"

The sudden order only caused her to step on the brake pedal harder than she normally would have, and her raspberry-colored Plymouth Sundance lurched to a halt just as the traffic light's yellow bulb turned to red. "Damn it, Mom! We could have made that!"

"OK, you are REALLY stressing me out!," Francine exclaimed. "We'll get there, and we'll get there safely! In the meantime, calm the F down! And buckle up, Sam. You never buckle up!"

She rarely had to use her "Mom voice" with Sam. But it came easily to her. Between her marriage, her job at the senior citizens home, and being a parent, she had been dealing with large male children in one form or another for way too long. But she did know how to handle them. "And one more thing," she added. "If we find out anything from Cindy -- and I mean anything at all -- we take it to the police. You got that?"

Sam nodded. His focus was on the light. The long light that was the last one on their route to get into the shopping center. It took an excruciating amount of time for it to turn green. After another 30 seconds of waiting, he pierced the tense quiet of the front seat and asked, "Seriously, doesn't the mall want any customers?!"

Finally it turned green and within a half-second of the change, Sam yelled, "GO!"

————

Cindy Ginty really hoped she would find a husband someday and someday soon. She hated her name. She didn't think it was a serious name, and she was a serious woman. Well, at least serious on the job. She thought of changing it, but getting rid of "Ginty" would crush her dad. She was an only child and no one would be carrying on the family name after her.

So, her father wanted to have it in existence for as long as possible. So, she kept it and had dealt with the snickers ever since elementary school.

Her friends from the apartment building rarely visited her at her place of business. They had no reason to. But when Francine called with her odd request, to meet with her and her son, Sam, to discuss Muffy McGregor, she was certainly intrigued. Nevertheless, she felt the need to keep her door open, so her nameplate wasn't immediately visible. Francine knew she was "Cindy Ginty," but they hadn't made reference to it in quite some time. It was definitely a hang-up of hers and a personal one. But she really wanted to be seen differently behind her gray, metal desk with all her closed-circuit monitors flickering behind her than how Francine usually knew her, with a glass of wine in one hand, a cigarette in the other, and talking about "Dallas" or "Dynasty" or any of the other TV shows she and Francine and their other friends obsessed over.

Francine and Sam came bounding through her office door with all the drama of two characters from a nighttime soap opera making an entrance. "Wow!" she exclaimed, from behind her desk. "I think my boring Saturday night just got a bit less boring."

Sam immediately spoke up. "Miss Cindy, do you have those two-way mirrors in the dressing rooms where you can watch people changing and trying on clothes to see if anyone's shoplifting? You know, like the ones on 'Good Times?' Like in that one episode where Willona was--"

"Yeah, I've seen the show, Sam. But I'm not going to share with you our store security procedures. And even if we did have those mirrors, I wouldn't let you watch people getting undressed and I certainly wouldn't--"

"No, I don't want to see people getting naked. I just want to ... wait, are you saying you really do have them? Wow, I should have applied here for the summer!"

Cindy scoffed. "Fool, men don't get to watch women. You'd be looking at other guys changing in and out of their drawers all day."

Francine dragged over a chair and motioned her son to sit down. She took the one seat that was positioned closest to her friend's desk in her cramped office, which was tucked away on the top floor of Hecht's department store, away from the shopping areas. Plopping herself in that chair with a groan and sigh, she then ordered, "Sit down, Sam. Sit down, and ask Miss Cindy what you came here to ask her."

Sam had called Cindy "Miss Cindy" ever since he and his mom had known her. He was 10 years old, and she moved into one of the apartments down the hall from them. He always found her to be a stern, humorless type until she got at least a couple glasses of wine in her. But, by that point, he had usually been ordered out of the room or shuffled off to his dad or one of his friends for a play date. Cindy didn't intimidate him, per se. He just had never been particularly close to her, even though they had carpooled into work a couple of times that summer. They had never shared anything more than small talk, though.

But Sam needed to have a big talk with her now. He was very eager. "Alright, look, this is a long shot," he began. "And I don't want you to violate any of Hecht's policies or rules. But if you can tell me some things about my friend, Muffy -- if you know them, that is -- I would really appreciate it, Miss Cindy."

Cindy looked at Francine, who gave a roll of the eyes. She then looked back at Sam and replied, "I'll help you if I can, Sam. But I've already answered a bunch of questions from the police and from that private detective who lost his shit on the news the other day. Despite all of our high technology -- the fancy cameras; yes, the two-way mirrors; and all the other things you see and don't see -- there's really not a lot that goes on here each day that's all that exciting. This is kind of a boring job actually. It's like watching really bad, boring TV sometimes. Even when the alarms do go off at the doors when someone walks out with a security tag, my staff barely react. Most customers just look back at their cashier all confused, and then we remove the tag they forgot to remove and send them on their way. Occasionally, you get a runner. And then, yeah, it's go time! But--"

"Miss Cindy, I don't think Muffy ever shoplifted. Can you share with me what were some of the questions the cops asked you?"

"No, I really don't think that would be appropriate."

"Well, then, what about Rabinowitz? Look, the guy left town all scared. He and I were friends, and he asked me to help him with this case from the high-school angle, because he wasn't comfortable with teenagers and all. But now he's left me with all these unanswered questions about my friend, and I'm frustrated."

Cindy hesitated for a moment. She briefly considered what her actual legal position was talking to the boy. The police had asked her a bunch of questions about her store's surveillance technology. They never asked to pull any of her tapes, which she thought was odd. But, at the same time, she really didn't have anything to share with them about Muffy. She barely knew of the girl until her death became front-page news. She'd seen her around the mall, because she worked there. And she was quite pretty. You definitely remembered her if you saw her more than once. And Cindy saw her several times just in passing.

"I really don't think I can be any help, Sam. All Rabinowitz asked me and my staff is if we ever saw Muffy with any guy anywhere in the store. He wanted to know about her boyfriends. And we all said, 'No.' We hadn't seen her with anyone. Not that any of us would remember anyway. We have hundreds of people coming in and out of the store every day."

"So, you never caught her in one of your dressing rooms? You know, like, fooling around with someone?"

"No, not once."

Sam immediately felt disappointed. It was a hunch, one of those he heard that cops and private eyes get all the time when they finally break a case. And it was exciting. Exhilarating even. He really thought he was on to something.

"I'm sorry, Sam," Cindy said.

"Me, too," Sam's mom chimed in, reaching over to pat her boy on his shoulder. "Can we go now?"

Sam thanked Cindy for her time, then he and Francine got up to leave. He held his head low, and Francine put his arm around his shoulders. Maybe now he could move on, she thought, and enjoy the rest of the summer.

But then he suddenly pivoted, and her arm dropped off his shoulders. Looking back at Cindy, he asked, "Did the cops and Rabinowitz talk to everybody on your staff?"

"Yes, Sam," she said confidently. "They talked to all of us."

Something intriguing had just happened, and Sam picked up on it immediately. Cindy's voice hesitated and trailed off at the word "us." She then had an odd look on her face, a look he couldn't quite place. Was it confusion? No. It was more like a sudden hint of uncertainty. "Miss Cindy, are you sure?" he pressed. "This is very important to me."

"Well," she said hesitantly, "there is Nikki."

"Nikki?"

"Nikki?" Even Sam's mom was intrigued.

"Yeah, Nikki. She's one of my watchers in the women's dressing rooms. She's been on vacation with her husband. Went down to the shore for about 10 days. In fact, today's been her first day back."

Sam's heart started to pound again. He immediately felt a rush of adrenaline. "Is she still here?" he asked excitedly. "Can I talk to her?"

Cindy checked the day's schedule, which was right there on her desk as the top page of a stack of papers. She ran her index finger down one of the columns and saw the hours. Sure enough, Sam was in luck. "Yeah, she should still be here. Come with me. You can't go into the dressing room area. But I can bring her out."

Just as Cindy was leading the two out of her office, they practically slammed into Sam's dad head-on in the small hallway that ran outside of Cindy's office and connected the bowels of the store with the store itself.

"Dad, what are you doing here?"

Calvin, face smudged with oil and still in his Lube Job uniform, immediately looked over at Francine. "Your mother called me, and I came right from work. She told me all about your hunch. Said I needed to be here. So, here I am."

Sam looked at his mom. He was legitimately surprised she extended his dad such a courtesy. Her tone, though, was stern. "Yes," she said, "unlike some people, I believe in sharing the parental responsibilities and information."

Sam didn't have time to referee. He looked past his parents' hard stares at each other to Cindy, who was already halfway to the dressing rooms area. He noticed she was about to turn a corner when he brushed past Calvin and Francine and ordered, "Come on! We gotta follow her!"

———

Nikki was a tall, slender woman who Sam found attractive. She wasn't his type at all. But her physical appearance surprised him. He thought she would look like one of his mom and Cindy's contemporaries, like a mother in carpool or PTA. But she was tan and athletic and surprisingly young. Probably no more than 25.

In his head, Sam was always putting people's backgrounds and connections to pop culture in order. If she was indeed 25, that means she was his age in 1975. So, that summer, she was a teenager when "Jaws" was in theaters, when "All in the Family" was the No. 1 show on TV, and when people listened to the Eagles and Captain & Tennille. And, according to Cindy, she was married. That means she was getting sex regularly, Sam marveled. To a 15-year-old boy, those were the jumbled thought patterns.

As it turns out, something else about Nikki surprised Sam. She spoke with one of the thickest Baltimore accents he had ever heard. "Hey, der boy, what can I do ya fer?" she asked upon emerging from her surveillance room.

Sam was briefly taken aback. He didn't anticipate that voice coming out of that mouth, that body. "Uh," he stammered, "my friend ... she was killed. And everyone's just trying to come up with some answers."

Nikki's face turned sad. "Oh, Muffy McGregor," she said, shaking her head at the tragedy. "I heard about her when I was down at the oh-shun eatin' some Polock Johnny's. Can't believe somethin' like that happened' rat here in Merlin. So sorry for your loss der ... uh, Sam is it?" Nikki looked over to her boss for confirmation of the name, and Cindy silently nodded affirmative.

Sam continued, still a bit taken aback by her voice, but also sheepish in what he had to ask her. He could talk to Chip and Buddy about sex and even his dad. But he always felt a bit uncomfortable talking about it with females. "Look, this is like so awkward. But Muffy was a bit of a wild thing. And she liked to fool around with her boyfriends apparently, like, all over the place. Even in store dressing rooms. And there's one of her guys unaccounted for, one who she apparently kept really, really secret."

Nikki got all wide-eyed at where Sam was headed. "Oh boy!" she exclaimed. "I heard da poh-lice was around here asking questions while I was on vay-cay. Wish I could've helped 'em, hon."

"Could you have helped them?" Sam asked urgently. "Could you help me now? Did you ever catch Muffy with any guy in one of your changing rooms?"

Nikki answered surprisingly fast. Motioning back to the dressing room area, she said, "You bet I had to shoo that girl outta der one time! She was with quite the stud, too. You should have seen this dude! Hung like one of dem ponies from the Preakness."

Sam slumped. "Ugh, Brent," he lamented, remembering a particularly eye-opening time in the showers after gym class. Unfortunately, Brent was no killer. He just wasn't the one.

"No, he didn't look like a Brent," Nikki shook her head. "More like a--"

"Like a Chet? Chet Robitaille?"

"From the Harmony Hut? No. Not him either. This dude looked more like ... well, like Ponch from dat show, 'CHiPs.' You know the one? He even had on a you-ni-form."

"He was a cop?!"

"No, not a poh-lice officer. He was more like a ... a..." Then, she looked over at Calvin, and she was suddenly very sure of what and who she had seen. "More like him!" she said, pointing to Sam's dad. Then, tapping his stitched-on name tag, she continued, "That same outfit, in fact. I'm certain of it. I remember laughin' at the Lube Job name. Hey, I've been meanin' to take my Chevy there. Good awl changes?"

"The best, ma'am," Calvin proudly replied.

Sam's eyes darted over to Calvin. He already knew what Nikki's revelation meant, but he somehow still needed his father to confirm. "Dad!" he exclaimed. "Is she talking about Alejandro?!"

Until Sam had said it, Calvin really hadn't put two and two together. But who else could it have been? A guy wearing a Lube Job uniform who looked like Erik Estrada. It could only be Alejandro. But a killer? "Yeah, I guess so," he answered quietly. "Oh, the irony. The guys at the shop, we'd always called him a 'lady killer.' Turns it out he was a ... bag lady killer?"

Francine immediately broke in. "Now, hold on. This doesn't mean anything. So, he and Muffy messed around in a dressing room. Who hasn't done that at least once in their life?"

"What?!" Sam and Calvin both exclaimed.

Francine put both of her hands in the air and made a quick "wiping the board" motion. "Never mind," she erased. "I'm just saying we shouldn't jump to any big conclusions here."

"But, mom!" Sam blurted, his mind made up. "We know Muffy was shacking up with her mystery guy at that motel. We know it wasn't Brent or Robitaille. We know this third guy wasn't white. And Dad, you and I both saw what Alejandro could do out on that paintball range. He was a bad-ass! After he lit every single one of those hillbillies up, we all whispered he must have had some kind of commando training somewhere. I mean, does anybody know anything about his background? Where's he from? What did he do before he came to the States?"

"I don't know much about his past, Sam. As you know, the guy could barely speak any English. All I know is he came over a couple of years ago, and he knew pretty much all there was to know about cars. We didn't have to teach him anything."

"You see!" Sam exclaimed. "He knew about cars! So, he probably knew how to wire 'em to blow!"

Calvin started to feel his throat go dry. His son was really on to something. "Yeah, I suppose that's possible. You know, he does kind of have an edge to him. Cool and suave one minute. Great with the ladies. But he has a temper. When something doesn't go right on a car, he starts ranting and raving and hollering like Ricky Ricardo when he'd get mad at Lucy."

"And a temper, too," Sam muttered. "Dad, you just came from the shop. Is he working there tonight? What time do you close?"

"Yeah, he was there. And we close at 9," Calvin said. Then, looking at the clock on the wall behind Cindy and Nikki, he observed, "About 25 minutes from now."

"We got him, Dad. We got him! You said you wanted to help me. Let's go, let's go!"

At that point, both Francine and Cindy stepped in. "Whoa there!" his mother said. "We're not going anywhere near this man if there's even a chance he's--"

"Yeah, Francine's right," Cindy added. "At this point, you have to get the police involved. Sam, if you're right, you're going to get the credit you want and deserve on this. You're gonna be a hero."

Sam considered this. But he still wanted to be there when it all went down. And he had both of his parents with him. So, at least, he had some measure of protection, right? He agreed to let Cindy phone Lieutenant Knox. But he also begged his mom and dad to at least drive to the Lube Job to keep an eye on Alejandro so that he didn't skip out before they arrived. He promised them that he and they would keep their distance.

"I just want to be there!" he pleaded.

Calvin and Francine looked at each other, and neither could turn him down. Deep down inside, if they were really honest with themselves and each other, they wanted to see how it was going to play out, too. On their way out of Hecht's, Sam thought of one more question he hadn't asked Calvin. "So, Dad, you said Alejandro 'came over' from somewhere a couple of years ago. Do you know where from?"

Getting into his own car with Francine in the front and Sam in the back, Calvin answered, "I'm pretty sure Portugal."

"Buckle up, Sam," Francine commanded, clicking her own belt into place. Then, shooting her ex-husband a look, she added, "And don't drive like an a-hole!"

Portugal? Criminal? Dangerous? Sam immediately thought of Pedro Machado Francisco. He had to be connected somehow. And for the first time since this whole thing all began, Sam felt a twinge of real and genuine fear. He felt like he was heading towards a situation that may turn quickly dangerous, possibly deadly. And his dad and mom were driving him there ... with their seatbelts on and doing the speed limit.

CHAPTER 15

To Sam's dismay, his father didn't drive them right up to the Lube Job. Instead, he parked across the street from the shop in the empty parking lot of the old A&P Supermarket that had gone out of business more than a year earlier. The landlord had yet to find a new tenant for the large space, so the building sat vacant and the lot's asphalt was starting to get weeds and cracks from the neglect. Sam thought it was silly keeping such a distance when they were literally the only vehicle in the lot, and their car could easily been seen from any window or bay at the car shop.

But at least his dad had gotten them there. At least he didn't chicken out and "let the police handle it." He wasn't even sure the cops were going to heed their call, even if it came from the head of store security at Hecht's. He had found Knox to be a bully and quite shifty. Could he really be counted on? Sam didn't know, but he was certainly eager to find out.

Sam and his parents sat quietly staring at the Lube Job for a good 10 minutes before any of them spoke up. "Aw, come on. Where's Knox? Why isn't he here yet?" Sam asked impatiently.

He knew he wasn't going to start hearing squad car sirens in the distance like in the movies or on TV. If Knox were to come at all, it wouldn't be to arrest Alejandro, only to question him. But just the sight of a police car pulling up to the shop might be enough to cause the man to panic and run if he truly was guilty, which Sam was sure of the more he thought about it all.

Francine could feel how antsy her son was from the front seat. He bounced up and down every 30 seconds, which made the car bounce up and down, too. Not a lot, but enough to be felt. "Relax, Sam," she assured. "Who knows if Knox was even on duty when the call came in? I'm sure he'll be here soon."

A good half-minute passed before Francine heard her son respond, "He better be."

As another couple of minutes passed and the time drew very near to the 9 o'clock closing hour, it was Francine who noticed something that her male passengers had not. They had stared at the Lube Job across four lanes of two-way traffic for quite a while. In that time, they had seen Vallone helping a customer in one of the bays. They had seen DeFao driving another car out of the second bay and around the store for a customer pick-up. Even Mr. Liepens could be seen every once in a while through the glass door that led into the waiting area.

But there was one man who she hadn't seen at all. And she knew him by face. The few times she had to go see Calvin at his work, she could never forgot a chiseled, handsome face like Alejandro's. "Uh, guys," she spoke up, "it's probably nothing, but I think the question should be asked. Has anybody seen--"

Both Calvin and Sam completed her question. "Alejandro?!"

"Well, he's kind of an important player in all this, don't you think?" she said. A slight hint of sarcasm was in her voice. Looking over at her ex-husband, she asked, "You are sure he was working tonight?"

"Hell, yes, I'm sure. He was there when I left the shop to come see you guys."

Sam wished he had binoculars. He had been at the Lube Job many times, and there were all sorts of small spaces where a man could be working and not seen from where they were parked. He might have been underneath a car this whole time. Or he could have been in the supply room, taking stock of what was needed to be ordered for the following week. Or quite possibly he was behind the shop where some of the auto detailing happened.

Nevertheless, Sam was eager for even a glimpse of the man. The shop was completely lit up, and its exterior was illuminated, too. If the man was on the job, there were no shadows to conceal him. Only those spaces that couldn't be seen from where they were parked. "Dad, I think we should go over there and check it out ... before Mr. Liepens closes for the night."

"No, we absolutely shouldn't!" Calvin emphatically replied. He was not to be manipulated, especially in front of Francine.

"But the bays are all empty. They're closing up shop. Fifteen minutes from now, Liepens will be counting his money, Vallone and DeFao will be in a bar somewhere arguing 'Tastes great or less filling,' and Alejandro will ... he'll just be gone. For all we know, he might have even clocked out early after you left."

"So what if he did? All things considered, that wouldn't be the worst thing, Sam."

"My point is we don't want Knox and the cops showing up and thinking they'd been crank-called. That would just get Cindy in a whole lot of trouble, wouldn't it? Not to mention us."

Calvin let out an audible "Humph!" Since when did his son become so alternately logical and illogical? "Alright," he conceded. "I'll go over there and see what's up. But just me! You two stay here."

Sam reluctantly agreed. Calvin shot Francine one last tense, exasperated look; got out of the car; and slammed the door. They watched as he carefully crossed the four lanes of traffic. There was a surprising number of vehicles on the road that evening; cars, trucks, vans, and semis. Calvin had to do more than a bit of dodging without a crosswalk. But he made it over to the shop without incident.

Sam and Francine watched as he talked with Vallone and DeFao. There wasn't a lot of body language to try and interpret. A couple of shrugs from Vallone. A pointing of the finger back towards the street by DeFao. Then, Liepens came out from the waiting room area and briefly joined the conversation.

Calvin was there for maybe two minutes before he turned and started making his way back across traffic to the car. "That's not good," Sam muttered.

And it wasn't. Calvin got all the way inside the car and shut the door before relaying what he had just learned. "OK, Sam, you might be on to something," he began.

"What? How so?" Sam asked in exclamation. Francine also straightened in her seat, a look of intensity on her face.

"Apparently, a few minutes before we got here, what the guys think is Alejandro's daddy showed up in a big stretch limo. They think this because Alejandro called him 'Poppy' or 'Popeye' or something like that. It was one of the few words they could make out. Who knew Alejandro had family local? At any rate, the older man jawed at Alejandro for about a minute in Spanish or Portuguese or Klingon or some foreign language. Alejandro kept shaking his head and arguing back. And, then, two big dudes got out of the Caddy, grabbed Alejandro, and shoved him in the backseat. Then, they drove off."

"Drove off?" Sam repeated. "Where?"

"Vallone thinks he heard the daddy say B-W-I."

"The airport?" Francine questioned.

"Yeah. Vallone also said he saw at least two suitcases in the backseat. So, I guess Poppy or Popeye had Alejandro's bags packed for him already."

Sam hit the back of the passenger seat with his fist, causing his mother to jump. She briefly rebuked him and the boy apologized. He then used his fist to punch the door, then the window, then the seat next to him. They had been so close. But was there still a chance? And where was Knox?

"Dad."

"Don't say it, Sam."

"You know what I'm gonna say next, right?"

"Yeah, I know. Just please don't."

"We gotta go to the airport!"

That's when Francine started hitting things in the car. She had reached her limit. She had indulged her child long enough. "No!" she emphatically protested. "That is NOT going to happen, Sam! It is over! It's done, you're done, we're done. You got your answer. You solved the puzzle. Maybe not the whole puzzle. But ... hey ... Alejandro! Mystery solved. I'm sure Detective Knox is somewhere en route. If not, we can call him when we get back home. He can alert the police at the airport. And then it'll really be done. The authorities absolutely have to take over from here."

The car fell silent, but only for a few seconds. Francine was surprised at who the next voice was. "But Franny..."

It was Calvin! And those were the only two words he said. All whiny and disapproving. It was that tone that had driven her up a proverbial wall during their marriage. He'd gripe and gripe, just like a child. And she couldn't stand it after a while. "But nothing!" she retorted. "You are going to put this car in drive and take Sam and me back to our car at the mall."

Calvin didn't like her tone either. She spoke to him as if he she was talking to a child, drawing out her words and slowing her speech. Nevertheless, he obeyed and begrudgingly started the car back up. Then, he looked in the rear view mirror and saw the sight of his son, sad-faced and disappointed. Disappointed in the outcome, disappointed in the world, disappointed in him. "Franny," he said softly. "Never mind letting down our son. Put that aside. Doesn't at least a teeny, tiny part of you want to see this through to the end?"

Calvin looked into his ex-wife's eyes and could see only fury. She was up for a fight on this one, and she was visibly gritting her teeth. "OK, OK," he said, trying to stay calm. "Look, we've done enough fighting in front of the boy. If you're going to lay into me, why don't we step outside and discuss this."

"Fine," she spat.

The two opened their doors in unison. The two closed their doors in unison. It was the first time they had done anything in sync in a long, long time, Sam thought. But what happened next totally took him by surprise. In one motion, his father darted back into the driver's seat, locked the doors, put the car in Drive, and stepped hard on the accelerator. "Calvin, you son of a bitch!" he heard his mom yell as they sped away.

Sam looked back at the woman, her fist raised in the air. Then, he looked back at his father, a few beads of sweat already forming on his forehead. "Oh, Christ, I didn't run over one of her feet, did I?"

Sam shook his head negative. He was truly speechless at what his dad had just done.

"Before you ask, I didn't strand your mother. I told both Vallone and DeFao to keep a lookout ... that this might happen ... and to drive her back to her car if and when it did. She'll be alright. Are you cool with this?" He looked back in his rearview mirror to see his son no longer disappointed, but re-energized and yet still processing what had just happened. "Sam?" he repeated. "Are you cool with this?!"

"Uh ... y-yeah. Are *you*?!"

"I know there's gonna be Hell to pay. I know that. But, hey, it's not like I live with the woman anymore. What's she gonna do? Give me the silent treatment for a week? Make me sleep on the sofa? I promised you I was going to help you solve this thing, and that's what I'm doing!"

Sam rolled down the back window to get some air. His dad was driving fast and erratic, swerving in and out of lanes. He almost missed the town's I-95 highway exit towards Baltimore and BWI Airport. The fast swerve onto the on-ramp turned up Calvin's energy level and courage greatly. "Hey, Sam, do you have any idea what the land-speed record is between here and BWI?" he asked, a crazed, almost Griswold-esque look in his eyes.

"No," Sam answered. "Why?"

"We're gonna break it!"

———

What normally would be about a 20-minute drive from Laurel to the airport took Calvin about 15 minutes. He didn't drive like a madman. He pretty much got in the interstate's far left lane, stayed there, and drove at about 80 miles an hour unimpeded. They were about a mile from the turn-off when he began making his way back across the four lanes of traffic to the off-ramp. When he had made his exit from the highway, he asked Sam, "So, what airline do you think ol' Poppy is putting Alejandro on? Pan Am? TWA? Is there an Air Portugal? We're gonna do this, Sam. We're gonna do this together, you and me! And then we're gonna go get some Denny's!"

Calvin's mind raced as the questions and proclamations kept on coming. "Should we go to the international terminal?" Calvin asked. "Do they even have an international terminal? Man, I'd forgotten how much I hate airports. They're so confusing."

The whole way he kept checking his rearview mirror to see if Francine had found a way to alert authorities. He kept dreading sirens and flashing lights. But all was calm behind them the whole way. Actually, he had such a fear of his ex-wife, he half expected her to be pursuing them in some vehicle or even on foot like some crazed, mad superwoman. But there was nothing and no one.

As they drew closer to the terminal, Sam finally brought himself to fill Calvin in on the rest of what he'd been holding back. "Hey, Dad," he said. "I don't think we're going to find them at the regular airport. Look for something called General Aviation."

"General Aviation?"

"Yeah, it's the part of the airport where they keep the private planes. It's where all the bigwigs fly out of, like when rock stars come to town or pro sports teams. Remember when we welcomed back the Orioles from the road after they clinched the division in '83? Remember all the fans and their signs and we got to shake Eddie Murray's hand and high-five John Lowenstein. That was at General Aviation."

Calvin nodded his head. "Oh, yeah. Yeah! I remember that. And I know where that is. What makes you think Alejandro's family is that loaded? I wouldn't be working at the Lube Job if I came from private-plane money."

Sam hesitated, and Calvin could see it. "Sam," he said, a bit nervous. "What do you know that I don't? Do you know who Alejandro's father is?"

Sam nodded.

"Well, who is he?"

"Oh, he's ... uh ... he's definitely a rich and powerful man."

"How rich and powerful? What does he do?"

Just as Calvin made the turn into General Aviation, Sam filled him in on the rest.

"I think Alejandro's dad is Pedro Machado Francisco. He's some big local import-export guy. Rabinowitz says he's one of those American immigrant success stories. An entrepreneur. A self-made millionaire. I hear he's also a philanthropist and a real patron of the arts."

"And?"

"And what?"

"What does he import-export?"

"According to Rabinowitz?"

"According to you!"

"Oh, I don't know," Sam replied. In listing, he tried to slip it in there. "Furniture, cars, carpets, electronics, drugs, rugs--"

"Drugs?!"

"I said rugs."

"No, you said drugs! What the Hell, Sam? Is this guy a narcotics dealer?! Are you driving us right up to the airplane of Tony Montana?!"

For whatever reason, Calvin never braked during this entire exchange. It never crossed his mind. There were no VIPs from the sports or entertainment, business or political worlds scheduled to fly in or out that evening, so the General Aviation gate was open. Calvin didn't even realize that there was normally at least the one security checkpoint to pass through to get to the private airfield that sat just behind one small terminal building.

When he made the slight left around that building and was greeted by the sight of a limousine and one other car stopped near a line of parked private jets, that's when he finally tapped his brakes and brought the car to a stop. But it was too late. They had been spotted. On the edge of the runway stood Francisco and two very large men on either side of him.

They were talking to a fourth man. Sam immediately recognized him as Knox. The second car was indeed his police cruiser with its siren lights off. Sam looked to his left out onto the runway and saw what they were watching. A lone jet was taxiing and about to take off.

"Oh, your mother's going to slaughter me," Calvin lamented.

But Sam was brash, and he immediately jumped out of the vehicle despite his father's protests. Calvin also got out and tried to meet his son's hurried stride towards the men. He didn't know what to expect. Did they have weapons? Would they put him and Sam on a plane for somewhere? Would they put them on three or four planes for somewhere? And yet he was just as afraid to face Francine if they ever left that airfield alive. He was so glad she wasn't there right now.

Calvin had never met Francisco before. He had only known drug lords from the movies and episodes of "Miami Vice." But on first appearance, he was immediately surprised by how warm and unthreatening he was. He was downright cuddly, with a slight belly paunch, an old Baltimore Colts ball cap on his head, and a bushy moustache that draped down on both sides of his mouth. "Young Sam!" Francisco called out, with a smile. Calvin didn't like that he knew his son by name. "And Poppa Sam, yes? I so wish my son had as much gumption as yours does. Well, if you've come to say good-bye to Alejandro, you're just a bit too late."

Sam immediately pleaded with Knox. "Stop the plane, Knox! Alejandro killed Bag Lady Betty! And he intended to kill Rabinowitz, Chip, and me, but splattered Muffy instead! You can't let him take off! You can't--"

"Whoa, whoa, whoa Sam! Whoa!" Knox said, putting his hands on the boy's chest before he advanced any further. "Calm down. You sure have been lighting up my phones this evening. First, Cindy Ginty at the mall. Now, the station has just radioed and your mom's been frantically calling the last 10 minutes or so. I, of course, came speeding here. And let me say that Mr. Francisco here has been very cooperative. He assured me that his son could never take part in anything so horrible. And without any real evidence, of course, I can't do anything. But Mr. Francisco has guaranteed that when his son returns from his pre-arranged vacation, he will answer any and all questions that the authorities may have."

"What?!" Sam was outraged.

"In the meantime, the police will continue to investigate."

Sam couldn't help but be bitter. He knew exactly what was going on. Knox really was a thoroughly corrupt bastard. Sam didn't have to call him that to his face. What was not being said in that moment was obvious. Sam looked at the plane, which was starting to make its final turn out onto the runway. Defeated, he asked, "He ain't never coming back, is he?"

Knox's grin was small, but more than a bit self-satisfied. "'Ain't never coming back?'" he mocked. "Really, Mr. Eckert. Is that kind of incorrect, improper speak what you're paying all that money to send your kid to private school for?"

Calvin pretty much knew he was looking at corruption in its face, too. "What are you the grammar police or the real police?" he questioned.

"He's no police at all," Sam said. Turning to Francisco, Sam then asked, "So, can you at least tell me where you're sending Alejandro? Let me guess. Out of the country, right? Back to Portugal?"

"That *was* the plan," he answered.

Sam detected a bit of wistfulness in his voice. "Was?" he questioned.

Francisco moved closer to the edge of the runway. The slight smell of jet fuel was in the air, and he held up his hand to wave to the plane even though it wasn't possible to see in through the tinted windows. He wasn't sure his son was watching. He wasn't sure if he had recognized and appreciated the lengths he had just gone to in order to keep him safe. They had their differences. He was a very different man that Francisco was. But he respected Alejandro, especially on this night more than any other.

"Alejandro is now in control of his destiny," he said admiringly, "and his destination."

"But ... what does that mean?!" Sam inquired.

The last thing Sam needed at this point was some old man waxing cryptic. He needed to know. But Francisco was not cracking. He seemed in a daze, like he was walking away from a grand fireworks show or some other dazzling display. To Sam, he also seemed genuinely happy. Or if not happy, at least pleased. Proud even. In a fatherly tone, he touched Sam's shoulder and said, "It means go home, boy. It is now truly over for you."

"No, not without you telling me--"

Sam's real father then stepped in. "Sam, it's over."

For a moment, Sam wouldn't budge. He would not yield. And then Francisco's tone and demeanor changed in an instant. He leaned in close to Sam and said in a loud whisper that could still be heard over the not-so-distant revving of the private jet's engines. "I have another plane, Young Sam. Would you and your father like to also go on a little trip tonight?"

The two locked eyes, and Sam finally understood everything. He looked into this ruthless man's soul and saw what he was capable of. He looked over at Knox ... corrupt, bought-and-paid-for Knox. He next looked at Francisco's two muscle men. Maybe in a few years, he could take one of them. But not both. And then he looked at his father, who was pleading with his eyes for Sam to get back into their car.

Finally, he looked at the jet taking off into the night sky. And Sam swears he could feel the passenger inside looking back at him. He stared at the aircraft until it was just a couple of blinking red and white lights in the distant horizon.

It was indeed over.

CHAPTER 16

Sam, Chip, and Buddy were back in their usual positions at their favorite table in the mall's food court. It was two days later. Nothing had changed, yet everything had changed. Life seemed different to Sam. The mall seemed different. Collette was gone. Muffy was really gone. His faith in right and wrong, good and evil, had been shaken. There was a crime; multiple crimes, in fact. And, yet, no punishment. He had the truth, and that was something. But there was no resolution. He didn't quite know what to do with it all.

And here he was right back where he started at the beginning of the summer, jawing with Chip and Buddy about trivial things. Movies, bad summer TV, the week's Top 40 songs on the radio. Maybe it was a way to avoid talking about all of the serious things that had happened the last few weeks. Teenage boys, as a whole, never do go very deep. But Sam was a kid of deep feelings.

The one big thing all three kept coming back to that day was Sam's mom's reaction once she finally did see her son and ex-husband again after they had left her in that parking lot across from the Lube Job. "So, she really kicked him in the balls?" Buddy asked. This was the second time in the last five minutes he had posed the question.

"Yup, just opened the front door of our apartment, took one look at him, and booted him in the nuts. I was standing behind Dad, and I swear I saw her foot come through his trousers. I think she even put some special shoes on, too, because when I got inside, there were sandals and high heels and slippers all over the floor near the closet. I guess you gotta respect the thought and preparation she put into it."

Buddy chuckled, trying to imagine the scene. "You know, it's a sick thing to say, but I really wish I could have been there to see that," he said. "I mean, how many times in real life do you actually get to see someone full-on intentionally get kicked in the crotch. Happens in the movies all of the time." Then, turning to the way-too-quiet Chip, Buddy attempted to bring him into the discussion, "Real quick, Chip. Best Ball Kicking Scene in a Movie ... go!"

Chip took all of three seconds to answer, "'Fraternity Vacation!' When that chick they were all trying to bang fended off that slicky-boy douche from 'Dallas,' who got fresh with her while they were doing aerobics. Friggin' great sound effect, too! Sounded like a melon going splat after being dropped off the Arbitron building. Best of all, it was a knee to the balls, not a foot. The Nigerian judge gives her a 9.5 for that one."

Sam laughed at the memory. "Yeah, that was a good one!" he agreed. "Great line from the dude, too. He looks up at her and strains, 'Does this mean you want me to leave?' And then he doesn't even get up. He just crawls out the door. Classic."

Buddy immediately scoffed. "Classic?! Oh, ye of such limited imagination and exposure. That's not even in the Top 5. You wouldn't have even thought of it if it weren't for The Movie Channel playing it every other night after 11. I'll tell you what the number one is. 'Butch Cassidy and the Sundance Kid!' You know, when Harvey Logan challenges Butch to that knife fight to decide who will lead the Hole in the Wall Gang. 'Rules?! In a knife fight?! No rules!' And then CRUNCH!"

"Yeah," Sam agreed. "That scene is pretty awesome, too."

Chip rolled his eyes. "White people movies," he muttered.

Sam took a bite of his ham and cheese sandwich from the Between the Bread mall deli, washed it down with some soda, then continued. "Well, Dad took it like a man. At least she's not threatening to take him back to court to change their child custody agreement, which he was afraid of. He figures the kick to the groin was punishment enough." Then, Sam went quiet for a bit, contemplating what he had just said. "I guess everyone's getting off light on this one."

Chip and Buddy looked at each other. There wasn't much to say or debate. Sam had laid it all out for both of them earlier. All of the pieces did finally seem to fit together, and it thoroughly unnerved both of them. Neither Chip nor Buddy really wanted to know how corrupt parts of their little Maryland suburb were. The proverbial rabbit hole was a lot deeper than any of them had imagined.

Still, Chip was starting to once again look on the bright side of things. "Look at it this way, my man. Alejandro probably really cared about Muffy. It's pretty clear they were in the process of running away together. That second car bomb? Dude, he accidentally killed his woman. He may not be in a jail cell right now. But he's gonna have to live with that for the rest of his life ... wherever he is now."

Buddy nodded his head in agreement. "Good point, Chip-a-roo," he said. "In the end, justice *is* a bitch."

"Is that from a movie?" Sam asked, his mouth now full of sandwich. Through it all, he hadn't lost his appetite.

Buddy rifled through his pop-culture memories and factoids. "No," he marveled. "I don't think it is. I think that's a Buddy Bradford original."

"Well, then," Sam said. "Something game-changing actually did come out of all this."

The trio fell quiet once again. They each finished up their respective fast-food meals. Some chomping was heard. Some slurping on straws of nearly empty drinks. It wasn't an awkward moment. It was more like a pause. A nice, quiet, contemplative pause. Life had a chance of getting back to normal, it seemed. Finally, Sam spoke up. "So, what do you think this was all about?" he asked.

"Oh, don't make this something philosophical," Chip moaned.

"No, really! There are two people dead, right? Your boss Chet's career in retail is probably wrecked as a direct result of all this. Another guy quit his career altogether and left town with his wife and kids, probably never to be seen or heard from again. The bad guy wasn't caught. The good guy--"

"You?"

"Yeah, sure. Why not me? The good guy didn't get the bad guy. He didn't get the girl either."

"At least he didn't die," Chip reminded him. "That would have been a real downer ending."

"True."

"Hey," Buddy interjected, pointing to Chip. "At least his sidekick didn't die either!"

"You mean his black sidekick. Because the black guy usually dies, right?"

"Well," Buddy stammered, "the really and truly important thing is the endearing comic relief guy didn't die!"

"Endearing comic relief?" Chip chortled. "You?!"

"Come on. You gotta admit, I had a few good zingers throughout this whole thing. And I might even be the one to end it all by yelling 'Game over, man!'"

"What?!" Buddy and Chip both asked together.

Buddy's smile was broad. He was practically panting like a little yappy dog on a chain in sheer and utter excitement. "OK," he burst, "my dad and mom and the theater staff screened it late last night. 'Aliens!' It's coming out July 18, and me and you and you are gonna be quoting it ... like ... forever!"

"And 'Game over, man!' is an actual line in the film?" Sam asked.

"Yeah!"

"What kind of stupid line is that?" Chip mocked.

Buddy immediately went on the defensive. "You guys are dicks. I'm telling you, this is going to be one of the greatest movies of all time. And from now until you're 60, you're gonna be saying 'Game over, man!' and "Get away from her, you bitch!" and "We're on an express elevator to Hell, goin' down!" and--"

"Alright, alright!" Sam cut him off. "Don't ruin the whole freakin' movie."

"Zingers indeed," Chip scoffed.

Just then, Mel and Rodney sidled by to gossip. Both seniors were looking quite nimble that day. Mel had a cup of coffee in his right hand and a newspaper under his left arm. Rodney was sipping diet soda, a Roy Rogers logo on the cup. Mel spoke first. "Sam, I heard about Rabinowitz skipping town. Tough break, kid."

"Tough, tough break!" Rodney echoed, a bit more intense. "That Rabinowitz. I could have told him he was eventually gonna be a target. If he'd only come to me, I could have told him his car was next."

"You couldn't have told him anything," Mel shot back. "Rodney, when you say things like that, you sound like an ass. You sound like a damn ass!"

Mel's rebuke barely registered with the man. "Well, I could have told him," he muttered.

Mel shook his head, then turned back to Sam. "At any rate, I guess you're snoopin' days are over. Right, Sam?"

"Right, sir."

"Did you at least get a date with that big gal you were fancyin'?" Mel then motioned over to a table about halfway across the bustling food court. "That one over there, right?"

Sam had been so deep in his own thoughts and so caught up in talking with his buddies that he had failed to notice Barbara sitting with some other girls from school. She no longer looked traumatized, and he was glad. She looked like a normal high-school girl again. And she seemed to really be enjoying her other lunch companions, laughing and gabbing.

"No," Sam said wistfully. "It still hasn't happened for her and me. But who knows? Maybe one day."

Buddy surveyed the table. He had failed to notice her, too. As he watched Barbara interacting with the other girls, she seemed more than just happy. She was actually animated. She looked like she was performing for them, with her hands more demonstrative than usual. Buddy even noticed her eyes meet with Sam's ever so briefly. But she looked away dismissively almost immediately.

"Hey, Sam," Buddy said in a slow, measured voice. "Have you ever seen a movie called 'Personal Best?'"

"Never heard of it. Why?"

Buddy continued to watch Barbara for a few more seconds. Then, he answered, "No reason."

Mel was the next person to ask Sam a question. "Do you wanna keep snoopin', boy? 'Cause if you do wanna stay on this, we'll keep our ears to the ground for you. Young folks talk around old folks like Rodney and me all the time, figurin' we can't hear 'em. But we can. And, hey, if you wanna still work with someone in the know, there's that Detective Knox over there gettin' his daily scoop at the Haagen-Dazs. I'm pretty sure he's still the primary on the Muffy case. And I think he's the only cop in town who prefers ice cream to doughnuts."

Sam gazed over at Knox ordering himself a scoop of some tasty treat. He didn't think twice. Against Chip and Buddy's protests, Sam impulsively got up from his chair and went over to confront the man. Both of his young friends could only watch, with Chip lamenting to Buddy, "Car bombs, crooked cops, a drug kingpin. Man, my dad is right. This is one truly messed-up town."

Buddy agreed. "Yeah, I say we take off and nuke the entire site from orbit."

Chip, sure that Buddy was once again quoting from "Aliens," scowled, "Dude, if you've ruined that movie for me in any way..."

———

"Spending some of your 30 pieces of silver, Judas?" Sam asked, coming up from behind Knox as he pulled a few thin napkins out of one of the ice cream kiosks' dispensers.

Knox looked at the petulant boy and could only chuckle. He knew he'd run into this kid eventually. He was glad he had a scoop of his favorite

Butter Pecan in a cup. "If you ask me," he cracked wise, "Iscariot should have held out for more, all the grief he's gotten over the years."

Sam thought the comeback was clever, but he still had a lot of anger boiling up inside of him. So much so, that now that he was in front of the man, he didn't know what to say first. In the moment, the only word he could muster was "How?"

"Pardon?"

For whatever reason, Sam wasn't intimidated by Knox anymore. For a time after Muffy's real death, he thought the guy was the real deal, that he was on the case and was going to get to the bottom of everything. Now, he wondered how much he knew and when. Sam knew he'd never get that much information out of him. So, instead, he just went with the morals and ethics questions. "How do you have that badge and yet work for a guy like Francisco? How do you look the other way while a man like that deals dope and kills people?"

Knox circled Sam slowly. He surveyed every inch of the boy's body, scoffing at the sockless feet, the too-tight Tears for Fears concert T-shirt from a year ago that was clinging to his soft torso, and the jean shorts that hung way too high. In surveying his appearance, one thing was clear. "Well, you're obviously not wearing a wire," he said, "unless you got it taped to the underside of your ball sack. In which case, the only thing a recording would be picking up right now is your two testes whimpering, 'Release me, release me!'"

"Knox, I just saw you and came over! You owe me some answers, and I--"

"For the record, and you'll be surprised to hear this, Pedro Machado Francisco has never killed anyone nor has he ordered the death of a single human being. Most of his business is completely legit."

"Most?"

Knox smiled. "Most of McDonald's and General Electric's business is completely legit, too, I'd imagine. But dig deep enough, and--"

"Oh. So, that's how you rationalize it all? That everything and every-one is corrupt on some level?"

"That's not a rationalization, Sam. That's a realization. You still don't get it, do you? You're not ready for this, boy. Any of this. It's not safe out here. It's messy. It's complicated. It takes years to figure out all of the players and angles. And it's all interconnected, and yet it's all hanging together by the thinnest of threads. Come on. In the past few weeks, have you not come to see the world just a little differently? Have you not come to see just this mall a little differently? You have a record store manager who could have any woman his age he wants, yet he happily takes the jail-bait. You have a major department store chain spying on people through dressing room mirrors, invading their most personal of privacies. And what about you?"

"What about me?!"

"Weren't you and Rabinowitz and your friend over there willing to break into Francisco's office if we didn't leave it unlocked for you? Did you and your Pops not violate pretty much every traffic law past, present, and future to get from the Lube Job to the airport in record time the other night? How many lies did you tell your mother? How far were you willing to go, Sam? What would you have done to find out the truth and be the big man on campus for once? But, a more important question to ask yourself is: 'What *wouldn't* you have done?' The answer to that may just frighten you."

"But you're a cop, Knox."

"And a good one ... most of the time. And I'm a good husband and father. Look, the only thing you really need to know about Mr. Francisco and me is that he helped me once with a problem when no one else would. Mr. Francisco has helped a number of people around this town and state with problems when no one else would."

"It sounds like you admire him."

"Mr. Francisco is a remarkable man. If he sleeps with your wife, you don't get pissed that he took her to bed. You feel grateful he found her that attractive. As for his son..."

"Yeah, you say the Franciscos aren't killers. Look what that dude was capable of!"

Sam was going toe to toe with Knox and barely flinching. Knox was actually enjoying the back-and-forth. "I said Mr. Francisco was not a killer. But Alejandro? Who's to say? The young man has always been a bit of an enigma, even to his family. Rigging cars to blow? Who taught him that? All Mr. Francisco wanted to teach him was how to run a company. But Alejandro wanted no part of the family business. He didn't want to be like his old man in any way. Working at the Lube Job as a blue-collar grease monkey was his way of thumbing his nose at him. But you know what? In the end, he was just as ruthless as his father ever could be."

"How so?"

"Alejandro was going to be sent back to Portugal. The jet was all gassed up. They'd even packed his bags for him. But Alejandro had grown some real stones. He flashed those pearly whites at his daddy, showed him some papers, and the next thing you know Mr. Francisco's offering him a one-way, one-time open ticket to anywhere he wanted to fly. Funny thing is, Alejandro knew exactly where he wanted to go."

Knox made a move to leave it at that, to walk away from Sam and let a bit of mystery linger in the boy's mind. But Sam had grown brash. He actually put his hand on the police detective's meaty forearm and jumped in front of him to impede his stride. Knox didn't take kindly to the boy's aggression, yanking his forearm back towards his torso and almost spilling his ice cream.

Before he could get a threat out, Sam demanded, "Just answer me one more thing, Knox. One more thing, and I'll leave you alone forever. If not back to Portugal, then where? Where did Alejandro go?"

Knox smiled at the boy, then looked away contemplating whether he should answer his question. If he told him, would Sam somehow, someday go there? Was he that obsessed? And would telling him ever come back at him in any way, shape, or form? Knox shoveled another small spoonful of Butter Pecan into his mouth and savored the flavor. The prospect of this kid never bothering him again was too much to pass up. Sam was still a big nothing, in his book. But he could be an annoying nothing. He decided to take the risk.

He leaned in close to the kid, veering from his face to his right ear. And in a whisper, he said, "Alejandro went to beautiful, sunny--"

———

"Aruba, sweet Aruba!"

Collette had said those words several times in her mind ever since her plane had landed. And, for the first time, she said them aloud. She couldn't believe she was finally there. She had planned for this, this specific moment, for a long time.

Aruba. An outdoor bar right on the beach. The sights and sounds of the ocean. The best sun dress right off the 16 Plus rack. A steady island breeze tickling her bare shoulders. A strawberry daiquiri that she slowly sipped. Even the bar stool was more comfy than she had dreamed. Its cushioned bottom was thick and seemingly new.

She could sit there all day, ordering drinks and food, watching the locals and tourists frolic, listening to the festive instrumentals being piped in through the bar's speakers. She had made it. Even the bartender was cuter than she imagined. She briefly wondered if he liked women with a bit of weight to them. But then again, she didn't really care. She made eyes at him anyway.

"You look like a woman who has everything she wants," the bartender observed.

Collette smiled mischievously at the tall Aruban, with the big smile and open shirt. She was about to flirt with him further when a familiar voice called out from behind her. "She does now!"

Collette spun around on the bar stool, and there he was. Alejandro Francisco. He moved quick to kiss her long and hard on the lips, the face, the neck. Alejandro's English was indeed not that good. But it was better than he had led most people to believe back in Maryland. "Mulher bonita!" he exclaimed. "You thought you were going to make the hanky-panky without me?"

Collette's mischievous eyes ignited. "Of course not, my stud!" she exclaimed. Then, glancing over at the bartender, she slyly added. "Well, maybe a little panky."

Alejandro laughed. The woman turned him on like no other. "Oh, Bonita," he said, taking her again into his arms. "You and I were always better as three than two, no? Did I surprise you?"

Collette shrugged.

"I didn't, did I? Why no surprise?"

"Well, my hunk, my man, my Portuguese plaything," she said, slowly undulating in his hold. "When I reported to my new store yesterday, I wasn't on the job 15 minutes before my former stockboy, Sam Eckert, frantically called to warn me that the 'evil mad bomber of Laurel' was none other than Alejandro Francisco, and that he had escaped the country and fled to of all places ... Aruba! He warned me to avoid you at all costs. At all costs! Sweet, sweet boy. I think I actually had a little bit of a thing for him."

"You?" Alejandro teased. "No!"

"Yeah," she cooed, running her fingernails across his muscular back as they embraced tighter. "In my hands, he might have actually been something someday. He really doesn't know how close he came to putting it *all* together."

Collette, Alejandro, and Muffy's love triangle was torrid and amazing from the get-go. It had been going on for a couple of months, ever since they pulled into the Lube Job at the same time in separate cars, in different bays and Alejandro charmed both of them and got them to agree to a drink after hours. When too many people started catching on, they put a plan in motion. And that plan was working. Collette had gotten the company's approval for her transfer. Both Muffy and Alejandro had agreed to leave their restrictive families behind. Muffy, though, wanted her break to be more than clean. She never wanted to be found again. She could be a heartless girl. But then again, so could Collette. And Alejandro was willing to do whatever for the both of them.

Their Bag Lady Betty set-up worked better than the three of them had ever hoped. No one even questioned that it wasn't Muffy who blew up. But then Sam and Rabinowitz just couldn't stop their snooping. It was never part of Collette's plan to rig the P.I.'s car, too. Alejandro did that on his own. How deep was his regret, Collette wondered.

Exiting their embrace and settling back into her seat at the bar, she lowered her voice slightly to ask, "So, have you forgiven yourself for the Muffler?"

Alejandro was a hard man to read at times. He had become such a master at hiding things. And hid he did, behind his looks, his language. Collette liked to think he didn't hide from her. They shared similar passions for life, for adventure, escape, and change. They despised the norms and had seduced Muffy together. Not that it took much to seduce her. In many ways, she was more adventurous and open to new experiences and new possibilities than Collette and Alejandro were. It wasn't quite love the three of them shared. But there were feelings involved. They all thought they had years to explore each other.

Collette grew impatient with Alejandro's silence. "Answer me, stud," she demanded. "Where are you at?"

"I am here," he replied softly.

"That's a bit vague."

Alejandro cocked his head. He motioned to the bartender that he also wanted what Collette was drinking, then took the empty seat next to her. "Vague?" he questioned. "What does this mean? Vague?"

"The last we spoke, you told me to go to Aruba and live my life, and you'd join me when you could. I know the Muffler had become more than just a chew toy to you. Even I'd grown quite fond of the little bitch. You know, a part of me didn't think I'd ever see you again. But here you are. You did it. You broke away. How?"

"The Jew man's briefcase. I was making it to go boom, too, and inside were all these papers he had on Papai."

"Wait, let me get this straight. You also rigged Rabinowitz's case to blow?! Jeez, I created a monster. Did you kill him?"

"Don't know. I only know Papai had found out everything about Muffy, and he says to me, 'You fly back to Portugal!' But when he saw what I had on him, Papai said I could fly anywhere! And so here I am."

Alejandro took a sip of Collette's daiquiri while his was being made. The bartender's blender was loud. But the noise made Alejandro's mouth water in anticipation. When the drink finally came, the two clinked their glasses and toasted each other. Collette then offered a toast to Muffy. And again she asked, "So, have you forgiven yourself?"

Alejandro thought for a moment. Staring out at the ocean, taking in the breeze, the surf, the sight of lovers and singles and families frolicking, he really did feel at peace with everything he was and everything he had done. "Sweet Collette," he finally replied. "I will always miss the sounds our little Muffler made when we tended to her. But look around. We will find another. Life is, how do you always say it? Life is for the living."

"Yes, I did teach you that, didn't I?"

"Bonita, you have taught me everything I know."

———

It wasn't long before school began again for Sam Eckert. He finished out the summer at 16 Plus, but it wasn't the same without Collette there. Julianna was a good boss. But Collette made that store what it was. So, quitting to focus on his junior year studies and activities was not a problem. It was always the plan.

And he wasn't surprised that when classes resumed, little had changed for him and Chip and Buddy socially. Brent once again hung out exclusively with his football buddies and barely acknowledged Sam's existence in class, the lunchroom, or the hallways. He had moved on and was dating Muffy's good friend, Elena, who was more than willing to step in and be one-half of the new First Couple of Our Lady of Sorrows. Barbara had moved on with Elena, too, and seemed to be as close to her as she ever was to Muffy.

Not even the infamous newspaper was seen anymore. The principal had ordered it and most other remembrances of Muffy taken down so the school and its student body could heal and move on. Muffy was no longer seen as a sympathetic character either. Public opinion both inside and outside the school had turned against her. If you asked most folks, they'd say she got what was coming to her for faking her own death in the first place and setting Bag Lady Betty up to burn. As a result, there was little thirst to find out who set the second blast ... the one that actually killed her.

Chip certainly didn't care. He barely mentioned the events of the summer anymore, and Sam didn't bring them up. There were, of course, no more party invites for either of them. And without Brent's protection, Jason Mumma was just as bullying as ever, racking each of them in the testicles at least a couple of times a month in gym class and laughing heartily each and every time.

It wasn't until December, with the school's Christmas and winter break approaching, that Sam even made his way back to the mall. Except for the decor, little was different there either. Mel and Rodney and the rest of the "oldies, but goodies" still held court. His old store, 16 Plus, still drew more young shoppers from Columbia than from Laurel. Even Chet Robitaille had somehow survived and was still managing Harmony Hut.

Sam didn't linger long at the mall, buying a couple of small presents for his dad, his mom, and her new boyfriend, Bill. When he got home that December afternoon, he found a note from Francine taped to the refrigerator telling him his pot-roast dinner was inside the fridge and ready to be warmed up, and that Bill had surprised her with D.C. theater tickets and a late dinner at Trader Vic's. Sam wished he could have tagged along. He'd only been to the famous eatery once, but couldn't believe how much he loved its Polynesian island cuisine.

And when he thought of island cuisine, he thought of Collette. His idle hands that night found their way into his mom's collection of back issues of BBW Magazine. And, of course, his first choice was that beloved Christmas edition from 1981. Sam chuckled at the memory of Collette correcting him on the year of the issue. That first conversation seemed like such a long time ago now.

Then, Sam noticed something he had never seen before. There was a caption under the main photo featuring Collette, the one in the Mrs. Santa Claus nightie he found so sexy. It read: "Collette Stephenson, returning from our July issue, models the latest in Yuletide intimate apparel." The July issue?! Sam couldn't believe there was another photo spread of his former boss. How could he have missed it?

He rifled through his mother's boxes of old issues that she kept in her walk-in closet. She didn't keep all of the various editions anymore. But Sam was hoping she hadn't recycled this particular one. Considering that Francine kept them all in order of date, it took him less than a minute to find the July 1981 issue.

He thumbed through its pages, excited at what he might find. And, sure enough, there she was. She had her own standalone spread, modeling various patriotic wear in an obvious nod to the issue coinciding with the Independence Day holiday. There was a red, white, and blue dress that showed a generous amount of cleavage. Sam liked that. He also really liked the pics of Collette in an American flag nightgown and in a stars-and-stripes, one-piece bathing suit.

Interestingly, there was a considerable amount of text to go along with the pictures of Collette. The headline was certainly intriguing. "Meet Our July Bombshell Collette." As it turns out, the article praised her for her military service. This surprised Sam. She had never mentioned any stint in the U.S. Army. He wondered how long she had served, where she had been deployed, and what she did.

The article answered all three of those questions. She had joined the service right out of high school and was active for five years. "I learned how to pick up and move on a moment's notice," she stated. "I think that will serve me well going forward."

She had been deployed to Europe, serving on bases in West Germany, Spain, and Portugal. "I loved the Portuguese men," she cracked. "And bless their hearts, the Portuguese men loved me!" And when it got to the part of the article where it highlighted what her job was, Sam almost dropped the issue. "Explosive ordinance disposal specialist."

"Explosive ordinance disposal specialist?" he whispered. "Bomb squad?" Then, he thought some more.

"Portuguese men?"

"Alejandro."

"Aruba?!"

At first, he resisted the pieces finally all falling into place in his mind. He didn't want them to. And then he remembered something Collette once said to him that had somehow stuck in his mind. "Maybe you're too close, Sam, and you're missing something right in front of your eyes that you're never going to see."

As it turns out, "never" only lasted for about six months in late 1986. Sam Eckert had finally solved a puzzle all on his own.

ACKNOWLEDGEMENTS

I have to begin by thanking my wonderful wife, Bonnie, and my awesome daughter, Madeline. Writing this book definitely took some time away from them, and I so appreciate their support. Daddy needed this creative outlet! These were characters who had been in my mind for a long, long time, and it's so cool to finally be able to have them out of my head and into the "real world."

I really wanted to get this book out in 2016 to coincide with the 30th anniversary of 1986. It's a year I often find my mind drifting back to because of so many real-life things that happened that year as referenced in the book. Everything from the Space Shuttle exploding to Len Bias dying to "Ruthless People" and "Aliens" being released. The '80s were still in full swing. The party that was that decade for so many of us was only half-over.

There's no way to thank everyone who have inspired me and helped me along the way. And I apologize to anyone reading this who is not mentioned. Certainly, I thank God for the gift and responsibility of writing. I thank my parents for giving me life, and my wife's parents for giving her life. I thank my college English and Journalism instructor, Tom Nugent, for being the biggest influence on me choosing the writing lifestyle. And I thank all of the quirky, two- and three-dimensional characters I've met along the way -- the bullies and the bullied, the jocks and the nerds; the rebels and the basket cases; but, most of all, to the many, many others who defied labeling and categorizing.

And, lastly, I thank the muse and voice of the '80s generation, the late John Hughes. My original idea for this book was "What if John Hughes wrote a high-school murder mystery?!" I probably didn't even come close to doing the kind of job he would have done with such a story. But I hope I, at least, did this particular story and these characters who I love justice.

I once read an interview with Mr. Hughes, and he spoke of how he would listen to music before writing to get himself in the mood. To any Gen X'ers reading this, I don't know about you. But I find it harder and harder to feel that ol' '80s vibe the older I get. Thank God, the tunes of those times can still transport me back.

So, to anyone wondering, some of the songs I would listen to before sitting down to write this book included: Julian Lennon's "Stick Around," Icehouse's "Electric Blue," Brenda Russell's "Piano in the Dark,"OMD's "So in Love," The System's "Don't Disturb This Groove," Hipsway's "The Honeythief," Flock of Seagulls' "Wishing (If I Had a Photograph of You)," Simple Minds' "Alive and Kicking," Red Rockers' "China," and the great Run-DMC/Aerosmith collaboration "Walk This Way."

I hope you, the reader, found this book totally awesome. Thank you!